CARROLL & GRAF

THE EROTIC READER

THE EROTIC READER

ANONYMOUS

Carroll & Graf Publishers, Inc.
New York

First Carroll & Graf edition 1988
Second Printing 1990

Carroll & Graf Publishers, Inc.
260 Fifth Avenue
New York, NY 10001

ISBN: 0-88184-425-X

Manufactured in the United States of America

Contents

Pauline the Prima Donna

You must have found me very serious as you read the end of my last letter, but that is just another trait of my character. I always seem to be able to foresee the way a chain of events will unroll, and take into account the various impressions, feelings and experiences that go to make it up. Even the most violent intoxication of the senses has never been able to make me lose my critical facilities, and today, in fact, I am beginning a chapter of my confessions which will prove this statement.

My affair with Franz continued. I was always very prudent and so my aunt suspected nothing and our rendezvous were secret from all those around us. In addition, I refused to be alone with Franz more than once a week. The day of my debut was drawing near and Franz was becoming more and more rash. He thought he had obtained some rights over me, and he was becoming too domineering, like all men who believe themselves sure of an undisputed possession, but this was not how I intended it to be, and I immediately conceived a plan. At the beginning of a brilliant career was I to connect myself with a man of no importance, one to whom I was, on all points, superior? To leave him on bad terms, however, would have been dangerous, for I would then be at the mercy of his indiscretion. It was necessary to be very clever, which I was, for I succeeded in ending our liaison so opportunely and so deceptively that Franz still believes today that if chance had not separated us I would certainly have married him.

The 'chance' was my doing. I had informed my professor that my accompanist had pursued me with his declarations and that I was ready to break off the course of my artistic career in exchange for love in a cottage. However, the good man, who was extremely proud of his pupil and who was counting heavily on my debut, grew very angry. I begged him not to make Franz miserable, and so I reached my goal while Franz reached the Budapest Theatre Orchestra by special engagement. We bade each other a tender farewell; I had broken off my relations without anything to fear.

Shortly after our separation I gave my first performance at the Theatre of the Kärntnertor, and you know how successful it was. I was more than happy. I was surrounded and besieged. Applause, money and celebrity poured my way and I had plenty of suitors, admirers and enthusiasts. Some thought to reach their aim with poems and some with valuable presents, but I had already observed that an artist cannot give in to his vanity or his feeling without risking everything in the game. This is why I pretended to be indifferent. I discouraged all those who came near me and soon acquired the reputation of a woman of unassailable virtue. Nobody had any idea that after Franz's departure I turned again to my solitary joys on Sunday evenings and to the delights of the hot bath. However, I never yielded more than once a week to the call of my senses, although they demanded much more. A thousand eyes were upon me and so I was extremely prudent in my relationships. My aunt had to go everywhere with me and nobody could accuse me of a single indiscretion.

This lasted all winter long. I had a steady income, and I installed myself in a very comfortable and well-furnished apartment. I was accepted in the best society and found myself very happy with my new life. I only regretted rarely Franz's departure, and fortunate circumstances compensated me for it the following summer.

I had been introduced into the house of one of the richest bankers in Vienna, and I received from his wife all of the marks of the truest friendship. Her husband had paid court to me, hoping with his huge fortune to easily conquer a popular actress. When he had been driven away like all the others, he introduced me to his household, thinking to win me that way. Thus it came about that I could come and go there as I pleased. I consistently repulsed his advances and, perhaps because of that, his wife soon became my most intimate friend. Roudolphine, for that was her name, was about twenty-seven years old, a piquant brunette, very vivacious, lively, tender and very much a woman. She had no children and was quite indifferent to her husband, of whose misdemeanours she was painfully aware. The relationship between them was friendly, and they did not refuse themselves from time to time the joys of marriage. Yet, in spite of all, it was not a happy union. Her husband probably did not realise that she was a very warm-blooded woman, a fact she most likely concealed very skilfully.

At the approach of the fine weather, Roudolphine went to live in a charming villa at Baden where her husband used to visit her regularly every Sunday, bringing a few friends with him. She invited me to spend the summer there with her at the end of the theatre season. This stay in the country was to do me a lot of good. Until then we had only talked about clothes, music and art, but now our conversations began to assume a different character. The court that her husband paid to me provided her the opportunity for this. I noticed that she measured her husband's misbehaviour according to the privations which he imposed upon her. Her complaints were so sincere, and she hid so little the object of her regret, that I immediately concluded that I had been chosen as her confidant and decided to act like a simple and inexperienced friend. I had played my cards right and touched upon her weakness; she at once began to explain things to me, and the more innocent I pretended to be and the more I seemed astounded by what she told me, the more she insisted on fully informing me of what filled her heart.

In addition, she took great pleasure in revealing certain physical matters to me. She was utterly astounded at the surprise I showed at discovering these things. She could not believe that a young artist who was always playing with fire could be so unaware of everything. It was only the fourth day after my arrival when we took a bath together—practical instruction could hardly be left out after so many fine speeches—and the more I appeared clumsy and self-conscious, the more amusement she derived from exercising a novice. The more difficulties I made, the more passionate she grew. However, in the bath and during the day she did not dare go beyond certain familiarities, and I realised that she was going to employ all of her cunning to persuade me to spend the night with her. The memory of the first night spent in Marguerite's bed obsessed me in such a way that I was quite ready to yield to her wish. I did this with such a show of ingenuousness that she was more and more convinced of my innocence. She thought she was seducing me, but it was I who was getting my way.

She had the most charming bedroom, furnished with all the luxuries that only a wealthy banker can afford, and with all the taste of a room arranged for a wedding night. It was there that Roudolphine had become a woman. She recounted in detail her experience and what had been her feelings when the flower of her innocence had been taken. She made no secret of the fact that she was very sensual. She also told me that until her second confinement she had never found any pleasure in her husband's embraces, which were then very frequent. Her pleasures, which developed only gradually, had suddenly become very intense. For a long time I could not believe that, having been very ardent myself ever since my youth, but I believe it now. In most cases this situation is the husband's fault; he is in too much of a hurry to finish as soon as he enters, and does not know how to excit his wife's sensuality first, or else he gives up half way.

Roudolphine had compensations; she was charming and avid and only bore her husband's negligence with all the more bad humour. I shall not bother to tell you all the sports in which we engaged in her big English bed. Our revels were delightful, lascivious, and Roudolphine was insatiable in the pleasure she took in kisses and the contact of our two naked bodies. She enjoyed herself for two hours and hardly suspected that these hours were still too short for me, so much did I desire and so much did I pretend to yield only with difficulty and shame.

Our relationship soon became much more interesting, for Roudolphine consoled herself in secret for her husband's pranks. In the neighbouring town lived an Italian prince who usually stayed in Vienna where Roudolphine's husband looked after his financial affairs. The banker was the humble servant of the prince's huge fortune. The latter, about thirty years old, was outwardly a very severe and a very proud man with a scientific education and turn of mind; inwardly, however, he was dominated by the most intense sensuality. Nature had gifted him with exceptional physical strength. In addition, he was the most complete egotist I have ever met. He had but one aim in life, pleasure at all costs, and but one law, to preserve himself by dint of subterfuge from all the troublesome consequences of his affairs. When the banker was there, the prince often came to dine or to tea.

I had never noticed, however, that there was any affair between him and Roudolphine. I learned about it entirely by chance, for she was very careful never to breathe a word of it to me. The gardens of their two villas were adjacent, and one day when I was picking flowers behind a hedge I saw Roudolphine pluck a note from underneath a stone, conceal it quickly in her blouse and hurry away to her room. Suspecting some little intrigue, I peeped through her window and saw her hastily read and burn it. Then she sat down at her desk, I supposed, to compose the answer. So that she would suspect nothing, I hastened to my room and began to sing at the top of my voice, at the same time carefully watching the place in the garden where the note had been left. Soon Roudolphine appeared, walked along the hedge toying with the branches, then so swiftly and adroitly did she hide her reply that I did not catch it. However, I had noticed the spot where she had paused longest, and as soon as she had returned to the house, and when I was certain that she was busy, I dashed into the garden. I easily found the message hidden under a stone. Back in my room with the door locked I read, 'Not today, Pauline is sleeping with me. I will tell her tomorrow that I am indisposed. For you, of course, I am not. Come tomorrow, then, as usual, at eleven o'clock.'

The note was in Italian and in disguised handwriting. You can well imagine that everything was at once clear to me. I had already made up my mind what to do. I did not return the note to where I had found it, for I wanted the prince to come that night and surprise us both in bed. I, the *ingènue*, was in possession of Roudolphine's secret and I felt sure I would not come out of the situation empty handed. Of course, I still did not know how the prince would manage to get to Roudolphine's bedroom.

At lunch we had agreed to spend the night together, which is why she had refused the prince's visit. Over tea she explained to me that we could not sleep together for about a week, for she felt that her period was approaching. She thought this would delude me, but I had already woven my net around her. Above all, I had to get her to bed before eleven o'clock, so that she could find no means of avoiding, at the last minute, the surprise I had prepared for her.

We went to bed very early, and I was so frolicsome, so caressing, and so insatiable that she soon went to sleep out of sheer fatigue. Bosom against bosom, her thighs between mine, our hands reciprocally at the sources of our pleasure we lay there, she fast asleep and I more and more wide awake and impatient. Suddenly I heard the floor of the alcove creak, the sound of muffled footsteps, and the door opened. I heard someone breathing, getting undressed, and at last approaching the bed on Roudolphine's side.

Now I was sure of myself, and I pretended to be very deeply asleep. The prince, for it was he, lifted up the bedclothes and lay down beside Roudolphine, who woke up terrified. I felt her trembling all over. Now came the catastrophe. He wanted to ascend immediately to the throne he had so many times possessed. She stopped him, asking hastily whether or not he had received her reply.

Meanwhile, trying to get where he wanted, he had touched my hand and my arm. I cried out, I was beside myself, shuddering and pressing myself against Roudolphine. I was highly diverted by her fright and the prince's amazement. He had shouted an Italian oath, so that it was no use for Roudolphine to explain that it was her husband coming unexpectedly to surprise her. I overwhelmed her with reproaches and upbraided her with having exposed my youth and honour to such a dreadful scene, because I had recognised the prince's voice. The prince, a gallant and knowing man, soon realised, however, that he had nothing to lose. On the contrary, he was gaining an interesting partner. That was just what I expected him to think. After a few tender and amusing words he went to close the bedroom door, took out the keys, and returned to bed.

Roudolphine was between us. Now came the excuses, the explanations and the recriminations. But there was nothing to be done, nothing could be changed; we would have to keep quiet, all three of us, in order not to expose ourselves to the unpleasant consequences of so hazardous a meeting, a thing it would be hard to explain. Roudolphine calmed down little by little and the prince's words grew sweeter and sweeter. I, of course, was in floods of tears. By my reproaches I forced Roudolphine to make me her confidant and thus her accomplice in this illegal liaison. You can see that Marguerite's lessons and her adventures in Geneva were useful to me. In fact, it was exactly the same story except that the prince and Roudolphine did not realise that they were merely puppets in my hands.

Roudolphine, then, no longer tried to hide from me the facts of her long-standing liaison with the prince, but she also revealed to him what she had been doing with me, the innocent young girl, and she told him how I burned with desire to learn more of these matters. That excited the prince and when I tried to make Roudolphine be quiet she only talked with all the more ardour of my sensuality! I noticed that he was pressing his thighs between those of Roudolphine and was trying in this way to reach the desired goal from the side. From time to time his legs brushed against mine, and I wept, I burned with curiosity. Roudolphone tried to console me, but with every movement the prince made she became more and more distraught. Soon she too squirmed about, trembled passionately, and finally moved her hand to my body to try to make me share her pleasure. Suddenly I noticed another hand straying where hers was already so busy. I could not allow that to continue, for I wanted to remain faithful to the rôle which I had given myself, so I turned over angrily towards the wall and, as Roudolphine had immediately taken away her own hand when she encountered that of her lover on this forbidden path, I was abandoned to my sulking and I myself had to finish secretly what my bed companion had begun.

Hardly had I turned my back on them when they forgot all restraint and all shame. The prince threw himself upon Roudolphine, who opened her legs as wide as possible to receive the beloved guest easily and quickly, and the bed shook at every movement. I was so consumed with desire and envy; I could not see anything, but my imagination was aflame. Then at the moment when the two lovers were fused most closely and overflowed, sighing and shuddering, I myself let loose so abundant a burning flood that I lost consciousness.

After the practical exercise came the theory. The prince was now between Roudolphine and myself, although I do not know whether this was by design or accident. He did not make the slightest movement, and I seemed to have nothing to fear, but I was perfectly aware that I had to keep quiet in order to maintain my superiority, and I waited to see what they would do next. Roudolphine explained to me first that, since her husband neglected her and ran after other women, she had every right to give herself freely to a cavalier so pleasant, so courtly, and above all, so discreet. She was in the best years of her life and did not want, indeed she was not able, to miss all the sweetest of earthly joys, especially since her doctors had advised her not to attempt to repress her natural sensuality. In any case, I knew that she was a very warm-natured woman, and she was sure that I was not indifferent to love, but only afraid of the consequences. She said that she simply wanted to remind me of what we had been doing together that evening before the unexpected arrival of the prince. I wanted to put my hand over her mouth to shut her up, but I could not do this without making a motion towards my neighbour, who seized my hand immediately and covered it with tender little kisses.

Now it was his turn to talk. His was not an easy rôle as he had to weigh every word so as not to hurt Roudolphine's feelings, but I realised by the intonation of his voice that he was more anxious to win me as quickly as possible than he was concerned about upsetting Roudolphine. However, by this time she was obliged to put up with anything in order to keep her secret.

I no longer remember what the prince said to soothe me, to excuse himself, and to prove that I had nothing to fear. I only remember that the warmth of his body was driving me crazy, that his hand was stroking first my breasts, then the rest of my body, and finally the very centre of his desires and mine. The state I was in defies description. The prince advanced slowly but surely; however, I could not allow him to kiss me, for he would then have noticed how I burned with desire to return his caresses. I was struggling with myself; I wanted to have done with this comedy, to put an end to my affected modesty, and to surrender entirely to the situation, but if I did that I would lose my advantage over the two sinners, and I would have been exposed to the dangers of love making with this violent and passionate man; for the prince would not have known how to limit his triumph once he was the victor.

I had noticed how feverishly he had finished with Roudolphine. All my entreaties would have been in vain, and perhaps even a backward movement would not have helped me. Besides, how could I tell whether, at the last moment, I would have been able to restrain myself? My whole artistic career was at stake, but I held my ground and let him do almost anything to me without responding to it, only defending myself desperately when the prince tried to obtain more. Roudolphine was at a loss as to what to say to me, or what she should do herself. She realised that my resistance had to be broken that night if she were going to be able to look me in the eyes the following day. To excite me even more, which was really quite unnecessary, she lay her head upon my bosom, embraced me, licked my breasts, and finally hurled herself between my legs where she pressed her lips to the still-inviolate entry of the temple, and began a play so pleasant that I allowed her complete freedom. The prince had yielded his place to her, and he was now kissing me on the mouth.

Thus I was covered from head to foot with kisses. I was no longer making any attempt to resist, so he placed my hand upon his sceptre, and I permitted this familiarity unenthusiastically. My arm pressed between the thighs of Roudolphine, who was kneeling, and I noticed that the prince's other hand was now in the place where his sceptre had been revelling so short a time before. He taught me to caress it, to rub and squeeze it. The group we formed was complicated but extremely pleasant; it was dark and I was sorry not to be able to see, for one must enjoy these things with the eyes as well. Roudolphine was trembling, excited to the extreme by the kisses she was showering upon me and the caresses she was receiving from the prince. She was half senseless with delight and opened wide her legs, whereupon the prince suddenly straightened himself and took up a position which was thus far unknown to me, bending over and penetrating her from behind. I had pulled my hand away, but he seized it and brought it to the point where he was most intimately united with Roudolphine. He then taught me an occupation which I should never have dreamed of, and which enhanced the rapture of the two pleasure-seekers. I was now to squeeze the root of his dagger and now to caress the sheath which enclosed it. Although I pretended to be ashamed, I was in fact extremely zealous in doing this. Roudolphine kissed and licked passionately and, all three together, we soared quickly to the very summit of pleasure. It was so intoxicating that it took us a good quarter of an hour to recover ourselves. We felt much too hot, and on this summer night we could stand neither the contact of each other's bodies nor that of the bedclothes and we lay naked as far apart as we could.

After this passionate and sweltering action the discussion was resumed anew. The prince talked as calmly about this strange chance rendezvous as if he had organised a party in the country. Basing his assumptions on what Roudolphine had told him, he no longer took the trouble to win me, contenting himself simply with combating my fear of unhappy consequences. He was well aware that he would have no difficulty in convincing me. The virtuosity of my hand, the pleasure which I had tasted and which had been betrayed by my beating heart and the trembling of my thighs had revealed to him how sensual I was. He only had to prove to me that there was no danger and that is what he was trying to do with all the art of a man of the world.

For these reasons he imagined that it would only be a question of time. He therefore did not insist upon the repetition of such a night and soon left us, for dawn was in the offing. He was perfectly willing to sacrifice the length of time spent in pleasure in order to safeguard his secret and his safety. He had to go through the dressing room and a corridor, climb a ladder, go out through a window, crawl back in through a skylight before finding himself in his house again, from where he would have to creep steathily back to his apartments. The leave-taking was a strange mixture of intimacy, tenderness, timidity, teasing and deference, and when he had left, neither Roudolphine nor I felt like talking things over any more. We were so tired that we fell asleep at once. Later, upon awakening, I pretended to be inconsolable at having fallen into the hands of a man, but I was really furious that she had told him about our pleasures. She did not even notice how much delight I found in her efforts to console me.

Naturally, I refused to sleep with her the next night, telling her that my senses were never to lead me astray from my good resolutions another time, for I never wanted such a thing to happen again; I wanted to sleep by myself, and she was not to believe that I would ever permit the prince to do what she allowed him to do so easily. She was married and it would do no harm if she became pregnant, but I was an artist. A thousand eyes were upon me, and I did not dare do anything like that, which would bring me to disaster.

As I had expected, she then spoke to me about safety measures. She told me she had met the prince at a time when she was not sleeping with her husband because of a quarrel, and that consequently, she did not dare to become pregnant. The prince had calmed all her fears by using condoms, and she told me that I could try them too. She also told me she was quite sure that the prince was very level-headed and had perfect control of his feelings. In any case, he knew another way of preserving a lady's honour and, if I were very nice to him, I would soon learn about it. In short, she tried by every means to persuade me to surrender to the prince, so that I might enjoy the gayest and happiest of hours. I gave her to understand that her explanations and her promises did not leave me entirely cold, but that I was still rather fearful.

Towards noon the prince came to visit Roudolphine, a polite visit which also included me. But I feigned illness and did not appear. This gave them the chance to agree freely upon the measures to take to overcome my resistance and to initiate me into their secret games. As I did not want to sleep with Roudolphine any more, they would probably arrange to surprise me in my bedroom as quickly as possible, so as not to leave me time to repent, and perhaps to go back to town. My surmise proved correct.

All that afternoon and evening, Roudolphine did not mention previous nights to me. She came up to my bedroom that night, however, and sent away the chambermaid. When I was in bed, she went to lock up the anteroom herself so that nobody would disturb us. Then she sat down on my bed and tried to convince me anew.

She described everything to me in the most beautiful and seductive manner and assured me there was nothing to fear. Of course, I pretended that I did not know the prince was in her room and that he might even be listening from behind the door, so I had to be prudent and give in to her arguments little by little.

'But who is to guarantee to me that the prince will use the mask which you described?'

'I will. Do you think that I would let me do anything more with you than what I let him do with me at first? I promise you that he will not appear without a mask at this ball.'

'But it must hurt terribly. You know he guided my hand and made me feel his strength.'

'At the very beginning it may really hurt you, but there are remedies for that, too. You have some oil of almonds and some cold cream. We will smear his lance with them so that he can penetrate more easily.'

'Are you quite sure that no drop of that dangerous liquid can get through to bring about my misfortune?'

'Come now, do you think that I would have given in without that assurance? Everything was at stake then, as I had no contacts at all with my husband at that time. When I had made up with him I permitted the prince everything. But now I arrange things so that he visits me at least once every time the prince has been here. And so I have nothing to fear any longer.'

'The thought of that misfortune horrifies me. Besides, there is still the shame of giving oneself to a man. I do not know what to do. Everything you say charms me, and my senses are urging me to take your advice, but for nothing in the world would I put up with another night like the last, for I know that I should never be able to resist again. You are quite right. The prince is as gallant as he is handsome, and you will never know what feelings were aroused in me when I heard the sounds of your surrender there beside me.'

'I too had a double pleasure in letting you share, although very imperfectly, in what I was feeling myself. I should never have thought that pleasure among three could be as violent as that which I tasted myself last night. I had read about it in books, but I always thought that it was exaggerated. The thought of a woman sharing herself between two men is odious to me, but I think that the accord between two women and a sensible, discreet man is delightful; but of course the two women must be true friends. One of them must not be more timid and more fearful than the other, and that is still your trouble, Pauline, dear.'

'It is just as well that your prince is not here, my dear, to hear your conversation. I really shouldn't know how to resist him, for I am totally consumed by what you have been telling me. Just look how I am burning, here, and how I am trembling all over.'

As I spoke, I uncovered myself—part of my thighs—and placed myself in such a position that if anyone were looking through the keyhold he would not miss a thing. If the prince were really there this was the moment for him to come in—and he did.

As you might have expected of an experienced and perfect man of the world, he understood at once that no talking was necessary, that he should conquer first and talk about it later. By the way Roudolphine had behaved I could see that everything had been arranged in advance. I tried to hide under the bedclothes, but she pulled them off me; I started to weep and she laughingly smothered me with kisses. Although at last I expected the ultimate fulfilment of the desire which had been mine for so long, I still had to be patient, for I had reckoned without Roudolphine's jealousy. In spite of the necessity of making me her accomplice, in spite of the fear of seeing her plans come to naught at the last minute, she was not going to sacrifice to me the first fruits of this day's pleasure. With an expression on her face that I envied, but which I dared not unmask if I were to stay within my own rôle, she told the prince that I had consented and that I was ready to do anything, but that I wanted to be certain of the efficiency of the means used, and that she would like to submit to a demonstration in front of me.

It was obvious that the prince was not expecting such an offer, and that he would have preferred to have carried out this trial directly with me rather than with Roudolphine. She took several of the small bladders from her pocket, breathed into one to show that it was impermeable, then moistened it and put it on with many caresses and giggles. After that she quickly undressed and lay down on the bed beside me, pulling the prince down on top of her, and exhorting me to watch closely so that I would lose all fear.

And so I really did see everything. I saw the delight of this handsome couple. I saw his strength and his power; I saw him penetrate her, and I saw her rise to meet him, and I saw them forget everything around them as the ectasy grew until finally the flow took place amid sighs and shudders of delight.

Roudolphine did not relax the hold of her thighs before she had recovered her senses. Then with a beaming face she removed the condom and showed me triumphantly that not a single drop had overflowed. She took all the trouble imaginable to make me understand that which Marguerite had already explained to me so well, but which I had never been able to procure for myself. For in that case Franz could have used it, too.

Roudolphine overflowed with joy. She had demonstrated to me her supremacy and had gathered the first fruits of the prince, who had certainly been expecting another dish that evening. I decided that later I would take my revenge. The prince, however, was very kind. Instead of making the most of his advantage, he treated us both very tenderly. He took nothing, contenting himself with what we were ready to give him, and spoke with passion of the pleasure which divine chance had brought him in the persons of so charming a pair of women. Describing our relationship in the most glowing colours, he filled in the time that he needed to gather up his strength once more. He was no longer very young, but he was still valiant as a lover, and at last the moment arrived. He entreated me to trust myself to him absolutely. Roudolphine very prettily made the victor's toilet, while I watched, peeping through my fingers. The cold cream was lavishly applied, and at last the longed-for instant arrived: I was going to receive a man. For a long time I had been wondering how I was going to deceive the prince about my virginity, because the first time I had used Marguerite's instrument I had lost that which men prize so highly.

As I wanted to surrender myself and since I had consented to be the third person in their games, I felt that I should behave myself without false modesty, and I let my two companions do all that they desired to me. Roudolphine laid me down on the bed in such a position that my head was leaning against the wall and my two thighs were hanging over the side of the bed, parted as much as possible. With eyes of fire, the prince gazed upon the delights spread before his view. Searing my mouth with burning kisses, he moved my hand away and placed his lance in, sliding it up and down very gently in the font. Roudolphine followed his slightest movement with eyes full of desire. Then he thrust his lance in as gently as possible. Up till then a very sweet sensation had penetrated me, but I had not felt any real delight. As he pressed, however, I was really being hurt and I began to moan.

Roudolphine encouraged me by sucking the tips of my breasts and fondling the place where the prince was trying to get in; she counselled me to arch my thighs upwards as much as possible. I obeyed automatically and the prince suddenly entered with such force that he penetrated half-way. I uttered a cry of pain and began to weep in earnest. I was lying there like a lamb at the sacrifice; however, I had made up my mind to go through with it. The prince moved slowly, this way and that, trying to penetrate further. I felt that all was not well; a muscle, a little skin, something anyway, had stopped him. Roudolphine had stuffed a handkerchief into my mouth to stifle my cries and I was now biting it in pain. I bore everything, however, to attain at last what I had desired so ardently.

Something wet was trickling down my thighs. Roudolphine cried out triumphantly. 'Blood! It's blood!

Congratulations, prince, on obtaining this beautiful virginity.' The prince, who so far had proceeded as gently as possible, quite forgot himself and penetrated so vigorously that I felt his hairs entangled in mine. That did not hurt me too much, though, for the most painful part of the proceedings was over, but my expectations were not satisfied in the slightest. My conqueror became more passionate. Suddenly, I felt something hot flowing inside me, then the vigour relaxed and the member escaped. Really, I should be telling lies if I talked about pleasure. According to what Marguerite had told me, and according to my own experiments, I had been expecting something much greater than that. And I well remembered the enthusiasm my parents had shown too. At any rate, I was glad to see that my trick had succeeded and that I had not been wrong in my calculations.

As I lay there pretending to be unconscious I heard the prince talking enthusiastically about the visible signs of my virginity. My blood had, in fact, bespattered the bed and his dressing gown. This was far more than I had dared to hope for, especially after my wretched attempt with Marguerite's instrument; there was such a tremendous difference between that thing and the prince's mature virility! In any case, it was through no merit of mine that I had still been a virgin, but only through chance.

Virginity is actually a mythical thing anyway. I have often talked to other women about it and have heard the most contradictory statements. Some girls have so wide a membrane that there can be no obstacle to the first entry, while others have one so narrow that even after having several times participated in love bouts a man entering will still think that he is the first. In addition, it is very easy to deceive a man, especially if he believes that the girl is well behaved. This can be done by waiting until her period is about due before she surrenders, when she must moan a bit and twist around as if in pain, and the happy possessor swears that he has been the first, for a few drops of blood from a different source will easily mislead him.

But it was high time for me to awaken from my fainting

fit. I had had my own way, and now I wanted to take pleasure without leaving my rôle of the seduced girl. The most important part had been acted. The prince and Roudolphine found particular delight in consoling me, for they were sure that they had initiated a novice. They both undressed and got into bed with me, the prince in the middle. The bed curtains were drawn and a delightful and indescribable game began. The prince was nice enough not to talk about love, langour or nostalgia. He was merely sensual, but with delicacy, for he knew that this quality is a spice to love play. I was still pretending that I had been violated, but that I was learning all the more quickly.

His two hands were busy with us, and ours with him. The more complicated our kisses became, the more animated our hands were and the more restless our bodies. Our nerves trembled with pleasure. It is a very great delight to kiss such a man, and he would have had to be made of stone not to warm up again. Even so, the second ejaculation had tired him. Sometimes he played with Roudolphine, sometimes with me, but I never let him approach without first having made his toilet, although he was very sure of himself. He gave me his word that I could try without a mask, that I risked nothing, that he was completely in control of himself. But I was not to be so easily tempted from the path I had chosen. So he began with Roudolphine, who lost consciousness two or three times without his strength being diminished. Then he washed and came to me. It still hurt a bit at first, but soon pleasure began to prevail, and for the first time I experienced complete fulfilment.

To prove to me once and for all that he was entirely master of his body, he did not finish inside me, but pulled out without ejaculating while I was half fainting with delight. He tore the condom wildly away and threw himself upon Roudolphine. She told me to come and sit upon her face and that she would calm with her tongue what the prince had brought to fever pitch. I was very reluctant, but a damp cloth refreshed the object of my desires and a charming group was soon composed. While the prince mounted Roudolphine, I knelt with my thighs wide apart over her face. Her tongue had plenty of room for its revels, for her head was thrown back over the pillows. Completely naked, because the prince had pulled off my nightdress in his passionate impatience, I was face to face with this magnificent man who now crushed my breasts against his chest and kissed me unceasingly.

Two tongues revived the fire which had hardly been extinguished. My pleasure increased and my kisses grew more and more passionate as I abandoned myself completely to this double excitement. The prince was enthralled, assuring us that he had never before experienced such happiness. At the moment of the spasm I grew jealous thinking of that warm wave of rapture spreading through Roudolphine and so, pretending to faint, I let myself fall heavily to one side. As I had calculated, I threw Roudolphine's cavalier right out of the saddle, and as I fell I saw their organs disunited where they had been so closely linked before. How fiery red and excited his was, how wide and violently open hers was. It was quite different from anything I had previously seen, though not more pleasant. I frightened them by falling, and they had no thought of pursuing their pleasures further, but came to help me.

I had reached my goal and was not long in coming to my senses. I made no secret of being very happy that I had been initiated with such art into the mysteries of love, but I refused to begin again as I could not stand any more. The prince wished to show us that he could give up the greatest of pleasures if we could not all share it together. He said that he left it to us to content him. I did not know what he was expecting, but Roudolphine, more lascivious than ever, accepted at once. The prince lay back naked on the bed and I had to imitate Roudolphine, who provoked with her fingers the marvellous fountain. As I kissed him and played with the oval containers of his sweet balm, Roudolphine took the shaft in her mouth. Finally, the foamy jet sprang forth and fell upon us all. I would have liked to have taken the place of Roudolphine, who absorbed most of this burning fluid, but I still had to pretend to be inexperienced and just learning everything. You can understand why I cannot forget that incomparable night. The prince left us well before daybreak, and both Roudolphine and I, closely entwined, slept until after midday.

The Amatory Experiences of a Surgeon

It is one of the requirements of society that the feminine portion of it should wear, at least to outward gaze, the semblance of virtue; yet there is nothing in female human nature which is more difficult to adhere to.

Among the males, society tolerates vice of all kinds, which does not actually bring the perpetrator within the pale of the law; but with woman, one false step—nay, the very breath of slander—is sufficient to cast her, a degraded being, without the pale of its magic circle.

Can we picture a more pitiable position than that of a young woman, in the prime of her youth and beauty, condemned to await in silence the adventure of the opposite sex, with the knowledge that the person whom she is prevailed upon at last to accept may, after all, turn out to be an impostor, totally disqualified for performing those functions that are necessary to the happiness of married life.

We medical men are not ignorant of the secret pangs and unruly desires that consume the bashful virgin, and that society with its ordinances prevents her from finding a safe vent for. We have often the means of tracing all the passionate thoughts, and sometimes the secret wanton doings, of those whom kind society has condemned to disease, rather than to allow nature to take its own proper course and allay those symptoms so detrimental to young girls.

Who shall say how many victims have been sacrificed on the altar of mock modesty for fear that the disgrace of the only natural cure for their complaint should blast their characters?

I have alluded to the circumstances which have come to

my knowledge from time to time, with reference to the expedients made use of to allay those raging fires which in too many cases prematurely exhaust the constitutions of our young women; and one of these cases will suffice to prove how ingenious are the designs to cheat society of its whimsical requirements.

A young lady, not yet eighteen years of age, was under my care for a complaint of the bladder, in which the symptoms denoted the presence of calculus, or stone. An operation became necessary, which the patient underwent with unexampled fortitude.

I could not conceal a suspicion from the first that the young girl could, if she choose, enlighten us to the nature of the case; but strange to say, she absolutely preferred to submit to a painful and dangerous operation, with the knowledge that death might possibly ensue, rather than render us any information which might lead to a correct conclusion.

The operation was performed successfully. A mass of calculus was removed, and as these formations never take place without something to build up a 'nucleus,' we began to search.

We recommended the usual examination, only to discover that the formation had for its nucleus a hairpin, which must have been introduced by the fair hands of the young patient herself, doubtless not without a sufficient covering to render the insertion tolerably agreeable.

The result was that the inexperienced girl had allowed the hairpin to become disengaged, and instead of getting into the entrance she had intended, it had slipped into the urethra, and thence into the bladder, from whence the very nature of its shape had prevented its returning.

This instance is only one of a number I could give my readers, illustrative of the shifts young ladies are frequently driven to in order to satisfy, in secret and by illicit means those desires which they are prevented from openly exhibiting and which they dare not appease by nature's only fit and proper remedy, connection with the other sex.

I have promised in these pages a faithful recital of events that, having befallen me, have left a sufficiently warm interest in their remembrance to entitle them to a place here; and true to this promise I am about to relate my adventure in the case of the sisters before alluded to.

As I have already stated, they were daughters of an opulent resident in the town. They both inherited the pretty face and elegant form of their mother, who, when they were quite children, had committed them in her last hours to their father's paternal regard.

I was the medical attendant of the family, and as such it fell to me to be depository of such little complaints as there two young beauties had to make.

At the time I write, the elder was just sixteen.

I had of late observed in her those usual indications of approaching puberty that disturb the imagination of young girls, and I knew from her symptoms that nature was working powerfully within her to establish her claim to be treated as a woman.

One day on calling, I found that Mr H—— had gone out hunting, and would not return until late in the evening. It was then four o'clock in the afternoon of a hot and close summer day. The two young creatures were alone, and received me with the modest grace so captivating to a young man.

I stood and chatted until the time for paying my other visits had passed, and as none of them were pressing and could as well be paid the following day, I remained to tea.

After tea the younger of the two girls complained of headache, and after a little while she went upstairs to lie down, leaving her sister to sustain the conversation.

I played the agreeable with all my powers of attraction. I gazed on her with longing eyes. My looks followed every movement of her body, and my wandering fancy drew an exquisite picture of all her concealed beauties.

Gradually love grew into ardent desire—a desire so strong that I had some difficulty to keep my seat, while my rampant member stood beneath my trousers with the strength of a bar of iron.

Each moment only served to increase my fever, while I fancied I observed an embarrassment on her part, which seemed to hint that she was not ignorant of the storm that raged within me. Innocent as she was, and all inexperienced in the ways of the world, nature stirred within her powerfully and doubtless whispered that there was some hidden fascination in my gaze, something wanting to content her.

At length, tea things were sent away, and I could find no reasonable excuse to linger longer by the beautiful being who had so fiercely tempted me.

I rose to go. She rose also. As she did so, a certain uneasiness in her manner assured me that she had something to communicate. I asked her if she felt unwell, pretending that I observed an unusual paleness on her lovely face.

She said she had something to tell me, and proceeded to detail the usual symptoms of a first perception of the menses, which had occurred a few days previously and which had at first much alarmed her.

I assured her on this subject, explained the cause, and promised relief. And on taking my departure I requested her to come to my house on the following day, and said I would then investigate her case.

With what impatience I passed the interval may be easily imagined by any of my readers who have been similarly situated. But as the longest night must have at length an end, so did this, and morning broke to dispel the restless dreams of unruly passion that had held me enthralled.

I anxiously awaited the time of my young patient's arrival, and my heart danced with joy as I heard her timid knock at my street door.

She entered—heavens! how my prick stood—how beautiful she looked.

I stand even now when I think of that sweet vision.

Over a plain skirt of black silk she wore a mantle, such as becomes young ladies, with a neat little bonnet. Pale kid gloves set off her exquisite little hands, and I noticed that her feet were encased in boots any lady might have envied.

I hastened to make her take a seat in my study. I entered fully into the particulars of her case. I found, as expected, that she was experiencing the full force of those sensations which were never intended to be borne without relief, a relief I was panting to administer.

I told her of the cause of her own symptoms. I gradually explained their effects and, without shocking her modesty, I contrived to hint at the remedy:

I saw she trembled as I did so, and fearful of overreaching my purpose, I broke off into a warm condemnation of that state of society that allowed such complaints to blast in secret the youth and beauty of young girls like herself.

I went on to hint at the evident necessity there was for the medical man to supply those deficiencies that society left in the education of young ladies.

I spoke of the honourable faith they maintained in such cases, and of the impossibility of anything entrusted to them ever becoming known.

I saw that she was so innocent as to be ignorant of my purpose, and burning with lust, I determined to take advantage of her inexperience, and to be the first to teach her that intoxicating lesson of pleasure which, like all roses, is not plucked without a thorn.

I gradually drew near her. I touched her—she trembled. I passed an arm around her slender waist; the contact literally maddened me. I proceeded to liberties that to a more experienced girl could have left no doubt of my intention.

Upon her my touches had only the effect of exciting more strongly within her breast those sensations of which she already complained.

I was now fairly borne away by my passions, and throwing my arms round the innocent beauty, I covered her face and neck with fierce and humid kisses.

She appeared to be overcome by her feelings, and seizing the moment, I lifted her like a child from her chair and placed her on a couch. I removed her bonnet and without meeting with any resistance from my victim, for contending emotion had rendered her all but senseless.

I carefully raised up her clothes. As I proceeded, I unveiled beauties enough to bring the dead to life, and losing all regard for delicacy, I threw them over the bosom of the sweet girl. Oh, heavens! what a sight met my gaze as, slightly struggling to escape from my grasp, she disclosed fresh secrets.

Everything now lay bare before me—her mossy recess, shaded by only the slightest silky down, presented to my view two full pouting lips of coral hue, while the rich swell of her lovely thighs served still further to inflame me.

I could gaze no longer. Hiding her face with the upturned clothes, I hastily unbuttoned my trousers. Out flew my glowing prick, standing like a Carmelite's. I sank upon her body; she heaved and panted with vague terror. I brought my member close to the lips. I pushed forward, and as I did so, I opened with my trembling fingers the soft folds of her cunt.

I repeated my thrusts. Oh, heavens! how shall I describe what followed? I gained a penetration. I was completely within the body of the dear girl.

I sank upon her, almost fainting with delight, my prick panting and throbbing in her belly. Oh, the ineffable bliss of that encounter. My pen trembles as I revert to the scene.

What followed, I scarcely know. I pushed again and again, until I felt myself getting dangerously near the crisis.

I observed her soft and still gloved hand beside the couch; I seized it, and covered it with kisses.

Heavens! what fire ran through me. I burned; I was on the point of spending.

Not unmindful of her reputation, even at that intoxicating moment when I felt the approach of the blissful moment of emission, with fear I thrust once more. My prick seemed to traverse the full extent of her belly.

Then, groaning in the agony of rapture, I drew out my bursting member, and falling prone upon her, I drenched her little stomach and thighs with an almost supernatural flood of sperm.

I lay for some time so utterly overcome with the intensity of my feelings that I could only close my eyes and press the dear girl to my breast.

At length I rose; carefully removing the reeking trace of victory, I adjusted the tumbled clothes of my companion, and taking her tenderly in my arms, I placed her in an easy chair.

I shall not attempt to describe all the degrees she went through before she came finally to herself and to a full knowledge of her complete womanhood. That she never blamed me for the part I had acted was the best guarantee that she had not regretted the accomplishment of my pleasing conquest.

On recovering from the confusion and dismay consequent upon the event I have just narrated, my fair patient lost none of her volubility, but talked away on the subject of our recent encounter, and asked so many questions that I had hardly time to reply to them ere she puzzled me with fresh ones.

Before she left me, I had initiated her into the exact proportions and nature of that potent invader whose attack she had so lately sustained.

The handling to which my prick was now subjected in no way reduced its desire for a second engagement, but a consideration for the delicate state of my new-made disciple, and the tender condition which I knew her very little privates must be in, induced me reluctantly to postpone any further attempt, and she departed from my house, if not a maid, yet a perfect woman.

Nothing could exceed the caution with which we concealed our secret enjoyments from every jealous eye, and yet I trembled lest my indiscretion should become known.

There was only one thing for which we both panted, and that seemed too dangerous to be put into execution. Julia had often received the entire length of my large member in her little cunt, but that was the sum total of our bliss; to emit there was more than I dared.

Several weeks had elapsed since the commencement of

our intercourse, and during that period I had been unremitting in my attentions to the youthful charms of my new acquisition.

She pined for the enjoyment, but I knew the risk of indulging her in her desires.

Fear of getting her with child was with me always paramount, for although as a medical man I might have enabled her to get rid of the burden before maturity, yet I was alive to the dangers attendant on so serious an undertaking.

One day, as with many sighs and much regret on both sides we proposed to omit the most usual way of finishing the performance of the Cyprian rites, Julia gave vent.

Julia, worked up almost to frenzy by the sweet friction, refused to permit my withdrawal, and throwing her arms round my loins, she finally detained me, while with wanton heaves and every exertion in her power, she endeavoured to bring me to the spending point.

I was alarmed for safety, and vainly struggling to free my rampant prick from the warm, sticking folds that environed it.

The more I struggled, the closer she held me, and the closer I drew to the dreaded moment, the more she exerted herself to produce the feared emission.

'Stop, stop,' I cried. 'Julia, my darling girl, I shall do it, I know I shall. Oh!'

I could say no more, but with a violent drive forward I sank, spending on her belly; my prick fairly buried in her up to the hair, the semen spouting from me in torrents.

As for my wanton companion, she threw back her head, and received the dangerous fluid with as much enjoyment as if it were herself who was trembling in the rapturous agony of its emission.

Trembling in every limb, as much from the fear of the result as from the excitement of the act, I rose and helped the tender Julia to her feet.

As she got up, a heavy pattering sound announced the return of the fluid, which ran in large drops upon the carpet and ran in rills down her beautiful thighs.

A few days after this affair we were diverting ourselves with sundry little freedoms one toward the other, when Julia, seizing my prick in her soft, white, little hand, threw herself upon the sofa and, drawing me to her, commenced to kiss and toy with my member. This, as may be supposed, afforded me considerable pleasure, and I let her do what she pleased, wondering all the time what her next gambol would be.

From kissing she took to sucking, and this delicious touch of drawing lips soon inflamed me beyond all restraint.

Again she took it between her lips, and holding the loose skin tightly in her grasp, she made her hand pass rapidly up and down the huge white shaft until, heated to the utmost and almost spending, I jerked it out of her grasp.

'Ah, my lad, you were afraid it would come out, were you?'

I replied that I was only just in time to prevent it, upon which with a laugh and a smack on the ticklish part in question, she exclaimed: 'Well, then, my fine fellow, we shall see what we can make come out of that large head of yours.'

Then, suiting the action to the word, she again commenced the agreeable titillation, until with nerves strained to the utmost pitch of luxurious excitement. Jutting out my member before me, I heaved my buttocks up and down, and with a few motions of her hand Julia fairly brought me to the emitting point.

With a sigh of heavenly enjoyment I let fly the hot gushes of sperm on her bosom, while her fair hand, retaining hold of my throbbing prick, received a copious flood upon its dainty surface.

After this we would frequently lie down together on the soft hearthrug and, each with a caressing hand on prick and cunt, produce in one another those delightful effects which, say what people will, give a spur to the passions no man or woman can resist.

We would operate on each other in this way until prudence compelled us to stop for fear of the concluding overflow, and then, waiting for a few minutes, would once more bring our senses to the verge of the impending flood.

These hours were wiled away until a serious cause of anxiety arose to put an end to our security.

As I had feared, Julia proved with child; how could she be otherwise, with such an opportunity?

As soon as she made me acquainted with the fact, I prescribed for her, but without effect. The prolific juice had taken firm hold, and nature was progressing in the formation of the little squalling consequence of our amour.

My anxiety was now intense lest the discovery I saw impending should, in spite of our endeavours, overwhelm us.

Under the circumstances I determined to take a resolute course. I operated on my little Julia. I succeeded. I brought away the foetus, and removed with it all danger of discovery.

The result was not so favourable with regard to the health of my patient. Our overheated passions had put an end to youth's dream of uninterrupted enjoyment in a continual round of sensual pleasure, and Julia had now to reap the harvest of her indiscretion. She soon fell into a weak state of health, and I recommended immediate change of air.

Her father, alarmed at her indisposition, took her to Baden, and after a residence of some months there, the roses again revisited her cheeks.

At Baden she was greatly admired, and soon received an offer for her hand, which her prudent father did not feel justified in refusing; she became the wife of a Russian prince, who, if he did not get with her that unsatisfactory jewel, her maidenhead, at least became possessed of a cunt well practiced in all the arts of love and lechery.

Thus terminated my amour with one of the the most agreeable and most salacious girls I have ever known, and my prick still stands at the recollection of the various luscious scenes in which we were mutually carried away by the violence of lust in its most enticing form.

The Loins of Amon

Withdrawing into the gloom of his dungeon, Ineni slowly walked the few steps around the walls. His mind was lost in bitter thoughts, which, for the moment even clouded thoughts of survival and escape. If only . . . But what sort of commander thought after the event 'if only'? He clenched his fists in fury.

Looking again through the aperture, he felt the immediate hopelessness of his position. All weapons had been taken from him. He had nothing but his tunic and his two hands. The prison was impregnable. The guards were incorruptible in face of the might of the High Priest.

There had, of course, been talk of his harem. He returned to the bed and waited.

Some time later, the slight drone of the guards' voices stopped and there was the sound of soft footsteps beyond the oak door.

Ineni stood up and stepped swiftly to the aperture. Down the stairway, led by an officer of the guard, came his harem, anxious and afraid.

In the chamber they were halted and the guards were ordered to search them. Ineni watched the heavy hands of the guards moving over the soft bodies of the women outside their thin robes. Hands violated even between their legs and buttocks over the slight protection of the robes. The officer stood by to see that no impropriety beyond the embarrassment of the search, took place. These women were the harem of a nobleman—most of them of high rank themselves.

The officer called out in the gloom to the blank door.

'The women are here for your pleasure, my lord. Is it your desire that all should enter?'

Ineni surveyed them from his eye-hole. They were all there; the Palestinian, a dozen others and, looking unhappy and forlorn amongst them, his recent acquisition from Kadesh.

'The dimensions of my chamber would not permit of such lavish hospitality,' he called back. 'Have enter but one: the young Syrian girl on the end of the line.'

The guards immediately seized the girl, whose eyes darted, quick and frightened from one to the other as once more rough hands mauled her. This time, the officer, too, approached after the examination by the men, had the girl remove her robe and looked at her more thoroughly. His eyes were dull, inscrutable as he surveyed her pronounced charms, but the eyes of the guards, forgetful of the proximity of the girl's master, lit up with lust at the sight of such beautiful flesh, so thinly covered, it seemed, with a taut, filmy skin. As the officer's hand searched in turn between the girl's legs, one of the rough men licked his lips involuntarily.

'Right, she may enter,' the officer declared after a moment. 'Should she leave before the morning you will keep her here with you. On no account must she be allowed to gossip before the sacrifices are completed.'

The eyes of the guards were riveted on the girl while he spoke. They saw in her an image of sweet, innocent beauty so much intensified from her noble standing and her uncovering before them.

One of them moved with the girl to the door, eyes still fixed on the profile of her face so near to him as, re-clad in her robe, she waited for the door to be opened. The iron bar was withdrawn with an effort and with a grunting tug, the door was swung outwards and the girl slipped into the cell.

She stood just inside in the gloom, staring uncertainly towards the dim shape of Ineni, while the door was re-barred and the sound of the officer's footsteps dwindled. For a moment the guard stood outside the door, staring in through the aperture. But then he decided discretion was necessary from one of his lowly station, even in face of a a condemned man. There was the creaking of the rushes on the divan and a low resumption of conversation.

Ineni moved towards the girl who meekly waited. As he reached her and caught her in his arms, she suddenly clasped him with a furious pressure.

He drew her to the bed, pulling her down alongside him in the gloom. Only their vague outline could be seen from the door.

The girl's hands moved tenderly over his face, her eyes looked bewildered; lovely and bewildered in the twilight.

'What has happened?' she breathed at last and there was disbelief in her voice. 'Why are you here?'

With his lips close to the smooth warmth of her forehead, Ineni spoke quickly and quietly. The girl listened, her fingers digging in continual little pressures into his shoulder.

'The high priests are corrupt,' he explained quietly, intensely. 'They are afraid of my power with the people. They know that I hate their corruption. When I met you in Kadesh, I had been sent on a war mission which it was thought could end only in my destruction. But I returned and they were afraid. So I am here. Nobody knows I am here. But tomorrow I shall be sacrificed to the god Amon and corruption will continue unopposed in Egypt.'

'But—but what of the Pharoah?' the girl asked. 'His name flies throughout Syria. Is he not the lord of Egypt?'

'In name only,' Ineni whispered in reply. 'He is the tool of the priests. Their word is law and they could overthrow him with ease if he tried to shake off their yoke.'

The girl was silent for some time. Tears welled in her eyes and she tried to force them back, but failed, so that they suddenly flowed in profusion over her slim cheeks.

'I—I just don't understand?' she said. 'You were all-powerful in Kadesh. Everyone spoke in awe of your power. And here you are thrown, like a common thief into a cell.'

'The ways of corruption,' breathed Ineni. 'But keep your voice down or the guards will hear.'

'But what can we do—what can we do?' She clung to

him with a desperate longing.

'Whatever is to be done,' Ineni whispered, 'it will be very risky with only a small chance of success.'

'But we must do something?' the girl breathed intensely. 'I should die if you were killed. My life would be worth nothing.'

'A plan occurred to me as I watched the guards searching you,' Ineni went on quickly. 'It involves you and will mean death if it fails. It will also be unpleasant for you—but it is the only chance.'

'I will do anything,' the girl said firmly. 'If you die I shall not want to live anyway.'

Ineni kissed her gently and wiped away her tears with a corner of the hides.

'In a few moments we must pretend to make love,' he whispered. 'But it would be better if we didn't make love in fact so that we shall preserve all our energy.

'After this pretence, I shall send you away. The guards have orders to keep you with them if you leave.'

He hesitated for a moment, searching for the best words to explain his plan. The girl's body was pressed against him, her face pressed against his as she listened.

'Normally they wouldn't dream of touching you, no matter how acute their desire. You are a noblewoman and the wrath of the nobles and the priests would have them slain. But if, while you sit with them on the divan, you make advances towards them they will, if I am not mistaken, have great difficulty in controlling their desires.'

He paused again. The girl's breath was sounding slightly, close to his ear. She said nothing.

'This plan,' Ineni continued tersely, 'is our only chance and you must forgive me the indignity I suggest. You must try to force them to make love to you—and not much force should be necessary.

'One of them has a dagger in his belt. He must be made to see the necessity of keeping his tunic on in case somebody comes. In his passion you must withdraw the dagger from the belt and kill him.'

The girl's grip on his shoulder tightened to a long slow

squeeze and Ineni was afraid she would be unable to carry out his plan—unable through her unwillingness. But when she spoke, her words made him grip her with a burst of love and continue.

'What shall I do with the other man—there are two?' she asked softly.

'That is the difficulty,' Ineni said quietly. 'I can think of only one solution. In order to stab them both you must have them both very close to you, both off their guard. They must both make love to you at the same time.'

There was silence and then the girl said: 'Yes, I see.'

'It will be unpleasant for you,' Ineni added, brushing his lips along her brow, 'and I cannot force you to do it. But it is my only chance of escape.'

'And what after they are dead?' the girl asked.

Ineni felt a surge of hope pass through him at the certainty in the girl's voice.

'Then you will have to pull back the bar and we can escape together through the temple,' he whispered. 'There will be more guards in the temple, but I shall be free and armed. Once out of this cell we shall escape.'

'Where shall we go?' the girl continued her relentless questioning. 'How can we hide?'

'That we shall have to decide in due course,' Ineni replied. 'We will have most of the night before discovery and I know where we can get horses. Can you ride?'

'I was taught by my father.'

'Right. Enough talk. Now we must pretend.'

Outside the door, shadowing through the hole, was a flickering of light. Ineni got up and crept over. A brazier had been lighted in the outer chamber and the guards were sitting quietly on the divan. They appeared to be listening. They are hoping to bear aural witness to the passion of a prince, Ineni thought with grim humour. They shall not be disappointed.

He tiptoed back to the girl and removed her robe. He in turn took off his tunic and lay alongside her. Their bodies were fused together and his penis rose in spite of him, pressing with rigid pain against her thighs. The girl breathed heavily.

'Could we not make love?' she pleaded in a whisper. 'The plan might fail.'

'It will not fail,' Ineni said, quietly. 'It must not fail. We shall need all our wits and strength and one becomes listless after passion is spent. It is better that we deny ourselves until we are safe.'

'I shall long for our safety with all my heart,' the girl said.

'So be it,' Ineni echoed.

For the next half-hour they pantomimed the act of love. Lying in the gloom where their movements would be now undiscernable from the door. The rustlings of the hides, the heavy breathing, the muttered exclamations, the moanings, the whinings, the groan after groan of growing passion, the convulsive explosion of fulfilment. All were there for the benefit of the guards, quietly listening outside, picturing afresh the lush curves of the girl they had seen searched in her nudity.

After the final gasping of the act, they lay silent for some time. Then both dressed quietly.

'Tell them I am asleep,' Ineni whispered. 'And you must act as if you really desire them, as if you mean every movement of your body, every word of encouragement. My life—and yours if you fail—depends upon it.'

'I will do all I can,' the girl whispered back. 'And I shall be thinking of you with every act I make.'

'Amon be with you,' Ineni said.

The girl breathed a prayer and then walked to the door. She banged on the inside and a guard came over.

'My lord has bid me leave him. He is asleep,' she said.

The guard tried to peer past her into the cell but could see nothing. He called out to his companion.

'Our lady wishes to leave. Be ready with your spear.'

The other covered the door from a slight distance, spear raised. His companion eased back the bar and the girl slipped out into the chamber, the light from the brazier shadowing over her, outlining the creases around the fleshy parts of her body, where the robe clasped and offered them. The bolt slid back into place.

'You had better sit on the divan, my lady. It is more comfortable and we have been ordered to keep you here for the night,' one of the guards said, gruffly, embarrassed in the presence of a noblewoman.

The girl thanked them and sat on the divan, while the two soldiers drew away and squatted on the floor at the foot of it.

Very quietly Ineni rose from the hides and crept to the door. He stood back a few inches from the aperture so that he had a good view of the outside, but could not in turn be seen. No light came down the steps from above. It was full night.

Ineni's heart kept up a continued, abnormal thumping as he prepared himself for the events which would end in life or death for him.

The girl had surreptitiously eased up the hem of her robe and she leaned back against the wall, legs apart so the material stretched tightly across her thighs, revealing their bareness under the skirt of her covering up to the gloom of her crutch.

The guards sat with their eyes on the ground, afraid, perhaps, to look at the lightly protected beauty of the girl.

'How boring it must be for you to have to sit in this chamber all night.'

The men looked round. She had succeeded in attracting their attention to herself.

'It gives us no great pleasure, my lady,' one of them replied—and his eyes fell on the open, revealed gulf of her legs under the robe. His companion, too had seen the uncovered intimacy. Their eyes became glued on the dark, firm, muscled flesh of her thighs—and were stuck there. Neither, it seemed to Ineni, had the physical power to remove his eyes from the tempting view.

The girl pretended to be unaware of their lustful eyes, the colour which had flamed to their faces.

'Are no women ever brought to give you a little distraction?' she asked.

She moved her position slightly as if she were

uncomfortable—and succeeded in presenting the men with an even fuller view of the secrets under her skirt. Her thighs, wide under the robe were now all visible and to the furtively searching eyes of the guards, the soft lips of her vagina were there in sight. Their heads, on the level of the divan, were directly in line with her legs and their eyes feasted ravenously—and now almost openly—on the object they would have given their lives to possess.

'Never such luck,' one of them answered. And his voice came out gruffly and uncertainly in his passion so that he had to cough to hide his feelings.

'How inconsiderate of your commanders,' the girl continued.

She rose as if to stretch her legs and strolled around the chamber, clasping her robe about her, outlining her buttocks as she walked away from them. Her bottom seemed contained like a firm pudding in a thin cloth and at its extremeties it rippled out against the cloth.

The men exchanged glances and stared with fixed eyes at the buttocks which rounded and creased like live things before their eyes. The fire threw shadow and light on the ripples of flesh so that they seemed even accentuated.

The girl turned back towards them and in walking appeared to find something wrong with a sandal. A few paces from them she paused and bent in front of them, jostling her sandal with her hand. At her bosom, the loose robe opened out and fell forward so that the guards found themselves looking down a long ravine of cleavage, their hungry eyes roaming over almost completely revealed mounds of round, firm breast-flesh.

Ineni, watching them closely, was aware how hard put to it they were not to leap to their feet and start the rape of the girl, in spite of the penalties which would follow. So far she was playing her rôle well.

'I always feel a great sympathy for guards,' the girl continued. 'They have no fun, while frequently their prisoner has everything he could desire. It seems so unfair.'

'We are not the privileged, my lady,' replied one, tongue

slithering over dry lips.

'But nonetheless you have probably more power and capacity than those in higher places.'

The girl, churned up with nervousness inside, as Ineni well knew, was giving no indication of anything but complete self-possession far beyond her years.

For a moment the guards stared at her, racking their brains for meaning to put to her words, unable to believe the obvious.

'My lord within there, for instance,' the girl continued relentlessly, nodding towards the door behind which Ineni watched. 'He has no more power than to satisfy himself and leave me unsatisfied—and now he sleeps while I can only regret.'

Slow grins appeared on the faces of the guards, grins they were prepared to wipe off at the slightest sign. Now they were sure—but one could not be completely sure with a noblewoman.

The bulges at the loins of their tunics were unmistakable. The girl sat once more on the divan, robe drawn up to reveal several inches of smooth, silky thigh, and motioned to the men to sit with her.

'Is it not ridiculous?' she asked with a smile. 'Two fine men like you, unable to have a woman and a woman like me left unsatisfied because of my lord's weakness. And here we are able to do nothing but sit and dream and wish.'

Her slim fingers played with her thigh, as if absently and her big, doe-eyes swept the two men.

'It is a great pity, my lady,' one of the men replied. 'And anyone who could not spend a whole night with you but must needs send you off at its beginning is no man in my view.'

He had risked all on his remark. The other guard looked at the floor.

The girl eyed the man.

'You would not have done so?' she asked. 'You would have kept me the whole night?'

'And several more besides if it were my choice.'

The other guard had not yet looked up from the floor.

They were playing with dynamite.

'Then you would seem to be the man for me,' the girl replied.

The other guard looked up at last. He grinned. They both grinned. This was a noblewoman with a difference. One could laugh and joke and talk intimately with her. But yet neither consciously dared suggest—not even hope—for more.

'You are so beautiful that I should probably have kept you for life,' the guard added, warming to his compliments.

'Am I so beautiful?' the girl asked, raising an eyebrow and smiling provocatively.

'More beautiful than the lotus blossom,' declared the guard who had not spoken up to this point.

'Ah. You, too, are a man of taste.' The girl encompassed him in her smile.

'But surely you have seen more beautiful women?' She addressed them both.

'I have seen some as beautiful of face and a very few as beautiful as body, but never one of such virtue in both,' the first guard said, boldly.

'And how can you be sure that my body is so beautiful?' the girl asked with a smile.

'My lady, you cannot hide your beauty—and was it not revealed to us when you were searched?'

Both men were now getting obvious pleasure out of simply making suggestive remarks to such a beautiful and noble woman. The bulges in their tunics were enormous and they made no fruitless attempt to hide these gauges of passion from the girl.

'But that was for only a moment. You had no time to judge,' the girl laughed.

'It was enough, but indeed we could have wished for more,' the first guard said, with a ring of passion in his voice.

'Then you shall have it,' the girl declared.

And before the lustful eyes of the men—hardly able to believe what was happening—the girl slithered off the divan and slowly divested herself of her robe. It peeled from off her breasts, which soared into view like great balls of ivory, strongly pointed at their uttermost protrusion by the expanse of nipple. Down from her slim ribs and slimmer waist the garment slipped, clasped her tightly around the broader flesh of her hips a moment and then with an extra tug and wriggle, had flowed off her hips so that her delicately rounded abdomen shot into view, the little muff of dark hair at her pelvis and then the broad, tapering-to-slimness thighs.

The robe slumped to the stone floor in a soft swoosh.

Bending before them so that her breasts hung vertically like the suspended, heavy fruit of a tree, the girl drew the robe from off her sandals and stepped out of it altogether.

'Now you can judge', she said, with a deep lustful look at the men.

She came closer to them, as they sat, mouths open, breath escaping in painful jerks, bodies heaving irregularly with their efforts to control their breath.

Close in front of them she spun around. The firelight flickered on her flesh, shadowing the rounds and hollows of her buttocks, her breasts, her belly as she turned, throwing into relief the lightly moving muscles as they tensed sinuously in her arms and thighs.

So close were the two men that they were aware of the flesh as if the skin was throwing off a light, radiant heat which reached them. They could see the light down on her body, feel in their minds, the texture of the taut, soft-looking skin.

Still they did not move.

'Tell me now am I not beautiful?' the girl asked, gazing down at them.

'My lady, you are so beautiful that you come near to tempting us to sin against our duty, which bids us quietly guard the prisoner, and our class which bids us not to touch a lady of noble birth—save in the spoils of war.'

'Would you like to touch me?' the girl asked, flaunting her hips.

There was a moment's hesitation.

'I should like to stuff my rod into the very depths of you.' The words came out quickly in the coarse expression which was all the soldier knew. The girl smiled at him invitingly.

'And I told you how unsatisfied my lord left me—I give you that right. Stuff me, stuff me with all your might until you are exhausted.'

Both men squirmed with passion at her words—but neither moved.

'We would be killed if we were discovered,' one whispered after a while.

From his hiding place Ineni held his breath. Would their fear overcome their lust and ruin everything?

But the girl had moved up to the men where they sat, open-legged on the divan, great branches thrusting out from between their legs, lifting their tunics in a great undulation.

With a swift movement she knelt in front of them and grasped each great penis in a hand through the cloth, squeezing it, fondling it.

'I need to be satisfied,' she said passionately, 'and now you need to be. I offer you my body—a body such as you have never had. I offer you the nectar between my legs. I offer you anything you want of me. It is past midnight. Nobody will come now until the morning. You will never have this chance again.'

At the feel of her hands both men had writhed their hips uncontrollably and now the first guard, helpless against himself, leaned forward and pulled her roughly onto him, hands running voraciously, fiercely, over her body.

The girl pursued her bridgehead. Her hand slid under the guards' tunics, up their hairy thighs and then clasped, gently, the thick stiff organs she found there, clasped them and then drew soft, cool fingers up their hot lengths.

The other guard, too, not wishing to be left out, had moved in and was feeling the girl all over from a side position.

Her hands slid, relentless, down from their rods to the hot, soft expanses of their testicles. Both men groaned and wriggled in delirium.

'Come on, come on,' the girl entreated.

'Just a moment.'

The first guard tore himself away with an effort, snatched a blazing torch from the brazier and moved towards the cell door. Ineni moved swiftly and quietly back to the bed, lay down and feigned sleep. The torch flickered for a moment or two at the aperture, while the guard endeavoured to peer through the inner gloom. After a moment, satisfied, he moved away and the light receded from the door with him. Ineni rose quietly again and moved once more to the aperture.

The first guard had returned to the divan and was pawing the girl. He pulled her at him and crushed his lips on hers. From his grunt, Ineni could tell that she had slipped her little, lean tongue into his mouth. The man's hands caressed her breasts, clutching them so tightly that they bulged out around his fingers and red marks appeared on the skin as he slid over the smooth expanse.

The other man had, now, boldly slipped his hand between her open legs from behind and was fingering the slim folds of flesh, searching between them for the spot. His other hand stroked and pressed the firm, bamboo-texture of her buttocks.

For some minutes they continued thus, all three breathing fiercely.

And then the girl cried out in passion:

'Oh, put it in me. Quick, put it in me.'

She rolled off the man and flung herself down on the divan, legs wide apart. Both men moved, tunics rolled up above their loins, to get on her as she lay with eyes closed, moaning through open mouth.

Each tried to elbow the other away. Neither succeeded.

'Oh, don't fight over it,' the girl begged, voice broken with passion. 'If one of you can't wait, you can have me together.'

The men looked at her in surprise.

Quickly she rolled onto her side, reached behind her and spread the cheeks of her bottom with her hands.

'One of you must have my behind,' she said.

The two men were in no mood to argue about details. Each simply wanted to embed himself in this beautiful woman without delay.

'All right, I'll have her ass,' the second guard said through his thick breathing.

Falling over each other in their hot desire, each with an enormous penis sawing the air, they fell onto the divan on either side of the girl.

As the first guard, taking the more normal passage, pulled her legs on either side of his hips, Ineni, watching with a turbulent pang of upset in his stomach, thought: shades of the Queen of Arad—but what different circumstances and how much more depends on it.

Both men were coarse and brutal. There was no waiting, no question of finesse. Behind her, while his comrade arranged the girl's legs, the other—all reserve of class gone now—pulled apart her buttocks, spreading them with a great pull on either hand, pressing the anus open with his thumbs. An aiming. And then his fleshy organ barraged against the hole, rebounded on the first attempt, stuck on the second and with a third thrust had seared into her soft back channel to her cry of pain. He showed no gentleness, but, face screwed up in passion and fury, shagged with wild, rapid movements straight into her rectum, bursting in, with a few strokes, to the full length of his organ regardless of the girl's cries.

Meanwhile his companion, slower to get started, had succeeded in drawing up the girl's thighs on either side of him, so that one was crushed under him in the crook of his waist, the other strung limply over his hip.

Without more ado he caught her cool hand and placed it on his penis for her to place it in her vagina for him.

The girl seized it bravely and directed it into the opening of the aperture. Feeling the moist warmth around its tip, the guard heaved upwards with a flexing of his hips and his penis in turn burst into the girl in one great, gluttonous movement, forcing up and up, determined to feel the tight, painful pressure on his organ in one movement before the channel had adapted itself to his intrusion.

Another cry was drawn from the girl, but she held her own and was soon forcing her hips back at the spearing of her behind, forward at the penetration of her vagina with alternate squirms.

Her hands moved around the broad back of the first guard as he buried his organ of pulsing pleasure into her. Her arms encircled him, pulling him into her, thighs clasped him, cradling him warmly against her soft secret. Her hands roamed over his back, down to the belt until they rested on the leather sheath in which the dagger was enclosed.

For a moment, while Ineni started in a sort of hypnotised horror, she fumbled with the sheath, but was unable to unfasten it for fear of attracting attention.

Behind her, the second guard was well taken care of. Forcing his way in and in and in her tight back-passage which clasped his penis in a soft vise, he had no thought in his head but the sensual, almost unendurable pain down there at the protrusion of his loins.

The girl concentrated on the first guard, while her hand rested lightly on the dagger sheath.

'Come on, come on,' she pleaded. 'Stuff me as you said you would. Kill me, shove it in further, further.'

Goaded on, loins alight with the thrill of her coarse words, the guard stuffed and stuffed. His movements grew faster and faster until his body seemed out of control and his face was furrowed all over, his neck stretched and taut with veins standing out on it as if he were about to burst at any moment.

'Oh how wonderful! You're so thick and filling me! I can't stand it! Go on thrust your knob home.'

The girl's wild, coarse words assailed his ear, sharpening his passion, pointing it to a razor edge until it seemed that razor edges were flicking the tender extremity of his penis and then his mouth had opened in a great rough bellow as his loins opened and his juices flooded out through the phallic canal into the soft receptacle of her body.

Ineni muttered to himself, spurring the girl on. What

was she doing? In a moment it would be too late. Sweat stood on his brow and his jaw was taut as he watched.

But the girl had chosen the only moment in which success was inevitable. As the hot discharge shot in bullets into her opening and the guard's head and thoughts were filled with nothing but a furious, all-pervading thunder of release, she undid the clasp with deft fingers, drew out the knife and plunged it deep into his back all in one movement.

He gave an extra jerk which could easily have been one of passion, and let out a sharp cry of pain, which mingled with his roars of fulfilment.

The girl, her face set, eyes filled with horror, but determined in her horror, pulled out the dagger and thrust it into his back again.

Watching, his heart pounding, biting his lips, Ineni saw the little drama enacted fully. Saw the incongruity of a beautiful girl being buggered furiously, while the recent possessor of her vagina, penis still in her, clasped in her legs, gave his last twitches all unknown to his comrade. The blood flowed down from his back onto the divan while the girl wriggle uneasily free of the body. The great penis, wet and slippery with the dregs of sperm, dangled limply to the rush surface on which the body lay.

The girl held the dagger, dripping blood, in front of her. The body had swayed over onto its back. It might have been exhausted from the violent intercourse.

The girl held the dagger tightly, waiting. She didn't want to risk a false blow at the man behind her. In the meantime Ineni could see his great shaft appearing and disappearing with startling rapidity. His hands moved around to the soft belly of the girl, grasping fiercely the soft flesh, clasping and unclasping the slim folds of her abdomen.

His thighs moved up and under her, clasped her hips as his hips smashed at her in quick undulation, his penis skewering into her bottom from all angles, splitting her buttocks apart, still bringing little shrieks of sensual pain from her lips.

His mouth was open. He bit her neck so that she cried

out. His hands moved up, almost in a paroxysm to her breasts, pinching them, twisting them, digging into the nipples. His thighs twined and untwined, his hips undulated and moved in an almost rotary motion. Trying to hurry him, the girl extended her bottom at him, spreading her buttocks, straining her aperture as if she were emptying her bowels so that it met his upthrust in the middle of emptying, aiding his organ on its inward rush into her backside depths.

'Shag!' she whispered. 'Harder. You're making me sore. Make me sore. Go on, lose it in me. Push, push harder!'

Her words reached Ineni as a gentle echo in the chamber and, in passing, he thought he had taught her well, that she had played the rôle tonight well, that she had probably half-enjoyed it after the initial moments.

And then he heard the guard uttering a long drawn-out moan which grew in pitch until with a sudden convulsive thrust which almost hurled the girl onto the corpse in front of her, his penis had shattered its contents into her bottom. It continued thrusting into her in long forceful strokes and a sharp gasp at each painful release, until the reserve had dwindled and drained and the man rolled away from her, his penis sucking out with him, onto his back.

The girl turned over without a moment's hesitation and plunged the dagger into the man's heart.

Leaving it buried there she rushed to the cell door, struggled with the bar a moment and then grated it back from its staples.

Ineni pushed from inside and the door swung open and he stepped out into the chamber.

The girl flung herself, sobbing into his arms, overcome with the macabre horror of the rôle she had played. Her nerves, stretched to breaking point, had momentarily snapped.

Memoirs of a Young Don Juan

Berthe and I heard voices close by, outside the garden. We soon realised that they belonged to some servant girls who had been working in the field just beyond. Since it was now their lunch hour we stayed to watch them.

It had been raining the night before and the newly ploughed earth stuck to the girls' bare feet. Their skirts—they wore just one layer of clothing it seemed—just reached their knees. None of them were great beauties but, all the same, they were well-built sun-bronzed peasant girls, aged between twenty and thirty.

When these women had reached the stream they sat on the grassy bank and paddled their feet in the water.

While bathing their feet they jabbered away, their voices rising in competition with each other.

They sat facing us, no more than ten paces off, so that we could easily distinguish the difference in colour between their brown calves and their much whiter knees which were now completely on view. With some of them we could even make out a hint of thigh.

Berthe did not seem particularly enamoured of this exhibition and she pulled my arm for us to go.

Then we heard footsteps near by and we saw three workmen approaching along the path close to the spot where we had hidden.

At the sight of these men, some of the girls began to fuss with their clothes. One girl in particular drew attention to herself, there was something of the Spaniard in her coal black hair and clear grey eyes sparkling with mischief.

The first of the men, a dull-looking clod, took no notice of the women's presence and, standing directly in front of our hiding place, unbuttoned his trousers to pee.

He took out his member, which looked much the same as mine, except that his glans was completely hidden. He uncovered it to piss. He had lifted his shirt-tail so high that the hair surrounding his genitals was visible. He had also pulled his balls out of his trousers and was scratching them with his left hand while holding his member in his right.

I was as bored by all this as Berthe had apparently been when I had pointed out the peasant girl's calves to her, but now she was all eyes. The girls pretended not to notice him. The second man likewise unbuttoned his trousers and brought forth a prick which was smaller than his companion's, but brown and half-uncovered. He began to piss. At that the girls all burst out laughing, and their shrieks grew even more hilarious when the third also assumed the position.

By this time the first fellow had finished. He uncovered his prick completely and, shaking off the last drops, bent his knees slightly to replace the package in his pants. In so doing he let fly a clear, emphatic fart and gave an 'Aaah!' of satisfaction. Amongst the girls this gave rise to much derisive laughter.

The hilarity increased when they noticed the third fellow's joy-stick. He had placed himself on a slope, so that we could see both his member and the peasant girls seated beyond.

He raised it skyward and sent his stream arching high which set the girls laughing like lunatics. Then the men approached the maids, and one of the latter began to splash water playfully on the stupid-looking work-man. The third man remarked to the brunette who, upon seeing the men arrive, had settled her skirts:

'A lot of good it does you to hide it, Ursula. I've already seen that article you hold so dear.'

'There's plenty of things you haven't seen yet, Valentin! And a lot you'll never see,' Ursula replied coquettishly.

'You think so, do you?' said Valentin, who was now standing directly behind her.

Seizing her shoulders he forced her backward to the ground. She tried to remove her feet from the water, but neglected to keep her light skirt and blouse from billowing upward, so that she was completely exposed from the waist downward. Unfortunately, this enjoyable spectacle lasted only a few seconds.

Nevertheless it had lasted long enough for me to see that Ursula, who had already shown herself to be the proud owner of a pair of splendid calves, also possessed a pair of thighs which in themselves were worthy of the highest honours, and a bottom whose cheeks left absolutely nothing to be desired.

Between her thighs, at the bottom of her belly, lay a bush of dark hair which extended far enough to envelop both pretty lips of her cunt. But there the hair was more sparsely scattered than above, where it covered an area I could not have concealed beneath my hand.

'You see, Ursula,' said Valentin, by now quite excited, 'now I've seen your black pussy.' And without flinching he took the series of blows and insults which the girl, now really angry, rained upon him.

The second man wanted to pull the same trick with another of the girls as Valentin had tried with Ursula.

This second peasant girl was fairly pretty. Her face, neck and arms were so covered with freckles that it was almost impossible to distinguish the real colour of her skin. Her legs were also freckled, but the freckles there were larger and more dispersed. She had an intelligent look about her; her eyes were a deep brown, her hair red and crinkly. She wasn't really pretty, but nevertheless a tempting enough morsel to give a man ideas. And the workman Michel seemed to have a few. 'Helen,' he said, 'you should have a red mound. If it's black it means it must be stolen!'

'Dirty pig!' spat the lovely peasant girl.

He grabbed her as Valentin had done.

But she had had time to get to her feet, and instead of getting a glimpse of her pretty mound, Michel received such a hail of blows full in the face that he must have seen stars.

The other two girls joined in and began to pummel him.

At last he broke away and, pursued by the girls'

mocking laughter, ran to catch up with his companions.

The girls had finished bathing their feet and had left. Only Ursula and Helen remained, and they were getting ready to go.

They were whispering together. Ursula burst out laughing and, wrinkling her forehead, made a funny face. Helen was looking at her and nodding her head in assent.

The former seemed to be thinking over what the other had told her. Helen shot a glance around her to make sure that everyone had left, then quickly lifted her skirts in front and, holding them high with her left hand, slipped her right hand between her thighs at the spot where one could see a forest of red hair. By the movement of the hair, which was much thicker than Ursula's, one could see that she was squeezing herself between her fingers, though the thickness of her fleece prevented me from actually seeing the lips of her cunt. Ursula was watching her intently. Suddenly a stream shot forth from the bush of pubic hair but instead of falling straight to the ground, it arched and described a half circle in the air. Both Berthe and I were astonished to see it, for neither of us had ever imagined that women could piss like that. The operation lasted as long as it had with Valentin.

Ursula likewise seemed surprised, and apparently wanted to try it herself, but she gave up the idea, for just then the second and last bell for lunch rang, and the two girls set off rapidly.

Several days passed without anything of further note taking place.

Since the weather had turned bad, I spent most of my time in the library, where I had been pleasantly surprised to come across an anatomical atlas in which I found an illustrated description of the intimate parts of both sexes. The book also contained an explanation of pregnancy and of all the phases of maternity, none of which I had known before.

This interested me especially because the bailiff's wife

was then pregnant, and the sight of her enormous belly had greatly aroused my curiosity.

I once had heard her discussing the matter with her husband. Their quarters were on the ground floor right next to mine, near the garden.

Obviously, the events of that memorable day, when I had seen my sister naked, and afterwards the sport of the peasant girls and men, had been constantly with me. I thought of them ceaselessly and my member was constantly erect. I looked at it and played with it often. The pleasure I felt when handling it incited me to continue.

In bed I amused myself by lying on my belly and rubbing myself against the sheets. My feelings grew more and more sensitive every day. A week passed in this way.

One day when I was sitting in the old leather chair in the library, the altas open in front of me to the page describing the female genital organs, I had such an erection that I unbuttoned my trousers and took out my prick. From constant rubbing it now uncovered easily. I was as a matter of fact sixteen by now, and considered myself a man. My hair had grown thicker and resembled a handsome moustache. That particular day I felt such a profound and unaccustomed voluptousness as I rubbed it that my breathing grew short. I tightened the grip on my member, loosened it, stroking back and forth. I uncovered the tip completely, tickled my balls and my arsehole, then examined my glans, which was deep red in colour and as shiny as lacquer.

The pleasure I felt was beyond words. I ended up by discovering the rules for the fine art of masturbation, and stroked my dick regularly and rhythmically, until something happened to me that I had never experienced before.

The feeling was so voluptuous that I was forced to stretch my legs out in front of me and push against the legs of the table. My body slipped down and was pressing against the back of the chair.

I felt the blood surging into my face. My breathing was becoming difficult. I closed my eyes; my mouth dropped slightly open. A thousand thoughts raced through my mind in the space of a minute.

My aunt, in front of whom I had stood naked, my sister, whose pretty little pussy I had explored, the powerful thighs of the two maids—all these images flew across my mind. My hand stroked my prick faster and faster. An electric shock coursed through my body.

My aunt! Berthe! Ursula! Helen! . . . I felt my member swell, and from the dark red glans sprayed forth a whitish liquid, first with a powerful jet, followed by others less forceful. I had just discharged for the first time.

My engine softened rapidly. I now looked with interest and curiosity at the sperm which had spilled into my right palm. It both looked and smelled like the white of an egg, it was thick like glue. I licked it and found it to taste like a raw egg. I shook off the last few drops clinging to the tip of my member, which was now completely subdued, and wiped it on my shirt.

I knew, from what I had previously read, that I had just given myself up to the pleasures of onanism. I looked the word up in the dictionary, and found a long article on the subject, in such detail that anyone who had not previously been aware of the practice would inevitably have been fully enlightened.

The article had once again excited me. The fatigue resulting from my first ejaculation was past. The only tangible evidence of my act was a devouring appetite. At table my aunt and mother remarked upon my appetite, but dismissed it as merely due to growth.

I soon came to realize that onanism is like drink: the more you have, the more you want . . .

My prick was constantly hard, and my thoughts increasingly voluptuous, but the pleasures of Onan could not satisfy me forever. I thought of women and is seemed a shame for me to waste my sperm masturbating.

My tool became darker, and pubic hair a handsome beard, my voice deepened, and a few microscopic hairs appeared on my upper lip. I realized that I lacked only one experience of manhood: *coitus*—that was the term used in books for the activity that was still unknown to me.

All the women of the household noticed the changes that had taken place in me, and I was no longer treated as a child.

The next day, after my morning coffee, the bailiff's wife came in to clean up my room.

I've alrady mentioned that she was pregnant, and I carefully studied the enormous contour of her belly, and the unusual size of her breasts which swung to and fro beneath her light blouse.

She was a pleasant looking woman with pretty features. Until the bailiff had put her in the family way she had been one of the château's maids.

I had already seen women's breasts in pictures and on statues, but never in the flesh.

The bailiff's wife was in a great hurry. She had buttoned only one of her blouse buttons. When she leaned over to straighten my bed, this solitary button came undone, and I saw her entire bosom, for the vest she was wearing was very low-cut.

I sprang to my feet: 'Madam, you'll catch cold!' And pretending to help her rebutton her dress, I untied the ribbon holding it on her shoulders. As I did so her two breasts seemed to leap out of their hiding place, and I felt their bulk and firmness.

The buttons on each breast stood out, they were red and surrounded by a large brownish halo.

Her teats were as firm as a pair of buttocks, and as I fondled them with both hands I could have sworn they were a pretty girl's behind.

The woman was so astonished that I had time, before she recovered her wits, to kiss her nipples at leisure.

She smelled of sweat, but in a way that excited me. It was that *odor di femina* which, as I was later to learn, emanates from a woman's body and, according to the individual, provokes either desire or disgust.

'Oh, ooh! What are you thinking of?—No . . . that's

not right . . . I'm a married woman . . . not anything in the world.'

These were her words as I steered her towards the bed. I had opened my dressing gown and lifted my nightshirt, revealing my member in a dreadful state of excitement.

'Let me alone. I'm pregnant. Oh, Lord God, if anyone should see us!'

She was still resisting, but less forcefully.

As a matter of fact her gaze had not left my sexual parts. She was supporting herself against the bed on to which I was trying to push her.

'You're hurting me!'

'My dear lady, no one can see or hear you.'

Now she was sitting on the bed. I was still pushing. She lay back and closed her eyes.

My state of excitement was beyond all bounds. I lifted her dress, her petticoat, and saw a pair of thighs which fired my enthusiasm even more than had the peasant girls'. Between the closed thighs I caught sight of a small tangle of chestnut-coloured hairs, among which the crack was concealed.

I dropped to my knees, seized her thighs, felt them all over, caressed them, laid my cheeks upon them and covered them with kisses. My lips advanced from the thighs to her mound of Venus, her smell excited me still further.

I lifted her skirt even higher and looked with astonishment at the enormous bulk of her belly, upon which the naval was raised instead of hidden in a hollow like my sister's.

I licked her belly button. She lay motionless, her breasts hanging down on either side. I lifted one of her legs and placed it on the bed. Her cunt came into view. At first I was frightened by the big thick puffy lips coloured a reddish brown.

Her pregnancy gave me a chance to revel in that sight. Her lips were spread and when I darted a glance inside I discovered a real butcher's stall of moist red meat.

Near the top of the lips was the pee hole, crowned by a

small bean of flesh which I knew from my study of the anatomical atlas must be the clitoris.

The upper part of her slit was lost in the hair covering her overly fleshy mound of Venus. The lips were almost hairless, and the skin between the thighs was damp and red from sweat.

All in all it was not a very appetizing picture, but I appreciated it nevertheless because the woman was very clean. I could not help inserting my tongue into her crevice and licking it hastily before moving to the clitoris, which hardened under my passionate tonguing.

I soon tired of this sport, and since the crevice was by now well moistened, I replaced my tongue with my finger. Then I laid hold of her breasts, taking the tips in my mouth and sucking them by turns. I kept my finger on the clitoris, which grew harder and larger until it was as thick as a pencil.

At that point the woman came to her senses and began to whimper but without leaving the position into which I had forced her. I felt slightly sorry for her, but I was too worked up to really care. I talked to her cajolingly, trying to comfort her, and ended up by promising to stand as godfather for the child she was expecting.

I went over and, taking some money from the drawer, handed it to her. She had by then got herself decent again. So I lifted my nightshirt, but felt somewhat ashamed to find myself naked again in front of a woman, especially one who was married and pregnant.

I took her moist hand and placed it on my member. The touch was exquisite.

She squeezed, gently at first, then more firmly. I had grasped her breasts, which held a strange fascination for me.

I kissed her on the mouth, and she readily gave me her lips.

My whole being was attuned to pleasure. I placed myself between her thighs, but she exclaimed:

'Not on top of me. It hurts too much. I can't do it the front way any more.'

She got off the bed, turned round and bent over with her face on the bed. She said nothing else, but my instinct supplied me with the solution of the enigma. I remembered once having seen two dogs doing it that way. Following Médor's example, I lifted Diana's skirt—that was her name.

Her bottom appeared before me, a bottom such as I had never even dreamed of. Berthe's may have been pleasing, but it was really nothing next to this. My two cheeks put together wouldn't have made a half of one of these miraculous firm-fleshed buttocks. Like all beautiful breasts and thighs, her bottom was a dazzling white.

In the slit were some blond hairs, and the crack itself was like a chasm dividing her superb cheeks.

Below the colossal buttocks, between the thighs, lay the fat juicy cunt, in which my probing finger burrowed.

I placed my chest against the woman's bare backside and with my arms tried to encircle her elusive belly, which hung down like some stately globe.

I caressed her cheeks, then rubbed my member against them. But my curiosity was not yet satisfied. I spread her cheeks and inspected her arse-hole. Like her navel, it was elevated and though brown, was very clean.

I started to insert my finger, but she gave such a start that I was afraid I had hurt her, so I didn't press the point. I placed my burning prick in her cunt; it was like a knife cutting into a mound of butter. Then I went at it like a madman, slamming my belly against her elastic behind.

I was like one possessed. I was no longer conscious of what I was doing, but I reached the voluptuous climax, and for the first time in my life shot my sperm into a woman's cunt.

After the discharge I wanted to stay for a while in that agreeable position, but the bailiff's wife turned round and chastely arranged her clothes. While she was rebuttoning her blouse, I heard the sound of something dripping: it was my sperm running from her cunt on to the floor. She smeared it underfoot, and dried her thighs on her skirt.

When she saw me standing in front of her, with my red,

moist prick partly erect, she smiled, took out her handkerchief and meticulously dried it.

'Get dressed, now, Monsieur Roger,' she said. 'I've got to go now. And for the love of God,' she added, blushing, 'don't let anyone hear about what happened just now or I'll never forgive you.'

We embraced, exchanged kisses, and she departed, leaving me lost in a flood of new sensations.

Sarah

On the day in question I had no knowledge of my true self. I knew I loved Nature—flowers, animals, scents, textures; the spidery crawl of Grandmother's fine lace shawl on the back of my hand, the soft fur of Olive's old tomcat when he allowed himself to be stroked, indeed the feel of my own smooth flesh on the insides of my upper arms and thighs gave me pleasure. I handled my body with care and confidence but up till now I had let it live its own life and it seemed to get on pretty well without my worrying about it. My breasts were full and firm, my hips rounded and womanly and my belly swelled gently down to a tidy thicket of springy curls, a shade of brownish blonde just darker than the hair on my head. Of the uses to which my attributes might be put, and of the power and pleasure my body could afford me, I had as yet no knowledge.

This night there was no family dinner to arrange as the family was dining out. To my surprise the atmosphere in the servants' hall was far removed from that I had come to expect. On the table stood a collection of bottles which Jarvis was fussing over with a proprietory air.

'Sarah, my dear,' he called as I entered the room, 'come and join our little celebration.'

I approached the table with some trepidation. I had so far received little in the way of friendship from my companions below stairs. Although they had not been cruel to me, until now I had thought of myself as an outsider and tolerated out of necessity. Of the three, Jarvis had been by far the most kindly though our respective duties had thrown us very little into one another's company.

Now he pulled up a chair for me and poured me a

generous draught of liquor.

'Mr Jarvis,' announced Winifred for my benefit, 'has had a little fortune with the gee-gees.'

'A *little* fortune,' said Milly in an ironic tone which implied a weighty addition to the Jarvis coffers.

'A considerable stroke of luck,' cried Jarvis, 'for which I claim no credit beyond the happy accident of running into the only honest Irishman ever to have quit the Emerald Isle.'

'Be careful, Mr Jarvis,' I said, the taste of courage, in the form of gin, burning the back of my throat, 'my father was an Irishman and he was as honest as he was poor.'

'Then let us drink to the memory of your father,' cried Jarvis, holding his glass aloft, 'and bless him for bestowing on the world a lass with such a delightful pair of blue eyes.'

By this I took it that he meant myself and was thus totally disarmed. The other two hooted and made such noises as are the aural equivalent of a dig in the ribs. I had, of course, observed that all parties were ahead of me in terms of liquid refreshment and as a consequence were somewhat drunk. Winifred gazed on me with a motherly benevolence I had not thought possible from one usually so stern; and Milly was as friendly and solicitous of my comfort as she was habitually reserved. I downed my gin and observed that the glass was smartly refilled.

I must make it clear that, though innocent at this time, I was not totally ignorant of the ways of men with women. I was not unduly modest by nature. I knew that my face and my figure rarely went unremarked by the male sex. It would have been extraordinary had I achieved my present age without having to encounter advances. And encountered them I had, though mostly of a fumbling, immature sort and, once or twice, of a more direct but fortunately also drunkenly ineffectual nature. Thus far my swift feet and sober wits had preserved me from nothing more dangerous than a few beery kisses and some heavy-handed fumbling at my bosom.

I could see, of course, that Jarvis was giving me the glad eye and, though surprised by the sudden turn of events, I was not displeased.

He was a compact man, upright and well-formed, only recently past his fortieth year—or so I guessed—with a kindly face and, at the moment, an unmistakably lecherous grin.

'I propose a toast,' he said, 'to the sweetest pair . . . ' and here he looked at me ' . . . of lips . . .' here he turned to Winifred ' . . in the kingdom.' At this he seized her and planted a smacking kiss full on her mouth—which did not appear to displease her in the least. In truth, in the half light, with her hair and bodice loose, Winifred looked fully worthy of any affection he might care to bestow on her.

'And now,' cried Jarvis, 'a toast to the finest pair of . . . thighs.' And he launched himself at Milly. There was a squealing and giggling and the scrape of chairs on the floor as Milly sprang up to avoid this sudden assault—thus facilitating Jarvis's attempt to lift her skirts and display her legs.

'Oh, you filthy beast,' she muttered as he hauled her clothing up to her waist. However it seemed to me that she did not protest overmuch and she could surely have done more to prevent the display of her trim and shapely limbs. Jarvis had now successfully laid bare an expanse of creamy white thigh, prettily framed by the close cut legs of her blue drawers and the tops of her stockings.

Still holding her firmly around the waist, with her skirts cleverly pinned out of the way behind her, Jarvis allowed his free hand to stroke and play across her exquisitely exposed legs.

'Look at these pretties,' he urged us, 'did I tell you a lie? Hasn't she got the prettiest, smoothest, whitest pair of thighs? . . .' and so on, all the while running his hand up and over and down the girl's naked flesh. I watched in fascination as his hand crossed over from one leg to the other, fingers running down under her stocking tops, then up underneath the hem of her knickers; then pressing gently with his third finger on the junction of her thighs as his hand fluttered over her most secret triangle. Then two fingers lingered, searching for her very groove beneath the material of her drawers.

'Oh my,' said Milly to no one and laid her head on Jarvis's shoulder.

His hand was strong, stubby, coarse, with filed down nails, blunt fingers and black hairs sprouting between the knuckles. A plain gold band twinkled on the little finger—which now insinuated itself beneath the edging of Milly's underthings. Tantalisingly Jarvis opened the leg of the garment and lifted it up to expose a thatch of black nether-hair. He teased the curls, twined and toyed with the strands to reveal the pouting lips of Milly's most intimate portion. So slowly that I could almost feel its agonising progress upon my own skin, Jarvis's little finger slipped between those tender pink lips and into the very quick of her.

'Oh,' murmured Milly as Jarvis eased in up to the joint and then out and then in again. I watched without breathing as the finger withdrew and, moistened with Milly's evident excitement, slid up to that sensitive spot at the apex of her love-lips. Milly bucked and squealed and rolled her buttocks back against Jarvis's legs but he held her firm, determined, it seemed, to spur her agitation to fever pitch. The gold ring on his finger winked in and out of view, glistening with her juices. A heady smell hung in the air. As I leant forward to drink in the mesmerising sight, I crossed and uncrossed my legs.

Now Jarvis was running the slippery metal of his ring over the pink nub of flesh evermore protuberant at the top of Milly's slit. Faster and faster he rubbed as the girl's breath came in short gasps, now interspersed with an uninhibited string of words that I'm sure she was unaware of uttering:

'Oh, yes, ooh yes, faster, faster, please, frig, yes, frig, do me nicely please, oh Jackie, you beast, stop, don't let me come, poke me, poke me please, oooh, aaah, I want your cock Jackie, oh they're watching, God don't stop, oh so nice, in my cunt, cock, cunt, fuck me after—OH, OH . . .'

In a flurry of wriggling hips and quivering thighs Milly jerked and shuddered and, for a few seconds, seemed to quite lose control of her limbs—if Jarvis had not been holding her I'm sure she would have collapsed in a heap on the floor.

'And now,' said Mr Jarvis, fixing me with the eyes of a starving man, 'who's next?'

To my surprise Winifred said, 'I think it's time we saw exactly what our new girl is made of,' and she pulled me up from my chair.

Truth to tell, such was my state of agitation by this time that I would have happily thrown myself into the arms of Jackie Jarvis had we been by ourselves. But to display such intimate emotions as I had just witnessed before Winifred and the shameless Milly was too much to ask.

However the other participants in this scene of unbridled lechery had different intentions. At Winifred's suggestion Milly had roused herself from her swoon and now latched a firm hand round my wrist.

'Come on, Sarah,' she said, 'be a sport, let's see what's beneath that Goody Two Shoes pinafore.'

And before I knew it Winifred had my other hand and the two held me fast.

'Now Jack,' said Winifred in a voice of sobriety, 'I imagine you'd like to examine Sarah in detail to see if she measures up to the high expectations Lord Coddrington entertains of her.'

'Indeed I would,' said he, 'I know for a fact his Lordship is looking forward to a full report.'

Winifred had contrived to stand behind me and, using her advantage of height and weight, she had forced me up on to my toes with my chest thrust forward and my hands imprisoned behind my back. Milly now began to unbutton and loosen and untuck my clothing so rapidly that, held in the housekeeper's firm grip, there was little I could do to prevent her.

In seconds Milly had unbuttoned my pinafore and laid open the bodice to reveal just the simple undershift that lay between my bare bosom and the burning gaze of three pairs of eyes.

'Well, well,' said Milly, insolently running her hands

over my breasts and feeling them through the material, 'ain't you a well-built girl.'

It was not possible to remove my shift without releasing my hands but, to my dismay, Milly proceeded to slide the straps of the garments off my shoulders. Thus she insinuated the article down my body then, delicately sliding her hands beneath the material onto the naked flesh of my bosom, she lifted my breasts free of their flannel covering.

I knew myself to be rudely displayed, my flesh thrust out into bold relief by Winnie's pressure on my back; my big breasts white and trembling, my shameless nipples pinkly engorged.

They then proceeded to have their fun with me. First Milly stroked and handled my titties, making their delicate tips tingle in a disturbing way.

'Your skin is so smooth,' she said.

'Have you no shame, Milly?' I asked.

'No,' she said simply and kissed me on the lips.

Winnie was less gentle with me in her turn but her rough handling only seemed to fan the spark that Milly's softer ministrations had ignited. Though I was now allowed freedom of movement somehow I made no attempt to break away.

'Take off her clothes,' commanded Jarvis, 'I need to take a closer look at her for his Lordship's sake.'

They lifted me on to a chair in the full glare of the gas light. Eager hands pulled at the fastenings that remained intact. I made no protest and lifted my limbs as required to enable them to disrobe me. Very shortly they had reduced me to just my stockings.

They lifted me onto a chair in the full glare of the light. I tried to cover myself with my hands but Winifred commanded me to hold them behind my back—or else she would make me.

I felt so exposed! I was mortified to exhibit my body this way—yet it had the hypnotic quality of a dream: a dream I often had in which I was displayed naked to faceless strangers and made to adopt poses for their amusement. It seemed that there was a part of my nature that understood what was happening to me better than I did myself.

My audience was delighted with the spectacle I made and generous in their compliments. These remarks were nectar to my vanity. Though I knew that I was fairly made, I had never before been so brutally exposed nor so carefully scrutinised.

'Isn't she a tasty morsel?' asked the housekeeper of Jarvis.

'My eye,' said he in tones of approval. 'A right cracker, I'd say.'

They made me turn back and forth, hold my arms above my head, then turn round so they could feast their eyes full on the flesh of my backside. The nip of my waist, the curve of my hips, the jut of my breasts, the swell of my bottom—all seemed to please them greatly.

Jarvis told me to face him and place my feet apart.

'Open up, my dear,' he said, taking a seat next to the chair on which I stood. 'I have Lord Coddrington's business to attend to.'

'Oh sir,' I cried, 'his Lordship must never know of this! You wouldn't tell him surely!'

'I might and I might not,' came the reply. 'But I can assure you that his Lordship would be most interested in that extraordinary treasure you are attempting to conceal from me just at this moment!'

'Feet apart,' cried Winnie and, seizing my ankles, she forced me into a position of some indelicacy. With Jarvis seated as he was, my most intimate portion was but a few inches from his prurient gaze.

My shame was now nearly complete, for the air was thick with a scent which I knew must be my own and they could clearly see the dew that moistened my sexual parts.

'And now the most important question,' announced Jarvis, '. . . is she still a virgin?'

'I am indeed,' I cried, for it was true.

'I hope so, my dear, for I paid out a lot of his Lordship's money.'

I was hardly in a position to ask him to elucidate on

these mysterious remarks. Indeed I hardly heard them as he delicately ran a finger up the inside of my thigh, from my stocking top to the alert and tender skin adjacent to the triangle of blonde curls that covered my mount. There he delved his inquisitive digit into my moist and hidden groove.

'Oh,' I cried, my loins twitching as a dart of sensation shot through me. 'Oh sir, please don't. This is most indecent.'

But Jarvis had no mercy on my shame and, had he shown any, I dare say his accomplices in debauchery would have been cruelly disappointed. In truth the sensations in my private parts were such that I would have been a little disappointed myself.

Now his fingers were playing with me at will; nibbling and stroking and paddling in my sodden thicket, finding my most secret nub of pleasure and agitating it so sweetly and so knowingly that my knees gave way and I collapsed into the arms of his two lecherous handmaidens.

They laid me on the table, on my back, and spread my legs on either side of the seated Jarvis. It was a grotesque and yet most titillating arrangement—in which the man sat at table to feast on the most succulent part of my anatomy. On either side of me were Winifred and Milly who fondled my neck and shoulders and breasts.

Jarvis now had total possession of my trecherous sexual portion and proceeded to insinuate a finger right into me.

'She's tight enough,' he muttered as his insistent digit eased into my virgin orifice. Then its passage ceased, its progress inhibited by the natural barrier of my uncorrupted state. A broad smile broke across the manservant's features.

'Your mother's an honest woman,' he said to me, 'and so are you it seems.'

'So, she's a virgin, is she—are you sure?' With this Winnie plunged her hand between my legs in Jarvis's place.

Though I recoiled from her fumbling there was little I could do. Indeed I was past the point of any resistance at all. I was totally bewildered—by my humiliation, by this talk of Lord Coddrington and my mother, by the praise heaped upon my person and, above all, by the overwhelming sensations in my most secret parts. It was dawning on me then that my body was not the uncomplicated mechanism I had always believed it to be. At the moment it seemed to have a will and an appetite of its own. Even the coarse manipulations of a matron old enough to be my mother were as the exquisite fingering of a musician on the strings of a harp. And when she took her hand away I could have wept for another player to have taken up the tune. In such a state I was hardly aware of what they were saying.

'She's pure all right,' agreed Winnie.

'And she's a hot little filly, too,' came the reply, 'look at her jib her cunt up, she wants it that bad. For two pins I'd give it to her and his Lordship could go hang.'

But that was not to be my fate.

There was a sound of giggling and a slithering and flapping of clothes. I opened my eyes to see Jarvis, his garments at his feet, stark naked in the dappled light of the fire. His chest was matted with thick black hair, his simian arms hung by his sides and from the forest of hair in his loins sprung a thick staff, its head angry and glistening.

Milly now stood in front of me, her dark hair loose about her shoulders, the points of her breasts clearly outlined through the material of her shift. To my surprise she pulled my thighs apart and bent down to support her elbows on the table between my legs. Suddenly, it seemed, my thighs were captured in the crooks of her arms and her face was buried right between my legs.

'Oh, what are you doing?' I shrieked as Milly's thin warm lips sought out my agitated slit as eagerly as a pig after a truffle.

'She's going to gamahuche you, my darling,' whispered Winnie in my ear. 'You just lie back and enjoy yourself. Mr Jarvis is going to take her from behind so he can enjoy the adorable spectacle you will make. Now you see how much we love you!'

I knew enough not to trust the old bawd, but in one particular she was not lying for Jarvis had upped Milly's shift from behind and was dandling the buttocks now thrust saucily towards him.

With a shameless gesture he ran his fingers in the juice of her crack and anointed the tip of his bobbing organ. Then he positioned himself rudely behind her and slid his shaft smoothly home. I felt the tremor of his entry transmit itself through the gasp and tremble of her lips on my nether-mouth. It was as if the three of us were worms skewered on one pin, wiggling and thrashing in an indistinguishable erotic agony.

Winnie too was transfixed by the same passion. At Jarvis's direction she had unfastened the pinning of her dress so that her huge white dugs now billowed out of her bodice and her skirts were up to her waist exposing the creamy flesh of her belly.

'Frig yourself, Winnie,' commanded Jarvis and the matron needed no second urging. She plunged her hand between her legs and began to manipulate her capacious hole with practised dexterity, spreading her legs as wide as she could and pulling open the flaps of her cunt at Jarvis's instruction.

He now surveyed us all in a libidinous frenzy. To excite his lust still further he told me to place my hand on Winnie's love-hole and to frig her as I would myself. I was willing to indulge this lechery but I did not know how, never having even done it to myself. Winnie herself showed me by placing her hand over mine and directing the play of my fingers over her bewitching motte.

Thus did the four of us take our pleasures. Jarvis pumping into Milly's delectable rear end, she milking and nuzzling my aching nether spot and Winnie writhing and twisting under the eager ministrations of my novice touch.

Though until now I had been a stranger to these delicious pleasures, I knew instinctively that there must be a coming crisis of the flesh. I could feel an emotion building within me that must soon have physical release.

'Oh Lord,' I heard myself say, 'oh heavens, oh dear,'

and it seemed a chorus of cries burst from us all at the same time. Even Milly, with her mouth glued fast to the hungry well between my thighs, seemed to sing a song of ecstacy into my very vitals as a white wave surged through my entire frame and threw me up into a blaze of sunlight and onto a warm, soft bed of bliss.

I opened my eyes to find my head pillowed on the bountiful still-heaving bosom of Winnie the housekeeper. I knew now that the world would never be the same.

Debauched yet still virgin, I awoke the next morning to the knowledge that the world itself contained a world that I knew nothing of. It was strange to think that I had always carried with me the key to this mysterious and intoxicating land and yet only now did I realise how to unlock its secrets.

Lying on my narrow bed with the day not yet begun, I took stock of the events of the previous evening. It was now plain to me why Olive, my step-mother, had been only too happy to see me go. I wondered how much money had found its way into her purse to compensate her for my absence and my usefulness about her house. Yet the realisation that I had been sold for my virginity did not strike me with horror as it might other girls in my situation. The shame, the fear, the praise, the pleasure—this new knowledge had changed me irrevocably from the girl who had come to this house just a few days before.

So this was what men and women did! It explained a great deal to me, made sense of the way my step-mother with her heavy figure and slatternly habits had besotted my father. I had seen them lying together, on top of the bed one hot summer's day and he palping and patting the big moon cheeks of her arse. It made sense too of the way Lord Coddrington's eyes followed me, dwelling on every curve of my uniformed figure—and maybe also of how his children had regarded me in the drawing-room the previous day.

Here lay the crux of my present dilemma. It was obvious that I was shortly to be whisked into his Lordship's bed for his enjoyment of the charms which Jarvis had so reluctantly refrained from sampling. When, I wondered, was my defloration to take place? Now that I had been subjected to the intimate scrutiny of Jarvis and company I could only presume it would be soon.

I confess to an immodest confusion. Most chaste girls in my situation would have plotted their escape from this licentious house—or fainted dead away from terror. But I knew already that I was one of nature's libertines albeit, as I now think, a foolish one. My concern was not to preserve my virginity—or to sell it to the highest bidder—but to bestow it for love. I knew I did not want to yield my maidenhead to an old lecher, no matter how noble or wealthy. I wanted to give it up to William, he of the elegant bearing and warm smile.

I wondered what he would look like in the place of Jarvis in my reminiscence of the orgy in the servant's hall. Would his organ thrust, club-like, from his belly like that stiff, threatening sword of flesh that Jarvis bore? I could not picture it precisely yet the thought excited me. I recalled the way William had regarded me the day before and his words—'a remarkably pretty child'—surely he would accept from me the gift of my virginity?

As I teased at this prospect in my imagination, my fingers naturally strayed to that now mysterious spot between my thighs and made an exploration in the light of my new knowledge. I rubbed the coarse short hairs on my mound and gently pulled open the wings of my cunt to probe within. I traced the outline of a bearded mouth and rolled the tender lips between my fingers, feeling the tingle of remembered new pleasures as I did so.

With both hands now, my legs asplay, I felt inside my hot passage and tried to imagine the entry of such an instrument as Jarvis's. In my mind's eye the bright red plum of his staff took on enormous proportions. Surely such a big thing could not be inserted into the confines of such a narrow corridor? Yet was Milly made so differently to me? She had engulfed that monstrous organ to the hilt, to his hairy balls which had battered her buttocks as he thrust into her! It was such a mystery. A delicious, exciting mystery that held me in a spell I had no wish to break.

Thus, my fingers now stroking, fondling, encircling the nub of flesh at the stop of my split, I frigged myself into a frenzy. Yet I was clumsy. It seemed I was chasing something not quite within my grasp and though I was flooded with a sudden warmth I was not able to scratch at my real itch.

It was time to get up, to clear and lay fires and embark on my daily chores. If I failed to perform my tasks I was certain to be upbraided by Winnie but, after last night, when I had witnessed her puffing and wheezing in the heat of her passion, and when it was I myself who had dictated the ebb and flow of her lusts, I no longer felt fearful of her authority. Besides, evidently I had not been added to the household for my abilities as a drudge. The fires could wait, I had another scheme.

I upped and dressed as quietly as I could. Yet in my impatience I could not help blundering into the end of Milly's bed which lay between my own and the door. She called to me in a voice heavy with sleep, asking if it was time for her to rise. I bent and spoke to the mass of dark hair that fanned over her pillow.

'Go back to sleep,' I whispered. Her face was barely visible but it seemed her eyes were still shut. 'I'll take the teas up.'

I tapped gently on Miss Hilda's door. From behind the door came a muffled sound which I took to be a summons to enter. I did so, bearing the tea tray and with my excuses for Milly already half out of my mouth.

And there they remained, frozen on my tongue, as I regarded the tableau before me. Miss Hilda's bed faced the door so, on the threshold of the room, I looked directly at its foot. As beds go it was a large and sturdy article, as indeed it needed to be to support the vigorous activity that was taking place upon it. I gazed, it seemed, upon a human octopus at whose centre clenched and writhed and thrust a pair of naked male buttocks. The pale skin of this gyrating seat was downed in dark fuzz, growing thick and black in the rude seam which bisected it. Above this mesmerising sight waved, inexplicably, a female foot whose toes wriggled and flexed in dainty abandon.

As my eyes grew accustomed to the dim light I struggled to make sense of the strange shape. Amid the wreckage of the bed linen, the bedraggled sheets half on the floor, I made out the columns of a man's strong thighs as he knelt forwards, a sturdy brown back and a dangling pouch of skin which waggled coarsely beneath the muscular cheeks of that dancing arse. Now I could see that the man had Hilda's legs slung high about his neck and that he was supporting them both in this position, thrusting deep within her body with fiercely energetic strokes. I could hear their breathing, he with slow deep pants, she on a quicker note that indicated laughter—or tears.

My mind was in a turmoil. In my ignorance it seemed incredible that two people could accomplish such things. And Miss Hilda, so well-mannered and proper—and here so abandoned! Or was I witnessing the violent sack of her virtue? Was her bedfellow some crude ruffian who had broken into the house and was now raping my mistress before my eyes? Yet I knew this could not be the case, if only by the way her fingers were toying feverishly with the short black curls that grew at the back of his neck.

Convinced by now that the lovers were too transported to have noticed my ill-timed entrance, I began to edge backwards out of the doorway when Hilda spoke. Her voice was low and breathless but it addressed itself unmistakably to me.

'Put the tray down Milly, you little trollop, and run along. You've seen enough.'

Now did not seem the right moment to explain that Milly was indisposed. Indeed, I imagined that it would cause a degree of consternation were I to do so. Accordingly, my mind buzzing with the implications of Hilda's remarkable speech, I placed the tea tray on the dressing table by the door and turned to go.

As I did so I cast one last inquisitive glance backwards. To my surprise the man on the bed turned to look at me. Then he deliberately shifted position to show me his thick brown staff plunging hungrily into the pink-lipped nest now revealed between Miss Hilda's suspended thighs. For a moment he held it still, in full view, at the entrance to her wet and hungry passage and grinned at me in shameless masculine pride. Then, as her cries mounted to a higher pitch, he stuffed it home deep inside her.

I left the room with my heart hammering against my ribs. What I had seen was coarse, vulgar, obscene. Yet it had affected me profoundly and what disturbed me most was that I wanted this rude spectacle for myself. I wanted muscular arms round *my* body, a mouth fast like a leech to *my* mouth and a big engine like that one bolting between *my* thighs. I leant against the wall in the corridor outside the bedroom and closed my eyes as the blood raced crazily through my veins.

The swirl of passion had scarcely abated by the time I entered Mr William's bedroom, bearing yet another tray in my trembling hands. His room stood on the second floor of the house, facing east, and already early morning spring sunshine had pierced the gaps in the drawn curtains of the high windows. A broad hand of pale sunlight fell squarely across the bed and the still form that lay between its crisp white sheets.

Mr William was deep in slumber, his mouth half-open and a sleepy gurgle in his breath, whose regular respiration both reassured me and aggravated my fear of discovery. I had no conscious plan but it seemed my body had more knowledge of my purpose than my lust drunk brain.

I took hold of the hem of the top sheet and slowly pulled. With surprising facility the bed coverings yielded to my naughty purpose and fell away from the unconscious form that lay beneath. Already uncaring of the consequences, I drew the sheet back to reveal the object of my desires.

He lay on his back, his limbs spread wide, one arm tucked up underneath the pillow. He wore just a simple night-shirt, unbuttoned at the neck to reveal an expanse of tender, boyish chest and which, in the manner of such garments had ridden up during his night's repose and was now rucked high around his waist. Thus I could gaze with sinful fascination on his almost naked form. He was slender, pale, almost girlish in his making—so different from the brutish Jarvis and the coarse ruffian I had seen but recently lewdly frolicking in Miss Hilda's boudoir. This was no vulgar ape who would leer obscenely at a woman as he roughly violated her femininity. Here lay a beautiful angel who would—surely—divest me of my maidenhead with tenderness and consideration.

But let me not be coy. Of course my eyes were drawn, above all, to the junction of the man's thighs; drawn there first and last to scrutinise every fold of flesh, every mole, every downy hair—every aspect of the instrument which I hoped would disencumber me of my virgin state. And here, indeed, was cause for fascination. If there was a marked contrast between William and the other men I had observed in their natural state, then here lay its epitome. Though the other two manly organs I had seen had been engaged, so to speak, and this one was in repose, here surely was a different order of masculinity.

The article in question lay curled like a tiny sleeping mouse on a cushion of two blue pigeon's eggs. There was no hair there to speak of, just a transparent fuzz of down which I could only observe by sinking to my knees at the side of the bed and bending my head close to the root of my curiosity.

What interested me above all was the mysterious hood of skin which covered the head of this exquisite article and ended in a curl of pretty pink flesh. Where was the great red plum, the focus of Jarvis's battering ram, that had so inflamed my imagination? Could it be wrapped within that dainty fold of flesh, hidden and asleep just like its owner?

My inquisitive nature was in no state to be denied. I cautiously raised my hand and, as gently as I could, ran my forefinger down the length of the tiny organ. The skin was as soft and smooth as a new born baby's. I glanced anxiously at William's face. There was no change in his features or in his regular breathing. He slept on. I touched him with my finger again. And again.

It seemed to me now that the mouse was stirring in its sleep. Now, when I gently stroked the tender crest of flesh I could see that the animal was waking up, was growing miraculously before my eyes. Emboldened, I began to tickle beneath its chin and the head began to twitch. Then—oh my—the whole organ gave a leap and jerked upwards out of my hand. Mouse no more, it had metamorphosed into a stiff snake which pointed upwards against William's belly and danced with a life of its own.

And now I could see the answer to the conundrum that had puzzled me as a pink bulb of flesh stretched the tender rose of skin on the hood of the serpent and emerged into view. Here was the vision that had haunted me since the night before. To be sure, the article was smaller and slimmer than the weapon that had inspired and inflamed me but it was, nonetheless, a worthy recipient of my virtue.

With thumb and forefinger I encircled the neck of this pretty wand and worked the roll of skin beneath the head up and down. I wanted to make the pink nut disappear and reappear, to see again the trick that had so delighted me, but the skin was dry and would not slide freely at my touch. Unthinkingly—instinctively, I suppose—I wetted my fingers with my tongue and applied the lubrication. To my delight the skin rolled up completely to conceal the head, then down again to reveal it once more. It now glowed a deep red in startling contrast to the pearly white shaft on which it so proudly sat.

I leaned closer to drink in this male mystery, to savour the aroma of sleep and sex that rose from William's body. The fat red nut wagged just inches from my lips as I jiggled and fiddled with it, transported in my idiot lust.

What happened next, happened all at once and it seemed that I was powerless to prevent it.

'For God's sake,' said a voice, as a hand grasped the

back of my head, 'suck the bloody thing properly.'

And before I could protest, my gentle plaything was propelled between my lips, full into my mouth. There it leapt and jumped as I fought against the insistent pressure on my head which held me fast against his loins.

I could hear William's voice talking in fast, urgent breaths as I stared into his stomach and he thrust and bored and stuffed his truncheon into my mouth.

'I've been watching you, you little minx. I've been awake for a while, observing your tricks. By golly, now you'll have to take what's coming to you—'

And with a flurry of twitches and jerks his staff exploded in my mouth, flooding me with a salty, choking deluge.

Confessions of an English Maid

The days slipped into weeks, the weeks imperceptibly, into months, and almost before I realized it, a year had gone by.

Miraculously, I had escaped all three of the afflictions whose menacing shadows are ever close at the heels of those who traffic with their sexual favours: syphilis, gonorrhea and pregnancy, the Three Horsemen of the Prostitute's Apocalypse.

My health was good, and I had gained in weight, having added several pounds of flesh which improved my figure even though at the cost of some of the juvenile slimness which in the beginning had been such a valuable asset. Nevertheless, I had for some time been observing a gradual change in my physical orgasm which was becoming more and more pronounced, and the condition was one which is not common in the walk of life I frequented.

I will speak plainly. Sexual sensibility, which is that capacity to respond easily and actively to erotic excitation, diminishes rapidly in the majority of professional prostitutes who are obliged to exercise their sexual functions with a frequency far in excess of the provisions of Nature. The sexual act becomes a mere routine in which pleasure or orgasm is only simulated to satisfy the customer's ego.

They moan and sigh and murmur passionate endearments, but if their minds could be read, the hollow mockery would be apparent, for one thought only occupies them: a wish to be finished and rid of the man as quickly as possible.

This is the rule which should have applied to me, but didn't.

Desires which should have been appeased by all too frequent gratification were quieted but for a moment, and almost at once flamed anew with increased insistence. And the tendency was growing. Strange as it may seem, sometimes after having had orgasm effected as many as half a dozen times in a single afternoon and evening, I was obliged to masturbate before being able to sleep. Pathologically and physically, I was oversexed, designed, seemingly, by Mother Nature herself, to be a whore.

Now in this propitious moment there entered into the horizon of my life, for the first time, a really sinister influence. And though in that influence I myself sensed a spirit of perversity, I was drawn toward it like a moth to the candle. Knowing that the destiny it signified was evil, I had not wish to resist it.

Montague Austin—what memories that name evokes. Memories of passion, cruelty, horror, blended with the cloying and intoxicating poison of a transcendental lust which knew no law other than that of gratifying its own frenzy.

I was supposed to have been infatuated with the man, but I never loved him, nor thought I did. No, I did not love him, but I did love the mad transports, the exquisite torment of lust which he, as no other man before or since, had the power to awaken in me. As an addict to the scented dreams of opium, so did I become an addict to Montague Austin. He was to me a fatal drug which held me a willing victim in its embrace.

For the first time, in broaching the subject of a new patron to me, Madame Lafronde manifested a doubt as to the expediency of putting my youth and inexperience to the test which she clearly thought an alliance with Montague Austin would signify.

I had seen the man but once; he was not a regular habituate of Madame Lafronde's house, but her facilities for gathering information were such that within less than twenty-four hours his social position, resources, and such portions of his history as were available on such inquiry were known to her. All the information, excepting that which related to his economic situation, was unfavourable. She summed up her opinion in the one expressive word—otter. But he had money, and money covers an otherwise nexcusable number of objectionable qualities. Possibly by he exercise of tact and vigilance I could handle him.

As for myself, I was the last person in the world to doubt ny own capabilities, so Madame Lafonde finally and with patent misgivings, yielded to my complacent and optimistic self-assurance.

Now let us glance briefly at the man himself.

He was, at the time our paths crossed, thirty-four years of age. The younger son of a titled British aristocrat, he had inherited both money and social position. The social position had been forfeited by dissolute escapades, the money dissipated in part, but enough remained to qualify him still as a rich man. He was married, but according to umour his profligate ways had brought about an rreconcilable estrangement with his consort.

At first glance one would have marked Montague Austin s an extremely good-looking man. But a less cursory bservation would not have failed to disclose signs of a ynical and somewhat cruel character in his darkly andsome face and narrow mouth. A little above average eight and signally favoured with regard to other physical haracteristics, he was in truth a figure to intrigue feminine nagination.

A feeling of lascivious exhilaration was welling within ne as I groomed myself for our first rendezvous. I had ately noticed that the craving for more frequently repeated rgasm was growing on me. It seemed that no matter how ften I had it, the longing was never completely satisfied. Even the two or three patrons I had who were sexually potent now left me with the irritated feelings of a woman whose passions have been inflamed and then abandoned in smoldering state.

It was a little after eleven-thirty. I had slipped out of the arlour, abandoning for the night my role of cigarette girl, nd was making my toilette, preparatory to Mr Austin's romised call.

'How nice it would be,' I thought, as I fluffed violet talc
over my body, 'if this Austin would suck me French style
and then fuck me about three times afterwards.' My nerves
tingled at the luscious vision thus evoked and a warm
feeling crept through my body. The little scarlet tips of my
bubbies swelled up and in the upper part of my cunny
could feel something else getting hard, too.

A few moments after twelve there was a discreet knock
at my door and the maid appeared, inquiring whether
was ready to receive Mr Austin. At this moment I wa
standing before the mirror considering the dress I had
tentatively chosen for the occasion, having yielded to an
impulse to use one of the short black silk frocks which
Daddy Heeley had bought me. Just why it had occurred to
me to put on this juvenile costume on the present occasion
I could not say; some vague intuition probably, but as it
turned out, a fortunate one as far as the effect on my new
patron was concerned, though until the arrival of the maid
I was still debating, undecided whether to wear it or chang
to something else more in keeping with the circumstances

'All right, Maggie,' I answered, 'you may bring him up.

I tied my short curls back in a cluster with a band of
ribbon, sprayed them lightly with my favourite perfume
and was just adding a final touch of powder to my fac
when footsteps at the door announced the presence of m
caller.

The door opened to admit him, closed again, and th
steps of the maid receded down the hallway.

Mr Austin paused as he took in the scene which con
fronted him, then his face lit up approvingly.

After a brief exchange of pleasantries he proved that h
was a man who went promptly and without any unneces
sary circumlocutions after whatever he wanted. With jus
the same directness as that employed to overcome Madam
Lafronde's reluctance, he proceeded to take immediat
advantage of the opportunity which was now his.

Abruptly he gathered me up in his arms and carried m
to the bed. Seating himself on the edge he bent over me an
his hand began to rummage under my clothing. With jus

the proper simulation of embarrassment I offered to undress

'Not yet,' he answered, 'you're too pretty a picture just as you are.' But a moment later his questing hand encountered panties which, if not exactly finger-proof, were at least something of an obstacle to easy exploration. He fumbled with them for a moment, then flipped my dress up and on his own initiative set about to unfasten and remove the panties.

I laughed nervously as he pulled them down over my legs. Already I was on fire. My sensibilities were reacting to the brutally frank sexual influence which the man exerted, and covertly I glanced toward his lap. The cloth down the inside of one of his trouser legs was distended over an elongated swelling. It looked enormous. As though drawn by some inner force I placed my hand upon it. It throbbed to my touch and I squeezed it through the clothing which concealed it.

Whether the thoughts that occupied my mind while I had been preparing for his visit were due to a premonition or mere coincidence I cannot say, but the wish I had expressed in thought was converted into a reality.

My dress was up, my cambric panties had been pulled down over my legs and cast aside.

Monty, on the side of the bed, leaning over my knees and supporting his weight on a hand which rested on the bed between my open legs had caught his first glimpse of my naked cunny. His eyes glistened and a faint flush crept over his cheeks. With one sudden movement his face was between my thighs and his mouth nuzzling my cunny. A warm, soft tongue penetrated it, tapping, touching, caressing, and then moved upward. The hot glow of the caress thrilled my senses and I relaxed in languorous abandon to the delicious ravishment.

His lips clenched my clitoris; it pulsed in response to the tugging incitation so vigorously that I was obliged to draw away to avoid orgasm then and there. I was torn between two impulses; I wanted to let it 'come' and at the same time I wanted the delightful ecstasy to last as long as possible.

The problem was not resolved by me, however, but by Monty, who raised up, ripped his trousers open and sprang upon the bed between my trembling legs.

Hard, rigid and hot I could feel it in there, distending my flesh to the limit of endurance, inspiring me with a wild desire to work on it rapidly, violently, until it poured out the balm which the fever within me craved. For an interval he remained poised above me, motionless, looking down into my face. His body did not move but within me I could feel the muscular contractions of the turgid thing which penetrated me. They followed each other with regular precision and each time I perceived that tantalizing twitch my ovaries threatened to release their own flood of pleasure tears.

'Oh!' I moaned finally and, unable to resist the urge, moved my hips in pleading incitation. 'You've got me in such a state! Please do something!'

'All right! Come on!'

And in a second that rigid shaft was plunging in and out in a mad dance of lust.

'Oh! Oh! Oh!' I gasped, and as though incited by my fervour, the turgid arm drove home in shorter, harder strokes.

Higher and higher mounted the swirling tides, lifting me upon their crest, no longer resisting, but an eager, willing sacrifice, panting to yield up the store of passion with which I was surcharged.

I perceived the approach of the crisis, that delicious prelude in which one trembles on the brink of ecstasy, in which the senses seem to hesitate for one sweet moment before the breathless plunge.

And in that critical moment the throbbing weapon which was working such havoc within my body suddenly ceased its movement and was held in rigid inactivity.

Above me I saw a face which smiled sardonically down into mine and vaguely I comprehended that he had stopped his movements with the deliberate intention of forestalling my orgasm in the last moment. But he had stopped too late, the tide had risen too high to recede and with but a momentary hesitation, it swept onward and carried me, gasping, writhing and swooning in its embrace.

When the languid spell which always overcomes me after a hard orgasm had passed, I found him still crouched above me and his cock, as stiff and rigid as it had been at first, still inside me.

'Why did you stop just as I was coming?' I complained weakly. 'You nearly made it go back on me!'

'That's what I was trying to do,' he replied cynically, 'but you put it over anyway. You know the old saying, baby, you can't eat your cake and have it, too. I like to enjoy the cake awhile before eating it.'

'That's all very well,' I rejoined, 'but when there's plenty more cake in the pantry, there's no use being stingy with it.'

'So!' he said, smiling, 'there's plenty more in the pantry, is there? I'm glad to hear it. But tell me this, does the second piece ever taste as good as the first?'

'And how!' I exclaimed fervently. 'The second piece tastes better than the first, and the third better than the second. The more I eat, the better I like it!'

He burst into laughter.

'You sound like you really mean it. I'd imagine that after a few months in a place like this you'd be so fed up on cake it would almost choke you. You're a cute youngster. You're wasting your talents here. What's the story? Innocence and inexperience taken advantage of by some bounder, I suppose?' he added quizically.

'I'm here for two reasons,' I answered calmly. 'The first one is to earn money and the second one is because I like to do what I have to do to earn it.'

'Well, bless my soul!' he gasped. 'What refreshing frankness! And you really weren't seduced by a villain?'

'Seduced, nothing! I was the one that did the seducing.'

'Good for you! You're a girl after my own heart! You and I are going to get along famously, Tessie!'

'Not Tessie . . . Jessie!'

'Ah, yes; Jessie. Pardon me. Well, since you really like cake, how about another piece?'

'I'm ready whenever you are!'

'What do you say we get undressed, and really make a night of it? I didn't expect to stay all night, but I've changed my mind.'

'That suits me, Mr Austin. I'm yours . . . till tomorrow do us part!'

'Not Mr Austin . . . Monty, if you please.'

'All right . . . Monty!' I repeated, giggling.

Whereupon we untangled our respective anatomies, scrambled off the bed, and proceeded to disrobe.

That is, Monty stripped, but when I had got down to my hose and slippers he suggested that I retain these last articles of apparel for the moment. Odd, I thought, how so many men who get pleasure from the sight of a girl's otherwise naked body were so alike in preferring that she keep on the hose and slippers, and I murmured something to this effect to my new playmate.

'Very easily explained, my dear little girl,' he replied. 'Complete nudity may be as suggestive of cold chastity as obscenity, whereas, nudity supplemented by a pretty pair of silkclad legs and neat slippers is the perfectly balanced picture of aesthetic lewdness.'

'But suppose one's legs and feet are pretty enough to look good without stockings? Everybody says I have pretty legs!'

'It's not a question of beauty, but of eroticism. I'll make a clearer illustration. Suppose we take two girls, each equally pretty. One of them stands before us entirely naked. The other is dressed, but she raises her dress and holds it up so we can see her pussy. Which of the two is the most exciting sexually?'

'The one holding up her dress,' I answered without hesitation.

'Right. And that's the answer to your question. You look naughtier with your hose and slippers than you would completely nude.'

My attention was now distracted from the matter of my own nudity to that of my companion. His body was well formed and in admirable athletic trim. Smooth, round muscles rippled under the clear white skin, a pleasing contrast indeed to some of my other paunchy, flabby patrons. But most impressive of all was the rigid weapon which, during the conversation and undressing, continued to maintain its virile integrity, standing out straight and proud from his middle. I glanced at it admiringly.

'How did you ever get that big thing into me without hurting me?' I commented, as I considered its formidable proportions.

'It carries its own anaesthetic, baby.'

'It looks strong enough to hold me up without bending.'

'Baby, it's invincible. I could put you on it and whirl you around like a pinwheel.'

'I'll take the starch out of it and make it melt down fast enough.'

'That's a big order. You may lose a lot of starch yourself trying.'

'Ha!' I scoffed. 'I wager it will be curled up fast asleep in an hour's time.'

A prediction which, as things transpired, turned out to be about one hundred percent wrong.

I returned to the bed and Monty, followed me, placed himself on his knees between my outstretched legs. Gripping the cheeks of my bottom in his strong hands as he sank down upon me, he pushed home the lethal shaft.

Our previous encounter had hardly more than whetted my appetite, so, as soon as I felt his cock well inside, I raised my legs, hooked them over his back, and without loss of time began to work against him. Apparently satisfied with my initiative, he remained still and let me proceed unhindered.

Grinding my loins against him I could feel his pubic hair compressed against my cunny. Moving my bottom from side to side, then shifting into undulating, circular movements, I sought to capture a second instalment of the cloying sweetness with which Mother Nature rewards the efforts of those who labour diligently in her garden.

The first warning of the approaching crisis was manifested by the muscular quivering of my thighs, and Monty, still squeezing the cheeks of my bottom, commenced to raise and lower himself upon me with slow, deliberate thrusts. Now the length of the hot thing was entirely buried within me, distending my flesh to the utmost; I could feel it pressing my womb. Now, it was coming out, slowly, slowly, out until naught but the tip lay cuddled against the quivering lips of my cunny.

A pause, a teasing agony of expectation, and it was going in again, in, in, until the crisp hair at the base was again pressed against my clitoris. Orgasm was creeping upon me, I could feel it coming, and in a frenzy of impatience, I launched my hips upward to meet the thrusts, but, instead of continuing its trajectory, it remained poised midway in its course. My orgasm was trembling in the balance. In desperation I brought it to its fulfillment with a supreme effort and fell back, half fainting.

'What is that, Mister, a system?' I panted when I could speak. 'You played that same trick on me the other time!'

An hour later the suspicion was beginning to dawn on me that, in the realms of erotic prowess, I had met my master. Two hours later, I knew it for a certainty. I had experienced nearly a dozen orgasms while my partner's cock was still stiff and rigid as it had been at the start. On each occasion he had succeeded in making me have an ejaculation without himself rendering any accounting to Nature. It lacked but a few minutes to three.

'You look a bit fagged, baby,' he said smiling quizzically. 'Think you can stand one more piece of cake?'

'Yes!' I replied valiantly, although in truth I was beginning to feel like a squeezed-out sponge. For once in my life I had about had my fill.

This time he rolled me over on my side and with his stomach against my back and his legs pressed against mine, he put it into me from behind, spoon fashion.

I thought to turn the tables on him and, by lying perfectly still, oblige him to work himself into spending heat. But it was unnecessary. He was done playing with me and went right to work on his own accord. Before long the pressure of his arms tightened about me and tensed my body against the harder plunges as a hot flood was loosed inside me with such force that I could distinguish each separate gush as it flung itself against my womb.

I held rigid for a moment in my determination not to let myself go, but the feel of that hot stuff spurting inside me worked havoc with my intentions and about the time the fourth or fifth jet hit me, the brake slipped and I was off again!

The aftermath of this last orgasm was a feeling of extreme lassitude and I was entirely agreeable when my companion, having apparently no further immediate designs upon my person, suggested that we turn out the light and sleep. I dragged myself from the bed, attended to the customary hygienic requirements, divested myself of my slippers, and hose, put on a silk shift, slipped back into bed beside him, and in probably less than ten minutes was deep in sleep.

I slept profoundly, dreamlessly, but not for long.

Something was pressing against my face, brushing my lips, with an irritating persistence which defied my mechanical, sleep-drugged efforts to shake away. I endeavoured to turn my face on the pillow away from it, and the knowledge that it was imprisoned so I could not turn it gradually crystalized in my mind.

As one coming out of a bad dream tries to dispel the lingering shadows, so did I try to free myself of something which seemed to be oppressing me, weighing me down, hindering my movements. I could not do it, and awoke to complete consciousness with a frightened start.

In the dim light which filtered through the curtains from the street illumination was revealed the fact that my erstwhile sleeping companion was now straddled over me, a knee on either side of my body. His hands were under my head, which he had raised slightly, and against my lips, punching, prodding, trying to effect an entrance, was that invincible cock.

I struggled to raise my arms to push him away, and at the same time tried to twist my head sidewise. I could do neither. My arms were pinioned down by his knees, and his hands prevented me from moving my head. At my movements their pressure tightened, a sinister reminder of my helplessness.

Of course I realized what he was doing. He was trying to fuck me in the mouth, something I had never permitted any man to do.

In prostitution, just as in other circles of life, there are social distinctions. The cocksucker is at the low end of the scale and is looked down upon with considerable scorn by those of her sisters who have not yet descended to this level. If among the entertainers in a high-class bordello one is discovered to be guilty of accommodating patrons with her mouth she not only loses caste but stands convicted of 'unfair' practice which makes it difficult for other girls to compete with her without also resorting to the same procedure.

This does not, of course, apply to those places known as French houses where cocksucking is the accepted practice, or to other places of a low and degenerate character wherein nothing is too debasing to be frowned upon.

These, together with the fact that I was both sleepy and exhausted sexually, were the considerations which inspired my efforts to escape the inverted caress which now threatened me rather than those of a strictly moral nature. The man appealed to me greatly in a physical way; I had reacted to his sexual advances with more passion and enjoyment than I had done before with any other patron. Had he endeavoured earlier in the night to seduce me, with a little gallantry and coaxing, into sucking his cock, I might, under the influence of my exhalted passions, have yielded. But I have always been quick to resent anything smacking of impudence or effrontery and, as I have mentioned, I wanted at that moment but to be permitted to sleep undisturbed.

'I won't do that!' I hissed angrily, as I struggled to free myself from his embraces.

'Oh yes you will, baby!' was the confident and surprising rejoinder.

His legs pressed tighter against my sides, constricting my arms so that I could not move them. He lifted my head higher. The end of his cock, with the foreskin drawn back, was right against my mouth.

'You . . . you . . .' I gasped, inarticulate with rage, as I was forced to clench my teeth to keep out the invader.

'Open your mouth, baby!' he ordered coolly, and gave my head a shake to emphasize his words.

When I comprehended that my wishes were to be ignored and that my efforts to dislodge him were useless, full rage took possession of me. For a moment I was on the point of screaming, but sudden recollection of the penalty exacted of girls who permitted scandals or disturbances to arise in their rooms at night stifled the cry in its inception.

We were expected, and presumed to be qualified, to meet unusual situations and resolve them with tact and discretion. Nocturnal disorders were unpardonable calamities and justified by nothing short of attempted murder.

'Open your mouth, baby!' he repeated, and shook my head again, this time with more force.

'All right!' I hissed, 'you asked for it!'

I opened my mouth. His cock pushed in immediately, and as it did so I sank my teeth into it. The intent was vicious enough, but the tough, resilient flesh resisted any actual laceration. Nevertheless, the pain inflicted by my small, sharp teeth must have been considerable.

He jerked it out of my mouth and simultaneously, withdrawing one of his hands from under my head, he dealt me a stinging blow on the side of the face with his open palm.

'Open your mouth, baby!' he repeated, undaunted, 'and if you bite me again I'll knock you unconscious!'

The tears started to my eyes.

'Damn you . . . !' I choked. 'I'll . . . I'll . . .'

The hands subjecting my head were again holding it in a viselike grip. His thumbs were pressing into my cheeks, against the corners of my mouth, forcing it open.

There was nothing to do but yield or scream such an alarm as would arouse the entire household.

I chose the more discreet course and, though almost suffocated with rage, opened my mouth in surrender to the assault which was being launched upon it. The big, plum-shaped head slipped in, filling the cavity with its throbbing bulk.

For a moment I tried to keep my tongue away from it, but there was no space in which to hide. His cock was so big I had to open my jaws to their widest, and my lips were stretched in a round, tight ring.

Further resistance was futile and anymore biting would bring a swift retaliation. So, still boiling inwardly, I relaxed, and let him go ahead.

A faintly pungent taste filled my mouth; the head of his cock, from which I could not keep my tongue, was wet and slippery. Every few seconds it jerked convulsively, forcing my jaws further apart. Pretty soon he began to move it, a short in and out movement. The foreskin closed over it as it receded, leaving only the tip inside my mouth, allowing me to relax my distended jaws momentarily. As it went in, the foreskin slipped back and the naked head filled my mouth again, forcing my jaws apart.

This went on for several minutes, and all the time he held my head with his hands. His cock seemed to be getting wetter but whether from its own dew or the saliva of my mouth I did not know. I wanted to spit, but he would not release me and I was obliged to swallow the excess moisture.

Finally, with the head just inside my lips, he paused, and after holding it still for a few moments, shook my face and whispered:

'Come on, baby! What's the matter with you? Are you going to suck it, or do I have to get rough again?'

I knew nothing of the exact technique of this business, though of course the very title by which the art was known indicated that sucking was in order. Choking, gulping, I tried to suck as it advanced into my mouth. Taking cognizance of my awkward efforts he paused again, and as though for the first time taking into account the possibility that I was in truth a rank novice, queried:

'What's the matter with you? Haven't you really done this before?'

Mutely, I managed to convey a negative by shaking my head.

'Lord love me!' he ejaculated, and then in slightly apologetic tones, 'I shouldn't have been so rough. I thought you were just stalling, my dear! However, it's something every young girl should know, and I'm glad to have the opportunity to be your teacher. Now listen: don't try to strangle yourself! You can't suck while the whole thing is inside! Wait . . .'

He withdrew it until just the head was encircled by my lips.

'Now suck while it's like that, and run your tongue over it!'

'Well,' I thought in disgusted resignation 'the sooner finished the better,' and submissively I followed his indications. Vigorously, if not enthusiastically, I sucked the big round knob and rolled my tongue over its slippery surface.

'That's the way, baby!' he whispered tensely after a few moments. 'That's great! Now . . . hold everything!'

And while I remained passive, he worked in and out in short, quick thrusts. Thus, alternating from one to the other, sucking one moment, submitting to having it rammed down my throat the next, my first lesson in cock-sucking continued.

I was still filled with resentment, but the first fury of anger had spent itself, and my thoughts were now concentrated on bringing the ordeal to a conclusion as quickly as possible. To this end I now tried to make the caress as exciting and fulminating as I could. I sucked the throbbing glans, curled my tongue around it, licking, sucking, coaxing . . . and the effect upon my companion was soon apparent. He groaned with ecstasy and from time to time jerked away from me so that the sensitive glans receded within the shelter of its elastic covering of flesh.

Perceiving that this manoeuvre was designed to delay an orgasm, I redoubled my efforts and when he again tried to withdraw I followed him by raising my head and with my lips firmly compressed around the neck of the palpitating knob, I sucked and licked without pausing.

The muscles of his thighs and legs, pressing against my sides, were quivering. Suddenly he withdrew his right hand from under my head and twisting sidewise reached behind him, groping with his fingers for my cunny. This was insult added to injury in my estimation and I tried to clench my legs against the invading hand. The effort was useless; he forced it between my legs and with the tips of his fore and index fingers he found my clitoris and began to titillate it.

Now began a new conflict. With every atom of mental influence I could bring to bear I tried to force that little nerve to ignore the incitation, to remain impassive to the friction which was being applied to it, to stay inert and lifeless.

I may as well have tried to stay the tides of the sea in their course. The traitorous, disloyal little thing cared not a whit for my humiliation and refused to heed the mental commands I was hurling at it. Despite the fact that it should have been as sleepy as I had been, it came almost instantly awake, hardened, and stood up stiffly.

He rubbed it in a peculiarly maddening way, a soft, twirling movement with the erected button lightly compressed between the tips of his two fingers. The little thrills began to generate, and communicated themselves to the surrounding area, up into my ovaries, down, seemingly into the very marrow of the bones in my thighs and legs.

Why say more? There was only one possible ending.

When the ultimate capacity of resistance was reached and passed, and in the very moment in which my organism was yielding to the diabolical incitation, my tormentor, waiting apparently for this precise moment, loosened within my mouth a flood of hot sperm. I choked, gurgling and gasping, as part of it gushed down my throat and the rest, escaping my lips, ran in hot, sticky rivulets down the sides of my cheeks, over my chin . . .

No sooner had the torrent subsided than he flung himself from me and lay panting on the bed by my side.

With the viscid stuff still dripping from my lips and its peculiar starchy flavour filling my mouth, I sprang from the bed and fled precipitately to the bathroom. First with water, then with tooth powder and brush and finally with repeated rinsings I endeavoured to purify my mouth.

When this was accomplished I went back into the room, turned on the light, and flung myself into a chair where, for a few moments I sat silently glaring at my tormentor who, with drowzy indifference, contemplated me through half-closed eyes.

'Well,' I said frigidly, breaking the silence. 'Aren't you going to congratulate me on my graduation into the cocksucking class!'

He smiled dryly.

'Forgive me, baby. Word of honour, I'll behave quite properly in the future. Anyway, it wasn't so terrible, was it? Listen, I'll tell you a funny story. There was a young French girl just married and her mother was giving her some confidential advice. "Daughter," she said, "the ultimate object of marriage is to have babies. Without the little dears no home is complete. However, the bearing and rearing of children is a confining task which imposes arduous and continuous obligations. It is my advice to you, daughter, that you do not have any babies during the first two or three years. You will then, in after life, not be deprived of the memories of a few years of happiness and freedom from care to which youth is justly entitled." "Ah, mother dear," answered the blushing maiden, "you need preoccupy yourself no further on that score, I shall never have any babies!" "Never?" gasped the mother, "why do you say that you will never have any babies, darling?" "Oh, mother," answered the girl, hiding her blushing face in the maternal bosom, "I shall never have babies because I simply can't force myself to swallow the horrid stuff! I always have to spit it out!" '

'And, so what?' I asked caustically, refusing to unbend at the ridiculous story.

'Don't you see, ha, ha, ha, don't you get the point? She didn't even know there was any other way of doing it. She thought she had to swallow the stuff to get a baby!'

Despite my efforts to remain haughty, my better humour was returning. I have always been like that, quick to anger, quick to forget. There was something about this man which was irresistible. Even his impudence had a saving grace, an ingenuous, disarming quality. Only the memory of the slap he had given me remained to irritate me. He sat there in bed, smiling, a sheet draped carelessly about him, half-concealing, half-revealing the smooth white muscles of his torso. His hair in its ruffled disorder gave him a boyish aspect, throwing a well-formed white forehead into relief against the background of bluish-black curls.

After all, what harm had really been done? And, I suddenly recalled, had he not earlier in the night given me a most delightful ten minutes by putting his tongue in my cunny? The service he had required of me was no less intimate. I shivered involuntarily at the recollection of the short but delicious episode. The last remnants of my resentment faded away. I began to feel slightly ashamed of myself for having made such a commotion.

'Still peeved at me, baby?' he inquired quizzically.

'No,' I answered, my lips twitching into a smile, 'only it was kind of . . . well, startling to be waked up that way from a sound sleep. I suppose you don't believe me, but I never did that before.'

'Of course I believe you, baby,' he interrupted, 'it was easy to see you hadn't any experience. Honestly, I don't know what came over me. You gave me such a stand tonight it came right back on me after I'd been asleep a short time. I woke up, and lay there looking at your pretty little mouth in the dim light, and the first thing I knew I got into a fierce argument with myself about it.'

'What on earth do you mean, an argument with yourself about my mouth?'

'Well, it was like this. At first I said to myself, it's too small, and then I said, no, it might be a tight fit, but it could be done. And the argument went on, until finally it got so hot it had to be decided definitely one way or the other, and so . . . and so . . .'

'And so I got fucked in the mouth to settle it. Very well, Your Highness, shall we retire now, or is there any other way I can serve you?'

'Well, if it's not putting too much of a strain on your hospitality, I'd greatly appreciate a shot of brandy!'

I rang for the maid. After a long wait, she shuffled to the door half-asleep, took the order, and was back again in five minutes with the liquor. When this was consumed, we turned out the light and again composed ourselves for sleep.

When I finally awoke it was late noon and the echoes of some of these lurid dreams were still reverberating through my brain. I felt wet and sticky between the legs and my clitoris was in erection. When I had got my confused thoughts in order and separated the real from the unreal, I sat up in bed and glanced at my companion.

He was sleeping soundly and quietly on his back, his curly head high on the pillow, lips slightly parted over white even teeth. He had thrown the blankets aside and was covered only by a sheet. I glanced downward over the recumbent form. Halfway down its length the sheet rose sharply, projected upward in the form of a little tent. As I fixed my eyes on this significant pinnaclelike projection, I saw that it was jerking sharply at short intervals.

I lifted the sheet without disturbing him. That indefatigable, tireless cock was standing upright, as firm and rigid as a bar of iron. White and graceful the stout column rose from the profusion of dark and tangled curls at its base, its plum-coloured head half-hidden, half-revealed under its natural envelope of satiny skin.

Still holding the sheet up, I looked at his face. It was in the peaceful repose of sound sleep. I thought of my curious dreams and wondered if he too was experiencing rare delights with some nebulous shadowland houri; maybe, even he was dreaming of me!

The thought set me aquiver. Softly I drew the sheet aside. I extended my hand, my fingers closed cautiously around the pulsing column. For a moment I was content to hold it thus, then, watching his face carefully for signs of awakening, I moved my hand up and down, slowly, gently, so that the silken foreskin closed over the scarlet head and then, receding downward, revealed it in its stark-nakedness.

Twice, thrice, I moved it so, pausing after each movement to see whether it was going to awaken him. At the fourth and fifth movement he stirred uneasily, murmuring some incoherent word. I waited, motionless, until his even breathing assured me that he was still deep in slumber, and began again.

'When he wakes up,' I thought, 'I'll make him tell me what he was dreaming about that made his thing hard this way.'

My wrist slid downward, the white elastic skin descended, and again the scarlet head protruded nakedly. As I paused, holding it in this position, I saw a round, glistening drop of limpid transparency emerged slowly from the orifice at the tip.

As I observed this natural reaction to my manipulations a wave of lewdness swept over me, and in an instant I was in a state of passion bordering on nymphomania, dominated by but one thought, one driving desire, and that was to feel the rigid, pulsating thing plunging in my mouth, to suck it and lick it until the spurting essence brought relief to the frenzy which now possessed me.

I literally flung myself upon it, indifferent now as to whether he was awake or asleep, and engulfed the ruby head within the circle of my lips. In a regular fury of lust I sucked and licked and bobbed my head up and down to approximate the motions of ordinary fucking.

Of course, this violent disturbance aroused my companion instantly, but I was too engrossed in my own passion to be hardly more than aware that he was sitting up in bed, and that his hands were clasping my face as though to guide the movements of my bobbing head.

Indifferent to all else I sought to force the living fountain between my lips to pour out its elixir as quickly as possible. Instinctively I knew that when it spurted forth, my own organism would yield in harmony. It was trembling now in that delicious borderland of anticipation, and needed but the final inspiration to precipitate its own shower of lust.

Between my thrusting, encircled lips the muscular flesh seemed suddenly to grow more taut. It held so for a second, and then with mighty convulsions poured out its tribute, wave on wave of hot, pungent ambrosia. Gasping, choking with the deluge which threatened to strangle me, I writhed in the ecstasies of orgasm which came upon me in the same moment.

The reaction to this furious excess was a spell of enervating lassitude. As I came out of it and my chaotic thought took on a semblance of order, I was filled with amazement at the demoniacal frenzy which had taken possession of me. Next came the thought of what had become of the spurting jets that indomitable geyser had poured out. The odd, pungent taste was still in my mouth, but I recalled that I had almost choked with the quantity that had flooded it. When he had assaulted me the night before I had spat most of it out, though I had been forced to swallow some. I glanced at the bed to see if, unconsciously, I had ejected it. The bed was dry and clean. Seemingly, it had all gone down my throat.

I remembered the absurd story he had told me about the French girl.

'Well,' I observed, 'if it's true a girl can get a baby by swallowing that stuff, I guess I'm going to have one.'

The English Governess

With the month of June the full heat of summer descended on London. The dusty streets, now almost empty, baked in the glare of sunlight, and the air was parched and quivering; in Great Portland Street the few trees supplied only the scantiest shade.

The interior of Mr Lovel's sombre house had become metamorphosed by the clear, searching light which penetrated into corners and recesses; the shadows of winter, which had seemed so native to these large dark rooms, were entirely dispelled; the house, indeed, seemed to have a rather uncomfortable air, as if light and sunshine had really no business in it. Even the schoolroom had taken on a new aspect: the furniture of walnut and old oak had lost its grim and surly character, and the funeral black leather armchair, on which Richard had had so often to kneel, his loins bared to receive the cane or ruler at the hands of his strict governess, had an air of dullness and respectability.

The boy had just passed his sixteenth birthday. During the winter he had grown taller and gained some weight; but it was noticeable that the effeminacy of his appearance had increased also. Moreover, if his figure was still slim, his thighs and loins had taken on a further breadth, an amplitude which was emphasised by the close fit of the Eton jacket and trousers he still wore.

Since Harriet Marwood had definitively adopted the method of corporal punishment to bring him to her idea of perfection,—the end to which she was entirely devoted—scarcely a day had gone by without her having had recourse to the whip. His education in the matter of discipline had indeed progressed remarkably: by now, like any other English boy under the authority of a governess, he had learned to resign all judgment on his conduct to his instructress; and he had learned to suffer the most vigorous flogging without protest. Nor was this all. At least one evening every fortnight, strapped to his bed, he was made to endure the protracted torment of a triple correction with strap, birch and cane. These important occasions, however, were no longer announced to him beforehand by the sagacious Miss Marwood: so that for three or four nights a week the boy could not be sure what her nightly visit portended, the rapture of an evening kiss or the ordeal of a special punishment—and uncertainty which was only resolved, at the last moment, by her appearing either fully clothed and with an affectionate smile on her lips, or in her long hooded cape, bare-armed and with the terrible strap in her hand. Thus, his anticipations and even his emotions of pleasure and pain were confounded in a single framework of exquisite tension.

By such treatment he had been brought to an extraordinary height of sensitivity,— and also, it must be admitted, of sensuality. Living in a state of constant nervous trepidation, at the mercy of all the whims of his instructress, he had come to entertain a highly ambiguous attitude towards her. He feared her and he loved her,—but his love was as yet almost entirely sensual. Her hold on him was through the flesh; and it was maintained and increased by the bestowal of the exact contrary of caresses.

As for Harriet herself, her temperament seemed to find full satisfaction in the imposition of such a regime. Why, or how, we do not know. To bring a beaten and degraded look into a boy's face, to rend self-respect out of him in fear, is a sight not especially relished by the ordinary woman. But Harriet Marwood, whatever she was, was not an ordinary woman.

She had said to him one day, 'Richard, I wish you to be in my hands *perinde ac cadaver*,—"like a dead body." That is the motto of the Jesuit Fathers, and it will be yours, too. And to bring you to that condition, I shall not cease chastising and shaming you in every way. In time, you will be grateful to me . . . for it is only in subjection that a boy such as you are can ever know true happiness.'

He did not understand her words; but he was as if hypnotised by her, and accepted all she did without question. As for even dreaming of complaining to his father, that idea was farther than ever from his intention. Harriet herself had entire confidence in her pupil on this latter point,—but nevertheless she was sometimes uneasy concerning Mr Lovel's own possible perception of what was being done to his son. The man of business rarely set foot in the schoolroom; he saw little of Richard,—but nonetheless he noticed him, and it happened that he found the boy's appearance marked by fatigue and melancholy.

'Upon my word, it's simply extraordinary!' he said to Harriet one day. 'What do you make of it, Miss Marwood? Here is a boy who, from what he tells me, simply adores you. He has you constantly with him, he lacks for nothing, you tell me he sleeps and eats well, and I can see for myself his schoolwork is tremendously improved,—and yet, and yet,—what's the matter with him? Why has he that wretched, moon-struck air? And why is he so sensitive that when I press him about it—as I did only yesterday—he is almost ready to turn on the water-works?'

Harriet remained perfectly calm. 'Richard is a boy of a very delicate nature, sir,' she replied. 'In fact, he is so exquisitely sensitive that even yet the slightest reprimand leaves its mark on him for days. As it happened, you were questioning him just a few minutes after I myself had given him a light rebuke. That is the explanation for his nervousness, which is ready to find its outlet in tears.'

Mr Lovel looked at her in admiration. 'How well you understand him!' exclaimed the worthy man.

And one day, soon after this conversation, Harriet saw fit to further improve her position with her employer.

'It is now midsummer, sir,' she said. 'Living in town, in this heat, is not good for a boy of Richard's age and delicacy of temperament. We ought really to go to the country for a month or two. Did you not tell me, sir, that you had a small property somewhere in the country?'

'In Hampshire? Of course!' exclaimed Mr Lovel. 'In fact, why don't you go down to Christchurch with Richard? That will do him a world of good, upon my word! Exactly, Christchurch. An excellent idea, don't you think?'

Harriet cloaked a smile of triumph. When she broke the news to Richard, he too seemed deeply moved.

'We will go to Christchurch together,' she said. 'Down there, I shall have you under my authority even more firmly than here. I will make you a well trained boy indeed, Richard!' She looked at him affectionately. 'Well, are you glad to be going down to the country with me? To live there with me, just the two of us alone?'

'Yes! Oh yes, Miss!' he breathed.

She took him in her arms and kissed him with such warmth that his head reeled.

Mr Lovel wrote to the old couple whom he employed as caretakers of his house at Christchurch; and in a few days Harriet and her pupil were ready to set out.

She packed the boy's trunk with him; and she also made him carry a parcel containing the ruler and a new rattan: the first cane had long since been worn out, and already at least a half-dozen had succeeded it in turn.

'I think,' said Harriet with a kind of bantering gaiety, 'that we shall be able to find in Christchurch everything necessary to whip you with, but it is better to be on the safe side. I have packed my strap, and I may need the cane as soon as we arrive. On the way down, my voice and hand should be enough to keep you in order . . .'

The trip passed without incident, except that Richard leaned out of the train window and caught a cinder in his eye, and the governess declared, in the presence of two very elegant women in the same compartment, that he was a foolish boy and would be soundly thrashed for his imprudence as soon as they arrived at their destination. This announcement had the immediate effect of gaining the favourable notice of the two ladies who, extremely distant heretofore, at once entered into conversation with Miss Marwood without deigning to acknowledge any further the existence of her companion.

They arrived at Christchurch in the evening. Mr Lovel's house was situated a little beyond the outskirts of the town, in the middle of the country and not far from the Stour, the pretty river which flows into the Avon a short distance further on. The old caretaker was waiting for them at the station; Harriet left him to see to their luggage, and set out at once with her pupil in a hired fly.

As soon as they arrived she summoned Molly, the caretaker's wife, and gave her instructions in her duties. The governess had already planned their life in the country, and she now organised matters accordingly. Molly was to do the housework in the early morning and prepare the breakfast, and neither she nor her husband were to set foot in the house at any other time of the day. The old couple occupied the small lodge at the entrance to the grounds, and thus had no further business in the house itself. A caterer in the town was engaged to bring the meals twice a day; Harriet would simply plan the menu and leave her instructions. In this way she and Richard would be always alone and undisturbed.

While waiting for their luggage to arrive, the governess and pupil went on a tour of inspection of their new home, as pleased with it as if they were a newly wedded couple.

The house, standing in the midst of heavily wooded grounds encircled by a high brick wall, enjoyed the greatest seclusion and privacy. At the end of the garden the wall was pierced by a small door which led to the park itself, a pretty stretch of woods made up mainly of oak, ash and birch. From the lawn behind the house, where she was standing with Richard looking at the trees, Harriet observed the white satiny trunks of the birch-trees, and pointed them out to her pupil.

'See,' she said, with a little laugh in her throat, putting her arm around him, 'at least we shall not lack for rods!'

He sighed: it might have been a sigh of trepidation or of pleasure. He was still suffering from the cinder which had lodged in his eye, and he had not forgotten the promise which Harriet had given him in the train.

After the trunks had arrived, and under Harriet's superintendence, the clothes had been unfolded, shaken out and hung up; and the linen unpacked and laid out in the drawers, there was still a good half-hour before dinner.

'Now let us look at that eye of yours,' said Harriet, drawing Richard to the window of her own room.

She explored the under side of the eyelid, and after patient effort succeeded in removing the unlucky cinder; when this was accomplished, she bathed the eye carefully, and then, having dried his cheek with her own handkerchief, she murmured with a smile, 'But after all, I might have saved myself the trouble of bathing your eyes, since you will be shedding tears in a few minutes . . .'

He raised to her a glance full of anguish and appeal.

'Have you forgotten what I promised you in the train?' she said pleasantly. 'Your imprudence deserves a sound whipping, and naturally you are going to get one.' She looked around her thoughtfully. The cane and ruler were already unpacked and lying on the massive mahogany table placed in the middle of the comfortable old-fashioned room. 'Unless you are fastened to my bed,' she resumed, 'I can hardly see how to place you so I can whip you properly . . . No, wait: you will lean over this table and hold on to the far edge with your hands. That is the best way.'

He obeyed, whimpering; but when he was standing in front of the table, stripped to his shirt, he looked at Harriet pleadingly. 'Miss, please! I've never travelled on a train before . . . I didn't know—'

'That is doubtless an extenuating circumstance,' she replied. 'But simple common sense should have told you one does not lean out of railway coaches . . . Bend over at once, sir.—Very good. Now reach out and hold on to this edge. Excellent!' She stepped back and surveyed him with satisfaction. 'Suppose, Richard, that at the moment you put your head out, the train was entering a tunnel! You would have been decapitated, my boy,—just like that. The correction I am going to give you may serve to put a little sense in your head for the future. It seems indeed, Richard, that the whip is the only language you understand . . .'

During this brief lecture she had raised his shirt above his shoulders, and emphasised her remarks with a few ringing slaps which made his flesh shake and quiver. Then, picking up the cane, she proceeded to flog him vigorously for almost five minutes. He wept and writhed, but took good care not to release his hold on the table.

'Very well Richard,' she said at last, laying down the cane. 'You may get up now. And now come here and kiss me, and promise to be more sensible in future.'

His face still bathed in tears, he kissed her smiling mouth as she had ordered, feeling the same disturbance he always felt in bestowing this salute,—this kiss which was, in fact, designed at once as a stimulus to his adolescent sensuality and as a last refinement of humiliation.

His rooms adjoined hers, and Harriet took care that the door between them should remain open at night.

One evening, a few days after their arrival, she said to him, 'I hear you stirring in your bed a good deal, Richard. You toss and turn and fidget. Are you sure you are behaving yourself?'

He was taken aback, feeling a sensation of uneasiness and a certain shameful alarm. 'Oh yes, Miss,' he stammered at last.

'But you are a long time getting to sleep, are you not?'

He mumbled an inaudible reply.

'This evening you will come and read to me in bed. That will leave you tired and able to fall asleep sooner.

That night, after they had said prayers in her room, she put a novel of Mrs Sherwood's into his hands. 'I am going to bed now,' she said. 'You will remain here while I get ready, and then you will read to me.'

'Yes, Miss,' he murmured. He was obviously carried to the height of excitement by the prospect.

Harriet looked at him impassively, hiding the pleasure she took in his nervous disturbance. 'Leave your book on the table for the present,' she said, 'while you help me undress. Come here and unlace my shoes, please.' She sat down on the edge of her bed, drew her skirt up and crossed her legs.

Richard watched her in a kind of stupour.

'Well?' she said. 'Have you turned to stone? Down on your knees with you, and undo my shoes.'

He obeyed, and began to unfasten the laces from the highly arched foot which, encased in its high-heeled shoe of supple fawn-coloured leather, was swinging under his nose. He noticed the slenderness of her ankle; he saw her leg also, in its fine, transparent silk stocking, the lace of her drawers, the hem of a white petticoat. His hands trembled as he untied the shoelaces. When he drew off the shoe itself, his excitement was such that he let it fall on her other foot.

'Clumsy!' said Harriet, leaning over and slapping his face smartly. 'Pay attention how you take off the other, if you please.'

The warm, intimate odour of her unshod feet put his senses in a fever. He rose from his knees, trembling slightly.

'You would make a poor lady's maid,' smiled Harriet, standing up. 'Go and sit down over there, and wait until I am in bed.'

Calmly she began to undress, letting fall first her skirt, then her petticoat; she removed her bodice, and then, standing in corset and drawers, she let down her beautiful hair, shaking it out to its full length so that it fell in a thick wavy mass covering her croup whose firm outline appeared through the fine linen of her drawers; then she divided her tresses and swiftly plaited them in two long braids. When this was done she removed her corset, drawers and stockings, and stood in front of Richard in her shift. His eyes did not leave her for an instant.

'Bring me my slippers,' she said. 'You will find them over there by the window.'

He brought them from their place and laid them in front of her; but she stretched out her naked foot.

'Put them on,' she ordered.

He would gladly have kissed these exquisite white feet with their pink nails, but he did not dare. He fitted the slippers onto them, and then stood up.

Harriet stepped to the closet from which she took a long silk nightdress, and then deliberately let her shift, which was held only by two straps passing over her beautiful bare shoulders, fall to the carpet.

She had taken no precaution to shield herself from the boy's gaze. But he, despite the desire he had to see her, had not dared keep his eyes on her until the very end . . . It was only when she turned back towards the bed, clad from neck to heels in the long ribboned gown and holding her shift in her hand, that he realised that for a few moments she had been entirely nude in his presence. At the thought, his face suddenly glowed a deep red,—as if the display, far from having been accomplished by slow gradations, had been made all at once.

She laid the filmy garment, still warm and impregnated with the odour of her magnificent body, on the back of the armchair where he was sitting, and went into the bathroom.

No sooner had she left than he turned round, seized the shift whose light folds were brushing his nape, and plunged his face into it, breathing in with eager and trembling nostrils the subtle and disturbing perfume which clung in the soft linen creases, intoxicating himself almost to madness. All at once he heard a step behind him.

Harriet had re-entered the room quietly. As he saw his governess beside him, erect and severe in her long night-dress, her penetrating gaze bent on him, his heart seemed to skip a beat.—She saw me! he thought; and, mixed with his resignation to the punishment he knew was coming, he was conscious of a certain pride.

'Richard! What were you doing?'

He did not reply. She took his head between her hands and forced him to look in the face. 'What were you doing?' she repeated. Then she fixed him with a gaze that grew harder and harder. 'Yes,' she said. 'I saw you! You sensual, wicked boy! I have already noticed this side of your nature. I have said nothing, but I have been watching you! Come here, Richard.'

'Miss . . .' he mumbled. He was choking with a peculiar excitement.

Now, for some reason, he did not fear the pain of the approaching correction: he was as if drunk with the sense of his own subjection . . .

Gently, with movements slow and deliberate as those which are part of some ritual, she picked up her shift, folded it once to make a gag of it, and then bound it over his mouth and nose: the filminess of the material did not hinder his breathing,—but every breath was as if it were taken from between her breasts or thighs. Then she bent his body beneath her arm, drew him tightly against her, and raised his shirt; between then there was nothing but the thin silk of her nightdress. Her hand rose, and fell.

At last she drew him to the bed, and sitting down made him kneel between her feet; she leaned over . . . With an impression of ecstasy that was boundless, Richard abandoned himself to the touch of her hands. Never before had she acted thus, never before had he experienced such sensations!—With her head close to his, so that he breathed the heady fragrance of her hair and the perfume of her breath, she was speaking softly in his ear: 'This is how I shall correct your wickedness, Richard . . . Do not mistake this for a caress! This is a punishment, a shameful punishment . . . Whenever I see that you are becoming too fond of me, I shall inflict it on you after I have whipped you well . . . Do you understand, you wicked child!—Now back over my knee with you! I am going to beat you again . . .'

Once more, in the warm, dimly-lit room, was heard the slow, regular cadence of a palm striking flesh: it continued a long time . . .

At last she stopped, sighing deeply; she removed the gag from his face, and then, taking him in her arms, pressed her lips to his in a long, shuddering kiss.

'Try to behave yourself, now!' she said, pushing him away abruptly and slipping between the sheets of her bed. 'Hold your book in your left hand, and put your right hand in mine. Just so, my dear. I wish you to have the constant impression of being in my power, of being in my hand . . .'

He was burning with a fever of the senses, he had no more strength than a two-year-old child. He abandoned his hand to Harriet and began to read.

The reading lasted a long time. In order to turn the pages, he placed his book on the edge of the bed and used his left hand . . .

Harriet was falling asleep. From time to time Richard darted a swift glance at her, seeing her resting quietly, the two heavy braids of hair framing the noble head—the head beautiful as that of a goddess. An even breath raised her creamy half-uncovered breast, and he fought down a wild desire to put his lips to it,—or at least to imprint a kiss on the soft hand which still imprisoned his own and which had struck and caressed him so recently. Then the great grey eyes half opened and were turned on him.

'Close your book now,' she murmured. 'Say goodnight to me, and go to bed like a good boy. And think of what happened to you this evening,—will you not? You will think of it?'

'Yes, Miss,' he whispered.

He bent over her and respired her warm, perfumed breath as their mouths clung together in the evening kiss.

His face a little paler, his cheeks a little hollower than usual, Richard stole into Harriet's empty room. His governess had just gone out, leaving her pupil occupied with some schoolwork which she had set him as a holiday task.

'You will not leave your room while I am gone, Richard,' she had told him. 'If you do, you will be well caned.'

He had obeyed the order, at first: then, despite the warning and the wholesome fear it implanted in him, he had dared to leave his work-table, to open the door, and at last, drawn by his overmastering desire, to enter the bedroom filled with the subtle perfume of the young woman.

His heart was pounding with excitement.—What had she just been doing there? he asked himself. He had no idea, could make no conjecture, but he was seized by an intense nervous disturbance at finding himself alone, for the first time, in this room where she lived, where she slept, this room haunted by the intoxicating fragrance of her clothing, her sachets, her body itself.

He approached the bed, and shivered slightly. On the silk coverlet, beside the pillow, the governess had left a cane whose end was split and beginning to fray.—That cane, he knew it only too well. The previous afternoon he had been whipped with it, as a punishment for his slovenliness in not having replaced a broken shoelace. His flesh was still tender from the effects of this punishment; but the remembered sting of the rattan only intensified the ardour of his desire,—that mysterious and uncertain desire which betrayed itself by an irrational wish to be mastered, scolded, shamed and whipped by his governess, and to touch and breathe the odour of every object belonging to her,—above all, those objects consecrated to her most intimate use.

He picked up the cane with a trembling hand, and pressed his lips to the end which had felt her grip, imagining he could still detect the warmth and scent of the strong hand which had held it. Then, replacing the instrument of his torment, he let his gaze rove around the room. He was uneasy, oppressed, almost stifling, but the desire was stronger than everything else. Trembling in an access of precaution, walking on tiptoe as if he feared to awaken someone in the empty house, he made the circuit of the chamber.

All at once he stopped, riveted to the spot. On a low, straw-bottomed, high-backed chair, whose form recalled that of a *prie-dieu*, a tiny handkerchief of fine batiste was lying, crushed almost flat. In front of the chair stood a pair of high-heeled shoes, from which Harriet had apparently changed before going out.

His throat dry, his heart beating wildly, he bent over and knelt down; he took the handkerchief and carried it to his lips. It exhaled a subtle perfume, the same perfume which he had breathed on that unforgettable evening when his governess had undressed in front of him before going to bed. And this handkerchief was at once crushed and flattened! Immediately he understood that in order to change her shoes Harriet had seated herself on this chair, and therefore—on the handkerchief: the little square of batiste was thus doubly precious to him . . . He kissed it once more, long and passionately, and then hid it under his shirt, against his skin, against his heart.—What delicious hours he would pass that night, he thought, when he could bury his face in it! Already, he was shaken with the thrill of anticipation.

But perhaps even more than the handkerchief, the shoes attracted him. He picked them up, smelled them, covered them with such kisses as a lover would bestow on the body of an adored mistress; he stroked them tenderly, drew back the tongues and tried to kiss the inside, gazed at them with love and reverence and pressed them passionately to his breast. He felt in a confused manner the pointlessness, the madness of these endearments bestowed on inanimate objects,—but then he began to ask himself if they were really so inanimate: he was dimly aware that there resided in this supple leather something more than the idea of the charming foot it had clasped, more than the sweet and intoxicating perfume it gave off, some immaterial essence which he was unable to explain and which, though he did not conceive or clothe the idea in comprehensible terms, was for him the symbol of an exquisite feminine domination . . .

He was about to rise, when a sound behind him chilled him to the marrow. He turned around and saw Harriet.

She was smiling, her thin lips parted in that terrible curve which he knew so well.

As if stricken by paralysis, all the strength fleeing from his body as the blood gushes from an open wound, he could not move for an instant. He tried to rise, but she halted him with a gesture.

'Stay as you are!' she said.

Deliberately, she took off her hat and gloves and laid them on the dressing-table. Then she approached the kneeling boy who, his eyes wide with terror and entreaty, watched her coming towards him without a cry, without a word or a movement.

'You were kissing my shoes, sir!' she said in a low voice. 'Yes, I saw you. You were kissing them . . .' She picked up one of the shoes and, seizing his long hair in her other hand, she rubbed the shoe vigorously against his face, which from being livid swiftly became as red as fire. 'So, you were kissing them!' she cried, her wrath bursting forth. 'So that is what you like, is it? Put your hands behind you! Behind you, I said. There now, kiss it,—kiss it again—you wretched boy! Again—again! Have you had enough of such vileness now?' Her anger suddenly mastered her, and dropping the shoe she slapped his cheek with all the strength of her arm: so hard was the blow that he would have fallen if she had not still held him upright by the hair. Deliberately, she slapped him again.

Her anger was perfectly genuine, evoked by the evidences of a perverted taste which was entirely at variance with her plans.

Released from her grip, Richard crumpled to the thick carpet and lay there prone, his face in his hands, sobbing and gasping weakly.

She regarded him calmly for a few moments; then, with her foot, she turned him over. Little by little, the sensuality of the punished boy was affirming itself now that his fright was receding. Harriet knitted her brows with determination.—I shall have to take further measures, she thought.

'Go to your room, undress yourself, and wait for me there,' she said coldly. 'I am not through with you yet, Richard.'

He obeyed. No sooner had he divested himself of his clothes than Harriet entered his room; she was bearing the leather belt and sleeves she had ordered from the saddler, and her face was stern. 'I did not know we should have occasion for the whipping-harness quite so soon, Richard,' she said quietly. 'Indeed, I had hoped it would not be needed for a long time. But your conduct has shown me that I must take the most extreme measures. You have disappointed me more than I can say . . .'

The note of reproach in her voice affected him even more painfully than the prospect of further chastisement. A great sob of anguish rose in his breast, and falling on his knees before her he burst into tears. 'Oh Miss, Miss,—I'm sorry,' he stammered. 'I—I couldn't help it . . . I'll never do it again! Only please, please don't be angry with me . . .'

'I am no longer angry with you, Richard. I am merely saddened to find such inclinations in you,—and I am, more than ever, resolved to root them out. The whipping you are going to receive will be as much a corrective as a punishment of your wickedness. When it is all over you will be forgiven.—Come, get up and put on your harness!'

Under Harriet's direction he buckled the sleeves on his arms, fastened the belt and attached the strap. 'Very good,' she said. 'Now that you know how to put it on, I shall expect you to do so yourself whenever there is occasion for your wearing it in future.—Turn around now, please . . .'

He obeyed; she drew his arms behind his back, folded them tightly, and snapped the catches into place.

Richard, feeling himself rendered absolutely helpless, experienced a sudden emotion of panic; breaking away sharply, he began to twist and strain against the straps, bending and writhing ineffectually, his face pale, a hunted look in his eyes.

Harriet stood watching his struggles with a detached and impassive air; she well knew the effects of such restraint, and congratulated herself on their success in further breaking her pupil's spirit. For a while she followed his disordered movements without speaking; when they ceased and the boy stood crouched in front of her, panting and tembling, she began to smile.

'Come now, Richard,' she said, 'you see you must resign yourself. There is no use your struggling any longer, you will only tire yourself to no purpose.' She stepped forward and took him by the upper arm, supporting his body which suddenly became weak. 'Lie down on your bed now . . . Very good. I shall leave you now, and I shall not come back until the evening. It is then that we will settle our accounts . . .'

She pulled the coverlet over his trembling body, and drew the heavy curtains; then she turned away without another word and left the room, locking the door behind her.

For Richard, lying helpless in his bed, the hours until evening passed slowly. Outside, the world drowsed through the afternoon of a beautiful English summer day, the sunshine growing ever mellower and more golden as the sun moved lazily across a pure and cloudless heaven, lingering and prolonging itself as if unwilling to leave the quiet country landscape; the hours rang out faintly from the priory church in the town, and they too seemed to be deliberately spacing themselves more and more widely apart, in obedience to some timeless element of the day.

In the darkened bedroom of the house where the pinioned boy lay waiting, time seemed to have stopped altogether. Still tormented by a burning desire for something of which he had no conception, his imagination was tossed between thoughts of punishment and voluptuousness, prospects confused yet complementary, ideas inextricably entangled in a quivering, ambiguous sensibility whose only focus was in the image of the woman whom he loved. Indeed, he was a prey to such closely mingled trepidation and desire that he seemed to be awaiting, in the arrival of his beloved, at once the signal of a martyrdom and an appeasement.—Ah, how many of us, looking back on our own childhood, might not say that we too have been consumed at some time by such a curious amalgam of emotion? And how many would not admit that in such hours of anguished expectation was forged, more strongly than ever, the sensual link which so mysteriously unites the ideas of pleasure and pain?

Harriet herself, perhaps, had known such an experience. Of such a possibility we cannot yet speak with certainty;

but her understanding of the conditions under which the mind is at its most impressionable entitles us to say, at least, that she was a psychologist both profound and practical . . .

Let us look at our heroine for a moment, as she sits alone in the peaceful English garden, awaiting the hour of ordeal.—The far-darting light of the evening sun is touching the dark masses of her hair; a faint breeze stirs the folds of her light, clinging summer dress. Her hands are clasped in her lap, the dark eyelids, fringed with long upsweeping lashes, have half fallen over the lovely grey-violet eyes, her bosom rises and falls tranquilly as she gazes unseeingly towards the rich green woods whose leaves have just begun to curl themselves up at the approach of the summer night . . . A picture, you would say, of all that is sweetest and most ethereal in English womanhood. Ah, but what is it that causes the short, delicate upper lip to curl so charmingly? What thoughts are passing behind that pure brow? *Lector, nec scire fas est omnia!*

She had entered the room so quietly that he had not even heard the rustle of her cape. The cool, pleasant voice startled him.

'Get up, Richard.'

He struggled off the bed and stood before her; he saw the leather martinet doubled in her hand.

'No,' she said, as if reading his thoughts, 'you will not have the strap tonight. But do not congratulate yourself too soon, my dear. I am sparing you a strapping only so that you may make a long and thorough acquaintance with this new martinet.' She smiled, and shook out the heavy leather lashes in her hand. 'I think you will find that it is an instrument quite able to command your respect . . .'

Richard gazed at her and shivered. More even than her anger, he had learned to dread this pleasant, almost quizzical air; she was never, he knew, more merciless than when in such a mood. As the beautiful bare arm swung the lashes through the air again with a soft, hissing sound, the muscles of his loins and thighs contracted spasmodically.

'Bend over, Richard.'

He obeyed, hardly able to control the shaking of his knees as she stepped behind him.

The first blow drew a scream from him. The rounded, tapering thongs had seemed to cut into his flesh like hot blades.

'Oh . . . Miss! Please—I can't—I can't bear it!'

Harriet laughed indulgently. 'Ah, you will have to bear it, Richard . . . You have brought this punishment on yourself, you know.' The martinet lashed him again, drawing another wild scream. 'It stings, does it not?' she said quietly. 'It has a different sting, I dare say, than the sting of your wretched desires. Keep telling yourself that this good whip is driving out those evil inclinations, and be thankful for its virtue . . . Straighten your knees, please! We have just begun.'

Very slowly, very methodically, the correction proceeded.—He is really going to suffer tonight, she told herself, thrilling to the idea of his helplessness and her own power: ah, he will remember this evening for a long time.

Richard was indeed in such an agony as he had never known before. Accustomed heretofore to the keen but superfical smart of strap and cane, he was receiving with a terrified amazement the strokes of an instrument whose bite seemed to penetrate his entire loins, as if the thongs were literally tearing him to pieces. He tried with all his will power to retain his bent position, to keep his knees stiff, to present his loins to his tormentress in the way to which she had so carefully trained him . . . But as the minutes went slowly by he found himself weakening. It was not, he realised desperately, that his resolve was giving away, it was his limbs themselves that were refusing to obey him. He found himself swaying on his feet, his legs bending, his body involuntarily swinging from side to side.

'Richard!' said Harriet in a warning tone. 'You are forgetting your lessons. Do not make me angry with you, or you will regret it.'

'I—I can't help it,' he gasped, straightening up and

turning to her piteously. 'I'm trying, Miss . . .'

'You must try a little harder then,' she said. 'Bend over properly now, keep your knees straight, and let us have no more of this foolishness.—Your knees, sir, I said! Your knees!' She lashed him smartly in the tender hollows of his knees,—and with a sharp scream he straightened his legs convulsively. 'That is better,' she said. 'You will find it wiser to do as you are told. Have you not yet learned that?'

She resumed the task of discipline with an appearance of calm. But by now she was deeply stirred: the blood had mounted to her head, her mouth was dry, her breath was coming faster. With her left hand she drew the folds of her cape tightly around her hips, feeling the contact of the material against her bare flesh, stiffening her spine as if she were offering her own magnificent loins to some imaginary flagellant. She began to wield the lashes more swiftly.

But Richard had now reached the limit of his endurance. Absolutely motionless for the past five minutes, his knees locked, gritting his teeth, he had managed to maintain the required attitude. When his strength deserted him, it did so suddenly: almost before he was aware of if he found himself falling limply to the floor.

Harriet, as if balked at the last moment of some wished-for goal, gave an exclamation of rage. 'Get up!' she cried.

He struggled to his knees; but with his arms strapped behind him he found he could get no further. And then, suddenly invaded by an immense and overpowering weakness, he crumpled to the floor once again, sobbing with pain and exhaustion.

'So, you will not obey me?' said Harriet, her voice almost stifled with suppressed fury. 'So much the worse for you!'

She pulled the hood over her head; Richard, seeing the ominous gesture, gave a shriek of terror and closed his eyes. The next moment he felt the leather lashes cutting into him where he lay . . .

For the next minute the governess seemed possessed by a demon. Stooped over her pupil's writhing body, she plied the martinet with all her strength, bringing it down on whatever portion of his flesh presented itself; secure in the knowledge that the harness protected her victim from any injury, she was able to forget everything but her own crescendo of emotion. Under the savage blows the boy rolled and twisted helplessly on the carpet, his whole body doubling and straightening, his legs beating the floor, his pain and terror released in sounds like the insensate howling of an animal . . . Then all at once the tall caped figure drew away from him; the martinet dropped from a nerveless hand; the whole superb body, swaying and supporting itself against a heavy armchair, began to tremble, as long shudders passed through it from head to foot. A great breath, half sob, half groan, burst from her breast,—and prolonged itself slowly into a profound and quivering sigh. She dropped into the chair, her hands pressed to her bosom, and remained there for a full half-minute, breathing deeply.

Through the half darkness of the room, as if from far away, Richard's voice sounded, faint and almost strangled with sobs. 'Miss . . . Oh Miss—is it all over—now?'

'Yes,' said Harriet softly. 'It is all over, Richard.'

She rose and bent over him, unfastening his arms. 'Get up now and come over here,' she said.

With the release of his limbs, and hearing Harriet's tone of tenderness, he felt his fear passing away like a black cloud before a fresh and healing breeze. But more than this, added to his relief like some priceless pendant, he had heard a new note in his governess' voice, something carrying a different message than any ever before conveyed to him, a vibration in which he sensed the expression of a love deeper than any she had hitherto avowed, and with which was mingled the suggestion of some mysterious acknowledgement, of some gratitude . . . As she drew him gently onto her lap, he laid his head against her shoulder, and then, raising his lips to her ear, whispered through the folds of the little hood which still confined her hair, 'Oh Miss, Miss. I love you, I love you . . .'

Harriet tightened the embrace of her arm around the naked boy; in the darkness, her own lips, so recently curled and drawn back in all the ferocity of her ardour, trembled slightly. 'Yes,' she said, in a voice which she strove to render calm.

'I am afraid you care for me only too much, and in a way which I must condemn . . .' She felt the sudden throb which answered the pressure of her hand. 'Richard,' she said in a tone of warning.

He was seized by an uncontrollable trembling, filled once more with that mingled emotion of terror and desire; but it was the latter, now, that dwarfed the former into nothingness. 'Oh Miss,' he whispered, 'I can't help it . . . Please, please don't be angry with me!'

Harriet drew a deep breath; but when she spoke her tone was calm and even. 'Get up now, take off your harness and go to bed,' she said.

She remained seated while she obeyed. The room was now almost dark; outside, the moon had risen above the treetops and was penetrating faintly through the curtains.

Lying on his back, the coverlet pulled up to his chin, Richard watched the tall, silent figure in the chair. Then he saw her rise, and standing erect, draw the hood from her head; he saw the bare arm raised to her throat,—and the next moment, with a splendid movement of the beautiful shoulders, the long cape was slipped off and fell on the chair behind her. Harriet was absolutely nude.

She stood for a moment in the centre of the room, presenting to the boy on the bed a vision of such beauty that he was breathless with ecstasy; then she advanced slowly. He could see her face now in the semi-darkness, grave and intent; but he had no eyes for anything but this magnificent body which swam before him like that of some antique deity.

With a deliberate gesture she drew the coverlet aside, and sat down beside him on the bed. Once again, he felt the intoxicating pressure of her hand.

The two nude figures, shadowy and indistinct in the dark bedroom, remained thus for a few instants; a shaft of moonlight, peering through the narrow opening in the curtains, fell on the motionless white bodies, illuminating them like marble, turning them to a statuary group at once tender and pagan, a piece of sculpture in which was symbolised but one more variant of the ineffable aspiration of mankind, but one more aspect of that divine and multiform Eros who can do no wrong . . .

Her hands began to move slowly, slowly, etching on the boy's affections a message never to be forgotten, a sensual memory, a type and pattern of voluptuousness to which he might turn back with longing for the rest of his life, as if it were the indelible imprint of herself . . . She leaned over and joined her parted lips to his, receiving like a viaticum the breath of his young rapture.

Flossie

My intercourse with the tenants of the flat became daily more intimate and more frequent. My love for Flossie grew intensely deep and strong as opportunities increased for observing the rare sweetness and amiability of her character, and the charm which breathed like a spell over everything she said and did. At one moment, so great was her tact and so keen her judgment, I would find myself consulting her on a knotty point with a certainty of getting sound advice; at another the child in her would suddenly break out and she would romp and would play about like the veriest kitten. Then there would be yet another reaction, and without a word of warning, she would become amorous and caressing and seizing upon her favourite plaything, would push it into her mouth and such it in a perfect frenzy of erotic passion. It is hardly necessary to say that these contrasts of mood lent an infinite zest to our liaison and I had almost ceased to long for its more perfect consummation. But one warm June evening, allusion was again made to the subject by Flossie, who repeated her sorrow for the deprivation she declared I must be feeling so greatly.

I assured her that it was not so.

'Well, Jack, if you aren't, *I* am,' she cried. 'And what is more there is someone else who is "considerably likewise" as our old gardener used to say.'

'What *do* you mean, child?'

She darted into the next room and came back almost directly.

'Sit down there and listen to me. In that room, lying asleep on her bed, is the person whom, after you, I love best in the world. There is nothing I wouldn't do for her, and I'm sure you'll believe this when I tell you that I am going to beg you on my knees, to go in there and do to Eva what my promise to her prevents me from letting you do to me. Now, Jack, I know you love me and you know *dearly* I love you. Nothing can alter *that*. Well, Jack, if you will go into Eva, gamahuche her well and let her gamahuche you (she *adores* it), and then have her thoroughly and in all positions—I shall simply love you a thousand times better than ever.'

'But Flossie, my darling, Eva doesn't—'

'Oh, doesn't she! Wait till you get between her legs, and see! Come along: I'll just put you inside the room and then leave you. She is lying outside her bed for coolness—on her side. Lie down quietly *behind* her. She will be almost sure to think it's me, and perhaps you will hear—something interesting. Quick's the word! Come!'

The sight which met my eyes on entering Eva's bedroom was enough to take one's breath away. She lay on her side, with her face towards the door, stark naked, and fast asleep. I crept noiselessly towards her and gazed upon her glorious nudity in speechless delight. Her dark hair fell in a cloud about her white shoulders. Her fine face was slightly flushed, the full red lips a little parted. Below, the gleaming breasts caught the light from the shaded lamp at her bedside, the pink nipples rising and falling to the time of her quiet breathing. One fair round arm was behind her head, the other lay along the exquisitely turned thigh. The good St Anthony might have been pardoned for owning himself defeated by such a picture!

As is usual with a sleeping person who is being looked at, Eva stirred a little, and her lips opened as if to speak. I moved on tiptoe to the other side of the bed, and stripping myself naked, lay down beside her.

Then, without turning round, a sleepy voice said, 'Ah, Flossie, are you there? What have you done with Jack? (*a pause*). When are you going to lend him to me for a night, Flossie? I wish I'd got him here now, between my legs—betwe-e-e-n m-y-y-y le-egs! Oh dear! how randy I do feel tonight. When I *do* have Jack for a night, Flossie, may

I take his prick in my mouth before we do the other thing? Flossie—Floss*ee*—why don't you answer? Little darling! I expect she's tired out, and no wonder! Well, I suppose I'd better put something on me and go to sleep too!'

As she raised herself from the pillow, her hand came in contact with my person.

'Angels and Ministers of Grace defend us! What's this? *You*, Jack! *And you've heard what I've been saying*?'

'I'm afraid I have, Eva.'

'Well, it doesn't matter: I meant it all, and more besides! Now before I do anything else I simply must run in and kiss that darling Floss for sending you to me. It is just like her, and I can't say anything stronger than *that*!'

'Jack,' she said on coming back to the room. 'I warn you that you are going to have a stormy night. In the matter of love, I've gone starving for many months. Tonight I'm fairly roused, and when in that state, I believe I am about the most erotic bed-fellow to be found anywhere. Flossie has given me leave to *say* and do anything and everything to you, and I mean to use the permission for all its worth. Flossie tells me that you are an absolutely perfect gamahucher. Now I adore being gamahuched. Will you do that for me, Jack?'

'My dear girl, I should rather think so!'

'Good! But it is not to be all on one side. I shall gamahuche you, too, and you will have to own that I know something of the art. Another thing you may perhaps like to try is what the French call "*fouterie aux seins*".'

'I know all about it, and if I may insert monsieur Jacques between those magnificent breasts of yours, I shall die of the pleasure.'

'Good again. Now we come to the legitimate drama, from which you and Floss have so nobly abstained. I desire to be thoroughly and comprehensively fucked tonight—sorry to have the use the word, Jack, but it is the only one that expresses my meaning.'

'Don't apologise, dear. Under present circumstances all words are allowable.'

'Glad to hear you say that, because it makes conversation so much easier. Now let me take hold of your prick, and frig it a little, so that I may judge what size it attains in full erection. So! he's a fine boy, and I think he will fit my cunt to a turn. I must kiss his pretty head, it looks so tempting. Ah! delicious! See here Jack, I will lie back with my head on the pillow, and you shall just come and kneel over me and have me in the mouth. Push away gaily, just as if you were fucking me, and when you are going to spend, slip one hand under my neck and drive your prick down my throat, and do not *dare* to withdraw it until I have received all you have to give me. Sit upon my chest first for a minute and let me tickle your prick with the nipples of my breasts. Is that nice? Ah! I knew you would like it! *Now* kneel up to my face, and I will suck you.'

With eagerly pouting lips and clutching fingers, she seized upon my straining yard, and pressed it into her soft mouth. Arrived there, it was saluted by the velvet tongue which twined itself about the nut in a thousand lascivious motions.

Mindful of Eva's instructions, I began to work the instrument as if it was in another place. At once she laid her hands upon my buttocks and regulated the time of my movements, assisting them by a corresponding action of her head. Once, owing to carelessness on my part, her lips lost their hold altogether; with a little cry, she caught my prick in her fingers and in an instant, it was again between her lips and revelling in the adorable pleasure of their sucking.

A moment later and my hands were under her neck, for the signal, and my very soul seemed to be exhaled from me in response to the clinging of her mouth as she felt my prick throb with the passage of love's torment.

After a minute's rest, and a word of gratitude for the transcendent pleasure she had given me, I began a tour of kisses over the enchanting regions which lay between her neck and her knees, ending with a protracted sojourn in the most charming spot of all. As I approached this last, she said:

'Please to begin by passing your tongue slowly round the edges of the lips, then thrust it into the lower part at full length and keep it there working it in and out for a little. Then move it gradually up to the top and when there, press your tongue firmly against my clitoris a minute or so. Next take the clitoris between your lips and suck it *furiously*, bite it gently, and slip the point of your tongue underneath it. When I have spent twice, which I am sure to do in the first three minutes, get up and lie between my legs, drive the whole of your tongue into my mouth, and the whole of your prick into my cunt, and fuck me with all your might and main!'

I could not resist a smile at the naîveté of these circumstantial directions. My amusement was not lost upon Eva, who hastened to explain, by reminding me again that it was 'ages' since she had been touched by a man. 'In gamahuching,' she said 'the *details* are everything. In copulation they are not so important, since the principal things that increase one's enjoyment—such as the quickening of the stroke towards the end by the man, and the knowing exactly how and when to apply the *nipping* action of the cunt by the women—come more or less naturally, especially with practice. But now, Jack, I want to be gamahuched, please.'

'And I'm longing to be at you, dear. Come and kneel astride of me, and let me kiss your cunt without any more delay.'

Eva was pleased to approve of this position and in another moment, I was slipping my tongue into the delicious cavity which opened wider and wider to receive its caresses, and to enable it to plunge further and further into the perfumed depths. My attentions were next turned to the finely developed clitoris which I found to be extraordinarily sensitive. In fact, Eva's own time limit of three minutes had not been reached, when the second effusion escaped her, and a third was easily obtained by a very few more strokes of the tongue. After this, she laid herself upon her back, drew me towards her and, taking hold of my prick, placed it tenderly between her breasts, and pressing them together with her hands, urged me to enjoy myself in this enchanting position. The length and stiffness imparted to my member by the warmth and softness of her breasts delighted her beyond measure, and she implored me to fuck her without any further delay. I was never more ready or better furnished than at that moment, and after she had once more taken my prick into her mouth for a moment, I slipped down to the desired position between her thighs which she had already parted to their uttermost to receive me. In an instant, she had guided the staff of love to the exact spot, and with a heave of her bottom, aided by an answering thrust from me, had buried it to the root within the soft folds of its natural covering.

Eva's description of herself as an erotic bed-fellow had hardly prepared me for the joys I was to experience in her arms. From the moment the nut of my yard touched her womb, she became as one possessed. Her eyes were turned heavenwards, her tongue twined round my own in rapture, her hands played about my body, now clasping my neck, now working feverishly up and down my back, and ever and again, creeping down to her lower parts where her first and second finger would rest compass-shaped upon the two edges of her cunt, pressing themselves upon my prick as it glided in and out and adding still further to the maddening pleasure I was undergoing. Her breath came in short quick gasps, the calves of her legs sometimes lay upon my own but more often were locked over my loins or buttocks, thus enabling her to time to a nicety the strokes of my body, and to respond with accurately judged thrusts from her own splendid bottom. At last a low musical cry came from her parted lips, she strained me to her naked body with redoubled fury and driving the whole length of her tongue into my mouth, she spent long and deliciously, whilst I flooded her clinging cunt with a torrent of unparalleled volume and duration.

'Jack,' she whispered, 'I have never enjoyed anything half so much in my life before. I hope you liked it too?'

'I don't think you can expect anyone to say that he

"liked" fucking *you*, Eva! One might "like" kissing your hand, or helping you on with an opera cloak or some minor pleasure of that sort. But to lie between a pair of legs like yours, cushioned on a pair of breasts like yours, with a tongue like yours down one's throat, and one's prick held in the soft grip of a cunt like yours, is to undergo a series of sensations such as don't come twice in a lifetime.'

Eva's eyes flashed as she gathered me closer in her naked arms and said:

'*Don't* they, though! In this particular instance I am going to see that they come twice *within half an hour!*'

'Well, I've come twice in less than half an hour and—'

'Oh! I know what you are going to say, but we'll soon put that all right.'

A careful examination of the state of affairs was then made by Eva who bent her pretty head for the purpose, kneeling on the bed in a position which enabled me to gaze at my leisure upon all her secret charms.

Her operations meanwhile were causing me exquisite delight. With an indescribable tenderness of action, soft and caressing as that of a young mother tending her sick child, she slipped the fingers of her left hand under my balls while the other hand wandered luxuriously over the surrounding country and finally came to an anchor upon my prick, which not unnaturally began to show signs of returning vigour. Pleased at the patient's improved state of health, she passed her delicious velvet tongue up and down and round and into a standing position! This sudden and satisfactory result of her ministrations so excited her that, without letting go of her prisoner, she cleverly passed one leg over me as I lay, and behold us in the traditional attitude of the *gamahuche a deux*! I now, for the first time, looked upon Eva's cunt in its full beauty, and I gladly devoted a moment to the inspection before plunging my tongue between the rich red lips which seemed to kiss my mouth as it clung in ecstasy to their luscious folds. I may say here that in point of colour, proportion and beauty of outline, Eva Letchford's cunt was the most perfect I had ever seen or gamahuched, though in after years my darling little Flossie's displayed equal faultlessness, and, as being the cunt of my beloved little sweetheart, whom I adored, it was entitled to and received from me a degree of homage never accorded to any other before or since.

The particular part of my person to which Eva was paying attention soon attained in her mouth a size and hardness which did the highest credit to her skill. With my tongue revelling in its enchanted resting-place, and my prick occupying what a house-agent might truthfully describe as 'this most desirable site,' I was personally content to remain as we were, whilst Eva, entirely abandoning herself to her charming occupation, had apparently forgotten the object with which she had originally undertaken it. Fearing therefore lest the clinging mouth and delicately twining tongue should bring about the crisis which Eva had designed should take place elsewhere, I reluctantly took my lips from the clitoris they were enclosing at the moment, and called to its owner to stop.

'But Jack, you're just going to spend!' was the plaintive reply.

'Exactly, dear! And how about the "twice in half an hour".'

'Oh! of course. You were going to fuck me again, weren't you! Well, you'll find Massa Johnson in pretty good trim for the fray,' and she laughingly held up my prick, which was really of enormous dimensions, and plunging it downwards let it rebound with a loud report against my belly.

This appeared to delight her, for she repeated it several times. Each time the elasticity seemed to increase and the force of the recoil to become greater.

'The darling!' she cried, as she kissed the coral head. 'He is going to his own chosen abiding place. Come! Come! Come! blessed, *blessed* prick. Bury yourself in this loving cunt which longs for you; frig yourself deliciously against the lips which wait to kiss you; plunge into the womb which yearns to receive your life-giving seed; pause as you go by to press the clitoris that loves you. Come, divine, adorable prick! Fuck me, fuck me, fuck me! Fuck me long and hard: fuck and spare not!—Jack, you are into me, my cunt clings to your prick, do you feel how it nips you? Push, Jack, further; now your balls are kissing my bottom. That's lovely! Crush my breasts with your chest, *cr-r-r-r-ush* them, Jack. Now go slowly a moment, and let your prick gently rub my clitoris. So . . . o . . . o . . . Now faster and harder . . . faster still—now your tongue in my mouth, and dig your nails into my bottom. I'm going to spend: fuck, Jack, fuck me, fuck me, fu-u-u-uck me! Heavens! what bliss it is! Ah, you're spending too, bo . . . o . . . o . . . oth together, both toge . . . e . . . e . . . ther. Pour it into me, Jack! Flood me, drown me, fill my womb. God! What rapture. Don't stop. Your prick is still hard and long. Drive it into me—touch my navel. Let me get my hand down to frig you as you go in and out. The sweet prick! He's stiffer than ever. How splendid of him! Fuck me again. Jack. Ah! fuck me till tomorrow, fuck me till I die.'

I fear that this language in the cold form of print may seem more than a little crude. Yet those who have experience of a beautiful and refined woman, abandoning herself in moments of passion to similar freedom of speech, will own the stimulus thus given to the sexual powers. In the present instance its effect, joined to the lascivious touches and never ceasing efforts to arouse and increase desire of this deliciously lustful girl, was to impart an unprecedented stiffness to my member which throbbed almost to bursting within the enclosing cunt and pursued its triumphant career to such lengths, that even the resources of the insatiable Eva gave out at last, and she lay panting in my arms, where soon afterwards she passed into a quiet sleep. Drawing a silken coverlet over her, I rose with great caution, slipped on my clothes, and in five minutes was on my way home.

The Diary of Mata Hari

Paris, 19 . .

In the beginning I liked the milieu I found at Madam Desiree's place very much; her clients consisted mainly of members of the middle class. She had, as she proudly assured me, an exceptionally 'fine' class of customer. 'They are all very well brought up; yes, most of them have had a good education.

'In my establishment you will not find those Apaches that scare a lady and trick her out of a few pennies, entirely aside from the fact that they try to use the material for free, and not only that, they work it too hard. Whenever such a man sleeps with a girl, the poor thing can't be used again for at least twenty-four hours . . .'

These prospects did not deter me in the least, on the contrary I would enjoy being worked over rather well. But the greatest attraction for me was being able to 'work' in Madam Desiree's house with my face hidden behind a mask. Madam Desiree insisted upon it, because she realised full well that this little 'trick' had its own special added attraction. Moreover I worked very cheaply. Anyhow, the set-up was cheaper than a piquant gown or real silk stockings. However, she did not object when the ladies used their own fineries when the overall effect would be enhanced by them. And after all, she was the one who made the largest profits from them.

Whenever I arrived I would slip through the entrance of a small café which was connected with a secret door to Madam Desiree's house. Drinks and other orders were also delivered through this door and the Madam of this fairly reputable, well-managed bordello made a good profit from them also. Once arrived, I would climb the small and very narrow spiral staircase till I reached my own little apartment on the second floor. It was my very own, tiny little bedroom with an even tinier little toilet. Both rooms were very clean and decorated according to the typical taste which one might expect in these small hidden shrines dedicated to the services of lustful Venus.

The moment I reached my room, I must admit that I quickly and happily divested myself of my clothes, especially my expensive lingerie. I draped a huge shawl, an exquisite piece of Turkish handwork, around my body, the long fringes clinging to my nude thighs. This shawl had the added advantage that it could be draped around my body in a thousand different ways, each one of them enticing, without ever hiding too much . . .

On other days I dressed in a tricot which consisted merely of holes; I mean that my flesh showed through a net whose mazes were almost two centimetres in diameter. Obviously I never forgot to wear a pair of black stockings worked with open lace. This particular costume drew the open admiration of Madam Desiree. 'Oh, Madam,' she was always very free giving us the title Madam unless she suddenly preferred to introduce us as her co-workers, 'you really do your best for my house, but believe you me, and I always tell the other ladies exactly the same, my profits are also yours!'

The most exciting moment, at least for me, was that of the 'selection', namely that particular moment when we were put in touch for the first time with the unknown person visiting this home of carnal pleasures to feast, however shortly, his physical senses. Actually 'putting in touch' is slightly exaggerated; this moment, in which we had to stand in line, forming a parade of more or less nude female bodies, was dedicated to feasting the eyes of the visitor. To look at us was supposed to put the guest in the proper mood; to suggest to me that we were there only for his pleasure . . . all he had to do was take his pick. The only thing he had to do really was to make up his mind which one of us would be his temporary true love.

These minutes of waiting always gave me a pleasant

tickling thrill—it was invariably me who was selected. And it was always my pleasure, because I had the right to look through a secret peephole at the unknown visitor and whenever I agreed to stand in line for the 'selection', it meant that his type would please me as a partner.

The more selection, the greater profit. Madam Desiree knew full well that not only did Paris have many women who were ready and willing to increase their small budgets by 'sacrificing' an occasional afternoon, but that there were many others who also had a small budget which they were more than willing to enlarge, namely the joys of the flesh—and some of them were more than willing to pay her for it.

I have spent many fabulous hours; the charm to be in a place which is dedicated to only one goal, exactly the same one for which the male visitors came to it, was in my opinion worth more than the few thousand franc notes I gave her. Even though I insisted firmly that 'my customers' handed over their money (it would have humiliated me not to be considered a good professional), I was never stingy toward my 'colleagues' or the owner of this for me so invaluable institution.

Ah, whenever the doorbell rang, whenever a happy hubbub of naked bodies ran to and fro to pick up something to cover themselves, then rushed toward the narrow staircase, laughing in anticipation—maybe today there would be a real good piece of ass—tumbling into the reception room to line up in sacred tradition . . . faces expressionless, standing erectly, waiting to be selected—oh, how entertaining this was for me!

And then the more or less excitedly inspecting gentlemen would point out one of us, one who conformed to his particular ideal of eroticism, one who in his mind could give him the delights he secretly hoped for, and with an imperceptible nod of his head he would select the person with whom he intended to have a delightful sexual bout.

As I said, I was most often the one who was selected. I am not trying to brag, but I was considered the queen-bee of our little group and frequently they put me in the most advantageous position. Whenever I had my gentleman it was the turn of the others; this was the established procedure. Madam Desiree never failed to congratulate my latest conquest on his good taste and excellent selection—'The lady is a wonderful companion, but I leave the final decision up to yourself!' she used to say.

I remember one visitor in particular as an exceptionally understanding partner. In the beginning I treated him like all the others; upstairs in my little room I threw my arms around his neck and whispered into his ear: 'Well, we are going to have ourselves a good time, aren't we?'

And I would grope into his pants, trying to open his fly as quickly as possible so that I could have a good look at the most important requisite for the following ceremony.

'What's your name, darling?' I'd ask, the moment I had his rapidly growing hard-on in my hands.

Most of the time they'd murmur just about any kind of a name, but this time my opponent said quite clearly, 'Call me Mimile—my real name is Emile . . . And what's yours?' His question was polite but firm.

'My name is Lolotte, my big darling!' I tried to copy the tone of voice of the true inmates to avoid any possible detection and to prevent my partner from getting the wrong picture.

'But come on, he is so beautifully hard and I'd love to have him in me as soon as possible.' With those words I pulled him toward the bed. We almost fell down upon it; in my enthusiasm I had pulled quite hard on the incredibly stiff instrument. The next moment this strange man, whose strong build had attracted me from the first moment I laid my eyes upon him, lay between my widely spread thighs and I felt his entire weight against my bosom. Since he pushed with all his force against my body, I could not do anything but guide his powerfully swollen prick toward my yawning crotch and let him disappear into it.

The moment this fantastically hot prick discovered its entry, Mimile started to jab and hump furiously, pinning me down on the bed. Since I had one hand free, I grabbed his big balls and started to squeeze them with the same rhythm in which his hard pole was pushing up and down. I completely forgot that these organs are to a man his most sensitive possessions. Mimile seemed completely unperturbed by my counterattack and paid no attention as he doubled the force of his jolts while voluptuously groaning and moaning. It is hardly surprising that his behaviour led me into true ecstasy and the hotly desired climax came much quicker than I had expected . . .

'Oh, you screw splendidly . . . fantastic . . . oh, please, fuck me as wild as you can . . . please, don't hold back darling, quick . . . *quicker* . . . no, really, you are not hurting me . . . *aah*, great—more, please, please . . . more . . . I have to . . . please go on . . . yes, yes, that's it . . . oh, you—now . . . *now* . . . aah . . . *aa-aa-aah*!'

I had made my first number. But Mimile was coming, too, and I felt his hot jism spurt into me at the exact moment that I reached my own climax.

'That's a pity,' he murmured rather dully. 'I came much faster than I had hoped—now it's all over and I just started to like you so well.' And with these words, my partner, who believed the game was over, was about to get up and put on his clothes. But he was mistaken. It was far from me to treat him like a professional trollop would have done and I had only one desire. I wanted to enjoy the pleasure he had given me with his well-proportioned pecker at least once more and, if possible, several times . . .

'Please, stay awhile, Mimile. Do you really want to go? Can't I play around a little bit with your big rod?' I smiled coquettishly at him and could see that he was rather bewildered about my request which is sort of unusual in a public house.

I took a towel and started to dry off his sopping wet love arrow. I noticed that it had lost some of its attractive hardness, but it was still pretty big and I was convinced that with the proper treatment I could make it stand up all over again. My experience told me that this was one of those men who had a considerable power of quick recuperation. And that pleased me enormously since it was the sole reason of my being in a place like this; to find a dong capable of performing something extra special . . .

Even while I was still playing around with the half hard rod, it started to get a new erection and when I suddenly decided to take the whole machine into my mouth it only took a few moments before it was as hard and stiff as it had been when Mimile came into my room a short while ago. It was a fantastic experience to feel how the proud man completely filled my mouth. Even though it was difficult, I succeeded to play around with the heavy knob and lick it with my tongue, causing it to throb excitedly and make Mimile cry out: 'You are driving me wild—come on, let's make another round, I've got to come once more . . . let me . . . I have to lay you . . . you've got a . . . I have to . . . you . . . I've got to put it into your cunt quickly . . .'

There was nothing I wanted more. But the moment Mimile wanted to pin me down again, I rolled away from under him. 'No, not this way . . . wait a moment . . . I want to get fucked from behind!'

I loved this particular position. Besides, I knew that my behind a work of art in itself—firm and round—fired every man whom I honoured this way to his greatest performance. The strength and intensity of the pushes I received in this position had convinced me completely of this.

It is fantastic to stick your behind freely up in the air and take in a prick slowly between your legs. So I pushed myself back and felt his hard lance shove into my hole. Almost immediately Mimile started to hump me thoroughly and the speed was, at least for the beginning, quite satisfactory. Slowly he pushed deeper and deeper into my body and I felt the instrument of my partner filling out my entire womb. Mimile worked without stopping. He banged with renewed vigour against my buttocks and grabbed alternately one or the other of my full, dangling breasts, squeezing them as hard as he could. Our bodies welded together in a beautiful curve; the knees of the man nestled themselves into the back of my knees and his hairy muscular chest pressed against my back. The big mirror next to my bed reflected our picture—I looked at it and was thrilled by what I saw. It never tired me to watch the frolicking of the two bodies working together in the act.

Throughout my life I have always had a weakness for mirrors. And especially whenever the mirror shows me a second couple busy with what is most important and most pleasant: a good screwing . . . Is it not far more pleasant to know that there is another couple busy with the same intimate occupation right next to you? Ah, even the mute couple in the mirror caused extra excitement; if it were only possible to see those parts in action which one feels, but it is so difficult to take a good look when the straining bodies start their voluptuous convulsions.

Mimile was not entirely disinterested in these same impressions; he turned around to look in the mirror at my beautifully rounded backside—and I made it even easier for him by turning slightly sideways—to convince himself optically that I returned every one of his jolts with one of my own.

'Are you very horny, Mimile?' I asked him, so that I could enjoy the pleasures of sound as well as those of touch and sight. 'Do you like my backside—yes? . . . I love to be fucked from behind . . . so very, very much . . . just push a little harder . . . I can stand it . . . ah, that feels good—that feels terribly good . . . ! Just go deeper if you can, Mimile—*aaaah* . . . *aaaah*! You've got to come here more often . . . always . . . ask . . . for . . . me . . . I want to feel your prick—every day—deep-inside me . . .'

Mimile banged with all his force against my ass. 'Just you wait, I'll screw you so hard that you won't know whether you're coming or going . . . you horny bitch . . . you would love to have a prick like mine in you all the time wouldn't you . . . It's all right with me . . . I'm gonna give it to you good, baby . . . you can have it any time you want to as long as you behave yourself . . . I'll fuck you all night . . . I—you—you . . .'

With these words, which had not failed to have their desired effect upon me and which made me enjoy the entire situation even more, the unfortunately independent human nature demanded its due—Mimile squirted his second load into my thirsty innards and pulled out without saying another word.

'But Mimile, please, don't do that . . . I haven't come yet . . .' I protested. 'Come on, quickly, put it back again . . .!'

'Aaaaah, that was fantastic my little Lolotte—dammit, I haven't enjoyed myself so much in quite a long time . . . What? You didn't come . . . ?' Mimile was quite surprised, and at the same time very flattered that the inmate of a 'house' was begging him explicitly to be satisfied once more by him. That had never before happened to him!

'You'll have more chances during the remainder of the night, little one . . . I'm sure you'll come at least once more,' he tried to reasssure me condescendingly.

'That's quite possible, but I want you to screw me, Mimile!' I had not yet given up hope.

'Well, you know I would love to—but look at it, you can see for yourself that I couldn't possibly bring it up!' and he looked down upon his rather droopy instrument with which we had made such beautiful music together.

'Bah, there is nothing wrong with it. It just needs a little extra excitement. Just wait, I have something for the gentleman which is guaranteed to put him in the proper mood again—yes, my dear Mimile, I have a weakness for you!' I really had a fantastic idea.

'I like you very much, too, Lolotte, and as far as I am concerned I'd never say "no", but I am afraid that for tonight . . .'

I did not listen to him. I went to the door, opened it slightly and called, 'Madam, could you please send Vivienne up to my room?'

And when I turned back to Mimile and saw his questioning expression, I explained what I had in mind. 'You will like her, little Vivienne is my younger sister, and her type is the absolute opposite of mine—if that does not excite you my darling . . . '

Mimile perked up his ears. 'Your sister? Really? That's

fantastic . . . and you both work in the same cathouse?'

I noticed that my little improvisation had the desired effect. At the same time Vivienne entered. I liked her best of all my colleagues and the two of us were quite intimate together. She was quite often my partner whenever one of the clients desired to cavort with 'two ladies at the same time', or when two couples had to be formed.

'Vivienne, may I introduced to you Mr Mimile—well, what do you say, dear friend, do you like my little sister, isn't she a real doll?' Unquestionably Vivienne's charms were very enticing; she was of medium size, very soft and she was a blonde, the particular silvery blonde hair which one only finds in the northern parts of France and in Belgium. Her eyes were large and blue like forget-me-nots. Her most visible charms were very pointed, not at all small breasts, which formed a piquant contrast to her otherwise frail figure; they bobbed up and down with every step. She forced them a little bit to do so, but the overall effect was so incredibly charming that one could easily forgive her this little mannerism. Even though she was already nineteen years old, she did not look a day over sixteen and, for this age an incredibly oversized bosom added extra spice which the real connoisseurs in our establishment considered a first-class titbit.

'Well, my dear Mister Mimile, so you are a little lecher, one of those people who can't get their fill with only one woman,' and Vivienne leaned against the big man, who put one arm around each of us, and looked with lustfully burning eyes from Vivienne to me and back. Mimile seemed to be content, but I had only one desire, and that was to speed up the proceedings.

'Take off your chemise Vivienne, and show the gentleman what you can do. I am sure that Mimile will show you in return the full impact of his virility—one favour is worth another,' I urged my little girl friend on. Now the three of us were sitting on the wide bed.

'Listen, Mimile, I will take your little brother into my mouth again and meanwhile you and Vivienne can start to get to know each other a little better; but when I have made him ready then you have to promise me to stick him in me again!' Said and done. The dangling thing already showed signs of getting up again. And, when I took it between my lips and at first very softly, almost superficially, then a little bit stronger and finally truly energetically started to suck on it, his erection began much quicker than I had hoped for. It stood up proud and stiff, with a hardness that promised fulfilment of my wildest desires. I would lie if I were to claim that I did not get pleasure out of trying to drive this huge cock into my gullet; however, I was afraid that Mimile would come too soon again, otherwise I would have played around with it much longer. And I was also very excited to notice the quivers that ran through Mimile's athletic body because of the unexpected pleasures and exciting new tricks that Vivienne played on him—aah, I knew them too, too well. My eyes burned passionately when I looked at those two. She pressed one of her pointed breasts into his face, at the same time Mimile was using one hand to fumble around with her firm buttocks and the other to squeeze her free breast. Then she started, because she knew full well what a greatly desired plaything her big bosom was, to put first one and then the other breast into his mouth, enticing him to suck the full, red and very hard nipples.

At the same moment I let the now hard and throbbing snake slide out of my mouth and decided that now my time had come!

I shoved Vivienne aside and straddled Mimile's big body. I took his big heavy prick in both hands and put it in position upon my crotch. As if he had waited for that signal, the sudden bucking of the man under me caused his magnificent arrow to pierce deeply into my waiting hole.

Vivienne knew exactly what I expected her to do. She threw her full weight upon Mimile's chest, pressing him down upon the bed in such a way that only his loins could move. He obliged with full force because the moistened crotch of Vivienne rested upon his lips and his wildly swinging hands had taken firm hold of my pulsating breasts. The combination of these feelings brought in me a complete frenzy. He no longer pushed against my down-pressing belly but raced up and down as if he were whipped by electrical jolts, quickly and regularly, driving his dong deeper and deeper into my sopping, longing cunt. Vivienne was rubbing her behind across his chest and I could clearly hear the smacking of Mimile's lips as he was trying to crawl around with his tongue in Vivienne's moistened hole. I tried to put off my climax as long as I could, but I was no longer master of my nerves and was unable to dam the flood that ran through me—it kept going on and on, releasing the sweetest feelings which pushed me three, no four times into seventh heaven . . . The other two also were reaching their climax. Vivienne's body stretched momentarily like a steel spring, floated away from Mimile's lips, stayed up in the air for just a second and collapsed, a small frail bundle of weakened flesh, resembling the fainted body of a very young girl. Our mutual partner bucked up high for the last time, releasing an enormous load of jism against my diaphragm and also collapsed. Without moving, the powerful body under me lay there like a dead lump.

This was one of those nights in which I got my money's worth at the house of Madam Desiree . . .

Teleny

Are we not born with a leaden cowl—namely, this Mosaic religion of ours, improved upon by Christ's mystic precepts, and rendered impossible, perfect, by Protestant hypocrisy; for if a man commit adultery with a woman every time he looks at her, did I not commit sodomy with Teleny every time I saw him or even thought of him?

There were moments however when, nature being stronger than prejudice, I should right willingly have given up my soul to perdition—nay, yielded my body to suffer in eternal hell-fire—if in the meanwhile I could have fled somewhere on the confines of this earth, on some lonely island, where in perfect nakedness I could have lived for some years in deadly sin with him, feasting upon his fascinating beauty.

Still I resolved to keep aloof from him, to be his motive power, his guiding spirit, to make of him a great, a famous, artist. As for the fire of lewedness burning within me—well, if I could not extinguish it, I could at least subdue it.

I suffered. My thoughts, night and day, were with him. My brain was always aglow; my blood was overheated; my body ever shivering with excitement. I daily read all the newspapers to see what they said about him; and whenever his name met my eyes the paper shook in my trembling hands. If my mother or anybody else mentioned his name I blushed and then grew pale.

I remember what a shock of pleasure, not unmingled with jealousy, I felt, when for the first time I saw his likeness in a window amongst those of other celebrities. I went and bought it at once, not simply to treasure and dote upon it, but also that other people might not look at it.

—What! you were so very jealous?

—Foolishly so. Unseen and at a distance I used to follow him about, after every concert he played.

Usually he was alone. Once, however, I saw him enter a cab waiting at the back door of the theatre. It had seemed to me as if someone else was within the vehicle—a woman, if I had not been mistaken. I hailed another cab, and followed them. Their carriage stopped at Teleny's house. I at once bade my Jehu do the same.

I saw Teleny alight. As he did so, he offered his hand to a lady, thickly veiled, who tripped out of the carriage and darted into the open doorway. The cab then went off.

I bade my driver wait there the whole night. At dawn the carriage of the evening before came and stopped. My driver looked up. A few minutes afterwards the door was again opened. The lady hurried out, was handed into her carriage by her lover. I followed her, and stopped where she alighted.

A few days afterwards I knew whom she was.

—And who was she?

—A lady of an unblemished reputation with whom Teleny had played some duets.

In the cab, that night, my mind was so intently fixed upon Teleny that my inward self seemed to disintegrate itself from my body and to follow like his own shadow the man I loved. I unconsciously threw myself into a kind of trance and I had a most vivid hallucination, which, strange as it might appears, coincided with all that my friend did and felt.

For instance, as soon as the door was shut behind them, the lady caught Teleny in her arms, and gave him a long kiss. Their embrace would have lasted several seconds more, had Teleny not lost his breath.

You smile; yes, I suppose you yourself are aware how easily people lose their breath in kissing, when the lips do not feel that blissful intoxicating lust in all its intensity. She would have given him another kiss, but Teleny whispered to her: 'Let us go up to my room; there we shall be far safer than here.'

Soon they were in his apartment.

She looked timidly around, and seeing herself in that young man's room alone with him, she blushed and seemed thoroughly ashamed of herself.

'Oh! René,' said she, 'what must you think of me?'

'That you love me dearly,' quoth he, 'do you not?'

'Yes, indeed; not wisely, but too well.'

Thereupon, taking off her wrappers, she rushed up and clasped her lover in her arms, showering her warm kisses on his head, his eyes, his cheeks and then upon his mouth. That mouth I so longed to kiss!

With lips pressed together, she remained for some time inhaling his breath, and—almost frightened at her boldness—she touched his lips with the tip of her tongue. Then, taking courage, soon afterwards she slipped it in his mouth, and then after a while, she thrust it in and out, as if she were enticing him to try the act of nature by it; she was so convulsed with lust by this kiss that she had to clasp herself not to fall, for the blood was rushing to her head, and her knees were almost giving way beneath her. At last, taking his right hand, after squeezing it hesitatingly for a moment, she placed it within her breasts, giving him her nipple to pinch, and as he did so, the pleasure she felt was so great that she was swooning away for joy.

'Oh, Teleny!' said she; 'I can't! I can't any more.'

And she rubbed herself as strongly as she could against him, protruding her middle parts against his.

—And Teleny?

—Well, jealous as I was, I could not help feeling how different his manner was now from the rapturous way with which he had clung to me that evening, when he had taken the bunch of heliotrope from his buttonhole and had put it in mine.

He accepted rather than returned her caresses. Anyhow, she seemed pleased, for she thought him shy.

She was now hanging on him. One of her arms was clasped around his waist, the other one around his neck. Her dainty, tapering bejewelled fingers were playing with his curly hair, and paddling his neck.

He was squeezing her breasts, and, as I said before, slightly fingering her nipples.

She gazed deep into his eyes, and then sighed.

'You do not love me,' at last she said. 'I can see it in your eyes. You are not thinking of me, but of somebody else.'

And it was true. At that moment he was thinking of me—fondly, longingly; and then, as he did so, he got more excited, and he caught her in his arms, and hugged and kissed her with far more eagerness than he had hitherto done—nay, he began to suck her tongue as if it had been mine, and then began to thrust his own into her mouth.

After a few moments of rapture she, this time, stopped to take a breath.

'Yes, I am wrong. You love me. I see it now. You do not despise me because I am here, do you?'

'Ah! if you could only read in my heart, and see how madly I love you, darling!'

And she looked at him with longing, passionate eyes.

'Still you think me light, don't you? I am an adultcress!'

And thereupon she shuddered, and hid her face in her hands.

He looked at her for a moment pitifully, then he took down her hands gently, and kissed her.

'You do not know how I have tried to resist you, but I could not. I am on fire. My blood is no longer blood, but some burning love-philtre. I cannot help myself,' said she, lifting up her head defiantly as if she were facing the whole world, 'here I am, do with me what you like, only tell me that you love me, that you love no other woman but me, swear it.'

'I swear,' said he, languidly, 'that I love no other woman.'

She did not understand the meaning of his words.

'But tell it to me again, say it often, it is so sweet to hear it repeated from the lips of those we dote on,' said she, with passionate eagerness.

'I assure you that I have never cared for any woman so much as I do for you.'

'Cared?' said she, disappointed.

'Loved, I mean.'

'And you can swear it?'

'On the cross if you like,' added he, smiling.

'And you do not think badly of me because I am here? Well, you are the only one for whom I have ever been unfaithful to my husband; though God knows if he be faithful—my husband; God knows if he be faithful to me. Still my love does not atone for my sin, does it?'

Teleny did not give her any answer for an instant, he looked at her with dreamy eyes, then shuddered as if awaking from a trance.

'Sin,' he said, 'is the only thing worth living for.'

She looked at him rather astonished, but then she kissed him again and again and answered: 'Well, yes, you are perhaps right; it is so, the fruit of the forbidden tree was pleasant to the sight, to the taste, and to the smell.'

They sat down on a divan. When they were clasped again in each other's arms he slipped his hand somewhat timidly and almost unwillingly under her skirts.

She caught hold of his hand, and arrested it.

'No, René, I beg of you! Could we not love each other with a Platonic love? Is that not enough?'

'Is it enough for you?' said he, almost superciliously.

She pressed her lips again upon his, and almost relinquished her grasp. The hand went stealthily up along the leg, stopped a moment on the knees, caressing them; but the legs closely pressed together prevented it from slipping between them, and thus reaching the higher storey. It crept slowly up, nevertheless, caressing the thighs through the fine linen underclothing, and thus, by stolen marches, it reached its aim. The hand then slipped between the opening of the drawers, and began to feel the soft skin. She tried to stop him.

'No, no!' said she; 'please don't; you are tickling me.'

He then took courage, and plunged his fingers boldly in the fine curly locks of the fleece that covered all her middle parts.

She continued to hold her thighs tightly closed together,

especially when the naughty fingers began to graze the edge of the moist lips. At that touch, however, her strength gave way; the nerves relaxed, and allowed the tip of a finger to worm its way within the slit—nay, the tiny berry protruded out to welcome it.

After a few moments she breathed more strongly. She encircled his breast with her arms, kissed him, and then hid her head on his shoulder.

'Oh, what a rapture I feel!' she cried. 'What a magnetic fluid you possess to make me feel as I do!'

He did not give her any answer; but, unbuttoning his trousers, he took hold of her dainty little hand. He endeavoured to introduce it within the gap. She tried to resist, but weakly, and as if asking but to yield. She soon gave way, and boldly caught hold of his phallus, now stiff and hard, moving lustily by its own inward strength.

After a few moments of pleasant manipulation, their lips pressed together, he lightly, and almost against her knowledge, pressed her down on the couch, lifted up her legs, pulled up her skirts without for a moment taking his tongue out of her mouth or stopping his tickling of her clitoris already wet with its own tears. Then—sustaining his weight on his elbows—he got his legs between her thighs. That her excitement increased could be visibly seen by the shivering of the lips which he had no need to open as he pressed down upon her, for they parted of themselves to give entrance to the little blind God of Love.

With one thrust he introduced himself within the precincts of Love's temple; with another, the rod was halfway in; with the third, he reached the very bottom of the den of pleasure; for, though she was no longer in the first days of earliest youth, still she had hardly reached her prime, and her flesh was not only firm, but she was so tight that he was fairly clasped and sucked by those pulpy lips; so, after moving up and down a few times, thrusting himself always further, he crushed her down with his full weight; for both his hands were either handling her breasts, or else, having slipped them under her, he was opening her buttocks; and then, lifting her firmly upon him, he thrust a finger in her backside hole, thus wedging her on both sides, making her feel a more intense pleasure by thus sodomising her.

After a few seconds of this little game he began to breathe strongly—to pant. The milky fluid that had for days accumulated itself now rushed out in thick jets, coursing up into her very womb. She, thus flooded, showed her hysteric enjoyment by her screams, her tears, her sighs. Finally, all strength gave way; arms and legs stiffened themselves; she fell lifeless on the couch; whilst he remained stretched over at the risk of giving the Count, her husband, an heir of gipsy blood.

He soon recovered his strength, and rose. She was then recalled to her senses, but only to melt into a flood of tears.

A bumper of champagne brought them both, however, to a less gloomy sense of life. A few partridge sandwiches, some lobster patties, a caviar salad, with a few more glasses of champagne, together with many *marrons glacés*, and a punch made of maraschino, pineapple juice and whisky, drunk out of the same goblet soon finished by dispelling their gloominess.

'Why should we not put ourselves at our ease, my dear?' said he. 'I'll set you the example, shall I?'

'By all means.'

Thereupon Teleny took off his white tie, that stiff and uncomfortable useless appendage invented by fashion only to torture mankind, yclept a shirt collar, then his coat and waistcoat, and he remained only in his shirt and trousers.

'Now, my dear, allow me to act as your maid.'

The beautiful woman at first refused, but yielded after some kisses; and, little by little, nothing was left of all her clothing but an almost transparent *crêpe de Chine* chemise, dark steel-blue silk stockings, and satin slippers.

Teleny covered her bare neck and arms with kisses, pressed his cheeks against the thick, black hair of her armpits, and tickled her as he did so. This little titillation was felt all over her body, and the slit between her legs opened again in such a way that the delicate little clitoris, like a red hawthorn berry, peeped out as if to see what was going on. He held her for a moment crushed against his chest, and his *'merle'*—as the Italians call it—flying out of his cage, he thrust it into the opening ready to receive it.

She pushed lustily against him, but he had to keep her up, for her legs were almost giving away, so great was the pleasure she felt. He therefore stretched her down on the panther rug at his feet, without unclasping her.

All sense of shyness was now overcome. He pulled off his clothes, and pressed down with all his strength. She—to receive his instrument far deep in her sheath—clasped him with her legs in such a way that he could hardly move. He was, therefore, only able to rub himself against her; but that was more than enough, for after a few violent shakes of their buttocks, legs pressed, and breasts crushed, the burning liquid which he injected within her body gave her a spasmodic pleasure, and she fell senseless on the panther skin whilst he rolled, motionless, by her side.

Till then I felt that my image had always been present before his eyes, although he was enjoying this handsome woman—so beautiful, for she had hardly yet reached the bloom of ripe womanhood; but now the pleasure she had given him had made him quite forget me. I therefore hated him. For a moment I felt that I should like to be a wild beast—to drive my nails into his flesh, to torture him like a cat does a mouse, and to tear him into pieces.

What right had he to love anybody but myself? Did I love a single being in this world as I loved him? Could I feel pleasure with anyone else?

No, my love was not a maudlin sentimentality, it was the maddening passion that overpowers the body and shatters the brain!

If he could love women, why did he then make love to me, obliging me to love him, making me a contemptible being in my own eyes?

In the paroxysm of my excitement I writhed, I bit my lips till they bled. I dug my nails into my flesh; I cried out with jealousy and shame. I wanted but little to have made me jump out of the cab, and go and ring at the door of his house.

This state of things lasted for a few moments, and then I began to wonder what he was doing, and the fit of hallucination came over me again. I saw him awakening from the slumber into which he had fallen when overpowered by enjoyment.

As he awoke he looked at her. Now I could see her plainly, for I believe that she was only visible to me through his medium.

—But you fell asleep, and dreamt all this whilst you were in the cab, did you not?

—There was, as I told you before, a strong transmission of thoughts between us. This is by no means a remarkable coincidence. You smile and look incredulous; well, follow the doings of the Psychical Society, and this vision will certainly not astonish you any more.

—Well, never mind, go on.

—As Teleny awoke, he looked at his mistress lying on the panther-skin at his side.

She was as sound asleep as anyone would be after a banquet, intoxicated by strong drink; or as a baby, that having sucked its fill, stretches itself glutted by the side of its mother's breast. It was the heavy sleep of lusty life, not the placid stillness of cold death. The blood—like the sap of a young tree in spring—mounted to her parted, pouting lips, through which a warm scented breath escaped at cadenced intervals, emitting that slight murmur which the child hears as he listens in a shell—the sound of slumbering life.

The breasts—as if swollen with milk—stood up, and the nipples erect seemed to be asking for those caresses she was so fond of; over all her body there was a shivering of insatiable desire.

Her thighs were bare, and the thick curly hair that covered her middle parts, as black as jet, was sprinkled over with pearly drops of milky dew.

Such a sight would have awakened an eager, irrepressible desire in Joseph himself, the only chaste Israelite of whom he had ever heard; and yet Teleny, leaning on his elbow, was gazing at her with all the loathsomeness we feel when we look at a kitchen table covered with the offal of the meat, the hashed scraps, the dregs of the wines which have supplied the banquet that has just glutted us.

He looked at her with the scorn which a man has for the woman who has just administered to his pleasure, and who had degraded herself and him. Moreover, as he felt unjust towards her, he hated her, and not himself.

I felt again that he did not love her, but me, though she had made him for a few moments forget met.

She seemed to feel his cold glance upon her, for she shivered, and, thinking she was asleep in bed, she tried to cover herself up; and her hand, fumbling for the sheet, pulled up her chemise, only uncovering herself more by that action. She woke as she did so, and caught Teleny's reproachful glances.

She looked around, frightened. She tried to cover herself as much as she could; and then, entwining one of her arms round the young man's neck—

'Do not look at me like that,' she said. 'Am I so loathsome to you? Oh! I see it. You despise me.' And her eyes filled with tears. 'You are right. Why did I yield? Why did I not resist the love that was torturing me? Alas! it was not you, but I who sought you, who made love to you; and now you feel for me nothing but disgust. Tell me, is it so? You love another woman! No!—tell me you don't!'

'I don't,' said Teleny, earnestly.

'Yes, but swear.'

'I have already sworn before, or at least offered to do so. What is the use of swearing, if you don't believe me?'

Though all lust was gone, Teleny felt a heartfelt pity for that handsome young woman, who, maddened by love for him, had put into jeopardy her whole existence to throw herself into his arms.

Who is the man that is not flattered by the love he inspires in a high-born, wealthy, and handsome young woman, who forgets her marriage to enjoy a few moments' bliss in his arms? But, then, why do women generally love men who often care so little for them?

Teleny did his best to comfort her, to tell her over and over again that he cared for no woman, to assure her that he would be eternally faithful to her for her sacrifice; but pity is not love, nor is affection the eagerness of desire.

Nature was more than satisfied; her beauty had lost all its attraction; they kissed again and again; he languidly passed his hands all over her body, from the nape of the neck to the deep dent between those round hills, which seemed covered with fallen snow, giving her a most delightful sensation as he did so; he caressed her breasts, suckled and bit the tiny protruding nipples, whilst his fingers were often thrust far within the warm flesh hidden under that mass of jet-black hair. She glowed, she breathed, she shivered with pleasure; but Teleny, though performing his work with masterly skill, remained cold at her side.

'No, I see that you don't love me; for it is not possible that you—a young man—'

She did not finish. Teleny felt the sting of her reproaches, but remained passive; for the phallus is not stiffened by taunts.

She took the lifeless object in her delicate fingers. She rubbed and manipulated it. She even rolled it between her two soft hands. It remained like a piece of dough. She sighed as piteously as Ovid's mistress must have done on a like occasion. She did like this woman did some hundreds of years before. She bent down; she took the tip of that inert piece of flesh between her lips—the pulpy lips which looked like a tiny apricot—so round, sappy, and luscious. Soon it was all in her mouth. She sucked it with as much evident pleasure as if she were a famished baby taking her nurse's breast. As it went in and out, she tickled the prepuce with her expert tongue, touched the tiny lips on her palate.

The phallus, though somewhat harder, remained always limp and nerveless.

You know our ignorant forefathers believed in the practice called *'nouer les aiguillettes'*—that is, rendering the male incapable of performing the pleasant work for which

Nature has destined him. We, the enlightened generation, have discarded such gross superstitions, and still our ignorant forefathers were sometimes right.

—What? you do not mean to say that you believe in such tomfoolery?

—It might be tomfoolery, as you say; but still it is a fact. Hypnotize a person, and then you will see if you can get the mastery over him or not.

—Still, you had not hypnotized Teleny?

—No, but our natures seemed to be bound to one another by a secret affinity.

At that moment I felt a secret shame for Teleny. Not being able to understand the working of his brain, she seemed to regard him in the light of a young cock, who, having crowed lustily once or twice at early dawn, has strained his neck to such a pitch that he can only emit hoarse, feeble, gurgling sounds out of it after that.

Moreover, I almost felt sorry for that woman; and I thought, if I were only in her place, how disappointed I should be. And I sighed, repeating almost audibly,—'Were I but in her stead.'

The image which had formed itself within my mind so vividly was all at once reverberated within René's brain; and he thought, if instead of this lady's mouth those lips were my lips; and his phallus at once stiffened and awoke into life; the glands swelled with blood; not only an erection took place, but it almost ejaculated. The Countess—for she was a Countess—was herself surprised at this sudden change, and stopped, for she had now obtained what she wanted; and she knew that—*'Dépasser le but, c'est manquer la chose.'*

Teleny, however, began to fear that if he had his mistress' face before his eyes, my image might entirely vanish; and that—beautiful as she was—he would never be able to accomplish his work to the end. So he began by covering her with kisses; then deftly turned her on her back. She yielded without understanding what was required of her. He bent her pliant body on her knees, so that she presented a most beautiful sight to his view.

This splendid sight ravished him to such an extent that by looking at it his hitherto limp tool acquired its full size and stiffness, and in its lusty vigour leapt in such a way that it knocked against his navel.

He was even tempted for a moment to introduce it within the small dot of a hole, which if not exactly the den of life is surely that of pleasure; but he forebore. He even resisted the temptation of kissing it, or of darting his tongue into it; but bending over her, and placing himself between her legs, he tried to introduce the glans within the aperture of her two lips, now thick and swollen by dint of much rubbing.

Wide apart as her legs were, he first had to open the lips with his fingers on account of the mass of bushy hair that grew all around them; for now the tiny curls had entangled themselves together like tendrils, as if to bar the entrance; therefore, when he had brushed the hair aside, he pressed his tool in it, but the turgid dry flesh arrested him. The clitoris thus pressed danced with delight, so that he took it in his hand, and rubbed and shook it softly and gently on the top part of her lips.

She began to shake, to rub herself with delight; she groaned, she sobbed hysterically; and when he felt himself bathed with delicious tears he thrust his instrument far within her body, clasping her tightly around the neck. So, after a few bold strokes, he managed to get in the whole of the rod down to the very root of the column, crushing his hair against hers, so far in the utmost recesses of the womb that it gave her a pleasurable pain as it touched the neck of the vagina.

For about ten minutes—which to her felt an eternity—she continued panting, throbbing, gasping, groaning, shrieking, roaring, laughing, and crying in the vehemence of her delight.

'Oh! Oh! I am feeling it again! In—in—quick—quicker! There! there!—enough!—stop!'

But he did not listen to her, and he went on plunging and re-plunging with increasing vigour. Having vainly begged for a truce, she began to move again with renewed life.

Having her *a retro*, his whole thoughts were thus concentrated upon me; and the tightness of the orifice in which the penis was sheathed, added to the titillation produced by the lips of the womb, gave him such an overpowering sensation that he redoubled his strength, and shoved his muscular instrument with such mighty strokes that the frail woman shook under the repeated thumps. Her knees were almost giving way under the brutal force he displayed. When again, all at once, the flood-gates of the seminal ducts were open, and he squirted a jet of molten liquid down into the innermost recesses of her womb.

A moment of delirium followed; the contraction of all her muscles gripped him and sucked him up eagerly, greedily; and after a short spasmodic convulsion, they both fell senseless side by side, still tightly wedged in one another.

—And so ends the Epistle!

—Not quite so, for nine months afterwards the Countess gave birth to a fine boy—

—Who, of course, looked like his father? Doesn't every child look like its father?

—Still this one happened to look neither like the Count nor like Teleny.

—Who the deuce did it look like then?

—Like myself.

—Bosh!

—Bosh as much as you like. Anyhow, the rickety old Count is very proud of this son of his, having discovered a certain likeness between his only heir and the portrait of one of his ancestors. He is always pointing out this atavism to all his visitors; but whenever he struts about, and begins to expound learnedly over the matter, I am told that the Countess shrugs her shoulders and puckers down her lips contemptuously, as if she was not quite convinced of the fact.

The House of Borgia

After the dissolvement of her marriage, Lucrezia withdrew to the Convent of San Sisto in the Appian Way—partly to escape the various items of scandal which were rocking Rome, partly to appear to act with the decorum her situation demanded.

She was to spend a period of some six months in her own private quarters, taking part with the nuns in daily prayers, joining with them in much of their work.

For some weeks she lived with them, praying, making baskets, carving small figurines in wood, walking in the quiet grounds, feeding their dozen hens. She was happy for a time to be free of the world in which she always felt a little as if she was living on the summit of a volcano that was likely to erupt unexpectedly.

But, at the end of that time, accustomed as she was to fierce and frequent intercourse, she began to feel an aching void in her loins, began to consider how to best soothe it.

During her walks in the grounds she had particularly befriended a young nun who had been in the convent only a short time before her. This young girl, whose name was Carlotta, was designated to show Lucrezia how to make the baskets and the little wooden figurines.

They got on very well and it soon became apparent to Lucrezia that the younger and unworldly Carlotta was quite fascinated by her.

Lucrezia managed, cleverly, to discover that the girl, who had never had a lover, was taking ill to her new and voluntary exile. She felt in her a need which she didn't understand, although listening to her confused explanations, Lucrezia was only too well aware of the trouble—the young girl needed a good fuck.

Carlotta was very attractive in her own way. She was dark, with a long face and slightly Jewish nose dominating long, well-defined lips. Her body was completely concealed under the shrouds of her long robes, but the melancholy attraction of her face was quite enough to excite Lucrezia in her present manless state.

Giving way to the girl's hinted-at curiosity, Lucrezia began, during their walks in the grounds, to tell her a few things about her sexual life. But always she exaggerated the brutality of the male, making him sound an utter, unbearable brute.

'I don't think I could stand to have a man using me in such a way,' Carlotta said one morning as they sat staring at the water lilies in the little stream which ran sluggishly through the lower reaches of the convent grounds. 'I should feel stripped of any sense of dignity I'd ever had.'

Lucrezia took the plunge.

'Yes. If the choice was between man and this convent, I would choose a cloistered existence within these walls,' she said. 'But, fortunately there are other things one can do.'

The girl raised her fine, dark eyebrows.

'What—other things in place of a man?'

'A woman, Carlotta. Women are much gentler and more loving than men. And they understand a woman's needs whereas most men are selfish and oafish in their lovemaking.'

'But . . .'

'I think,' Lucrezia went on quickly, 'much as I respect the Mother Superior and the individual right of choice, that any woman who locks herself away in a prison is betraying her function as a woman and displaying a fear of the world which belief in God should not justify.'

Carlotta stared at her, shocked. She had never dared to voice such sentiments, but they fitted well with her present mood of boredom and rebellion.

'You only have to look at the majority of the women here,' Lucrezia continued, 'and you see immediately that they're women who are too ugly or too witless to succeed in a competitive and natural world.'

She took Carlotta's hand.

'But you don't belong among them, Carlotta. You are lovely and full of life which won't allow itself to be kept in check forever.'

The girl was flattered and moved by the words which were spoken to her in such sincere tones. They sped her own unformed impulses along the channel that Lucrezia intended.

'I feel you are right,' she said. She glanced at the distant figures of the other nuns wandering in the upper part of the grounds among the trees. 'I'm beginning to wish I hadn't taken my vows.'

'You should make the best of things as they are,' Lucrezia said. 'We are both in the same cul-de-sac of frustration. We should help each other.'

'But what can we . . . ?'

'We can take the place of men for each other.'

The girl dropped her eyes and gazed down at the lilies. There was a silence for some seconds.

'I—I wouldn't know how . . . and—and I'm not sure that it's . . . '

'We all have deep centres in our beings which others may never reach,' Lucrezia cut in, 'but unless they do, unless we try to help them to, we all live lonely, unsatisfied lives, lives which wrinkle us up with bitterness, the feeling of having missed what was essential.'

Carlotta raised her eyes from the stream and found herself unable again to withdraw them from Lucrezia's deep, compelling gaze.

'Come to my quarters after evensong tonight,' Lucrezia went on, 'and I will show you what it means to reach that centre.'

The dull peal of a bell calling them in to prayer cut short any reply the young girl might have made. She stared at Lucrezia, dropped her eyes at last and walked away toward the building. Lucrezia smiled after her for a moment and then slowly followed her.

That evening, alone in her quarters—two rooms at the far

end of a wing of the convent—Lucrezia, garbed only in a dressing gown, waited for Carlotta to come. She was almost certain she would come although the girl had given her no answer. She knew how the possibility of sexual adventure could play on one's nerves, stimulating, frightening, exciting all at the same time.

For Lucrezia, too, this would be the first lesbian experience and the idea filled her with the same lustful chill of eagerness that her first fuck had—especially as she had been deprived of her conjugal and fraternal rights for some weeks now.

She found herself unable to keep still as the minutes went by following evensong. She rose time and time again and looked out of the sloping window down to the grounds. At last she sat on her bed and tried to concentrate on the pages of Boccaccio's *Il Decamerone* which she had smuggled into the convent with her.

As time passed she became more and more anxious. If Carlotta didn't come now she would die of frustration. She put down the book and stared out of the window again before walking into the next room where she studied herself in a small, silver-backed hand mirror.

Her heart leapt as there came a light tapping on her door. She ran to open it and almost clasped the young girl to her bosom as she drew her into her room.

Carlotta smiled at her briefly and stood uncertainly just inside the door while Lucrezia closed and bolted it.

'Make yourself at home', Lucrezia urged, turning around to her.

Nervously, the girl went to the window and looked out as if to reassure herself that the outside world was there, solid and unchanged. Lucrezia watched her pretending to interest herself in the exploration of the rooms, pretending to examine the few books, flicking pages over with a pointless speed.

'I was afraid to come,' she said at last. 'Wasn't that ridiculous—we are quite free to visit one another's rooms.'

'We are quite free to act as we please,' Lucrezia added.

'Yes,' the girl said uncertainly.

'I have another gown—why don't you make yourself more comfortable and put it on,' Lucrezia suggested.

She handed over the garment and Carlotta took it nervously.

Lucrezia turned away and studied *Il Decamerone*, listening to the rustle of clothes as Carlotta slipped out of them. She kept swallowing with nervous excitement.

At a well-judged moment she glanced around and caught her companion naked. Carlotta gazed at her with wide, embarrassed eyes and Lucrezia glanced back at her book immediately. But not before she'd had a glimpse of the girl's small, firm breasts, high up and dark, with the splodge of dark nipple giving them body, and her slim figure below it with the eye-catching fuzz of dark hair above her thighs. Lucrezia felt almost matronly beside the girl's small proportions.

She did not look up again until the girl came and sat beside her on the bed. Carlotta seemed to have lost some of her uncertainty. It was as if she'd reminded herself that she had, after all, come for a specific purpose and that there was no point in trying to pretend she hadn't.

Lucrezia replaced the book on a shelf over the bed and lay back on it, looking at her companion. Carlotta looked even more attractive out of her nun's sombre garb, and the long V-neck of the gown revealed a smooth stretch of her succulent-looking skin between her breasts. The beginning of their bulge on either side of the valley of flesh was heaving with a nervous emotion.

'You are really very lovely,' Lucrezia told her. 'It was a great mistake for a girl like you to get such a mad idea in her head that she wanted to pass the rest of her days in a tomb.'

The conversation brought a sense of normality with it and Carlotta's voice hid a trace of relief as if a spell had been broken.

'If you hadn't come, I might never have realised it,' she answered.

'Sooner or later you would have—but I'm glad it's through me that your revolution is to be achieved.'

Carlotta had again, as in the afternoon, become lost in Lucrezia's eyes. They seemed to hold her hypnotically. She came, as if Lucrezia had commanded her, and lay down on the bed beside her. Lucrezia touched the girl's cheek, lightly.

'Remember that this is the only way to liberate yourself from the horror and monotony of a death in life,' she said softly as her lips followed her hand.

Lucrezia was not very surprised to find that a relationship with a woman gave her as strong an erotic urge as with a man. It was as if it were something she'd always known, even when her conscious thought had included nothing but images of Cesare's, her father's, Giovanni's embraces. Now she felt the soft, smooth skin of the girl's cheek against her lips, a softness and a leafy fragrance which were missing in a man, and she felt her spirit stirred with the upsetting excitement of a new and forbidden experience about to come to fruition.

She slipped her hand into the girl's gown and Carlotta winced. Then her hand was caressing the small, firm breast with the lightest of touches. Her lips moved over the girl's face without losing contact—and found her lips. The lips were still, slightly reluctant and unsure. But as Lucrezia's hand moved from one breast to the other and tweaked the nipple, as her tongue played hide and seek with Carlotta's lips, the mouth opened with a sound which was near to a sigh, the lips relaxed and then kissed back.

Lucrezia's tongue gave up its game and lunged right out to fill the mouth which opened and spread at its assault.

Gently, her hand untied the belt of the gown. The material slipped slowly down to the bed off the glossy flesh of Carlotta's hips and thighs.

Lucrezia's hand rested on the girl's waist for a moment, the index finger playing with her navel. She noticed the girl was trembling faintly, like a leaf in the merest zephyr. She let her hand float away over the glassy expanse of flesh, lingering, unhurried, exploring every part while her tongue continued to caress the moist, heavily-breathing lips.

As her advancing fingers encountered the silky fan of

pubic hair, she slowed. She let her fingers course through it as through money. Under it she could feel the flesh swollen in a little mound, like a slight rise in the ground covered with a fine grass.

Carlotta wriggled her hips very slightly. She seemed ashamed of their movement, which was like an effort at escape.

Lucrezia sucked heavily on the lips which were trembling now in unison with the body.

With her free hand, she awkwardly unpulled her own belt and then pushed the plump flesh of her thigh against Carlotta's.

Slowly, as if stroking a timid animal, she allowed her fingers to continue on their downward progress. They moved down the rise and into the hot, little hollow between the oozing flesh of Carlotta's tightly-gripped thighs. Her path was barred for the moment by the instinctive inward pressure of those thighs. She stroked all the flesh she could reach and was rewarded with a sudden seepage of moisture around her fingers.

She moved her lips off Carlotta's and kissed her neck.

'Relax, darling,' she whispered. 'Open your legs.'

'I can't bear it,' Carlotta whispered back after a moment. 'It makes me jump every time you touch me.'

'All right—just let it go naturally. It'll come.'

Lucrezia went on with her gentle fondling. The hollow was very warm now and Carlotta was letting out an odd 'oh' every so often from deep down in her throat.

Moving her lips down the neck, over the slim shoulders, Lucrezia invaded the breasts which were taut and straining with sensation. She closed her mouth over a nipple and sucked hard and strong, bringing forth gasps of torment from the girl.

Carlotta's thighs relaxed and, awaiting her moment, Lucrezia was able suddenly to advance her fingers so that the texture of flesh changed and she knew she was in the beginning of the wet ravine formed by those nether lips. Carlotta clasped her thighs together again, crushing the tormenting hand, but Lucrezia bore the weight and tickled the wet flesh with her fingertips.

She drew on the nipple again with her lips, sucking in as much of the breast behind it as she could.

Carlotta thrust her breast at the lips which seemed to be drawing milk from her shapely udders. She arched her hips and gave way suddenly, opening her thighs, relaxing them so that the raping hand was suddenly right between her legs, the fingers in at their target.

Lucrezia moved a finger in the suddenly conquered vagina. Carlotta groaned in submission.

Slowly Lucrezia titivated and explored the flood-washed well. She pushed in through the tight ring of flesh, to the accompaniment of a little squeal from Carlotta. She thrust up, and then up again, feeling the hips withdraw instinctively, pull up away from the hand and then ooze back as they became used to the exquisite pressure.

Steadily Lucrezia sucked the breast, gnawed it, remembering all the things she liked a man to do and doing them with that greater finesse which was born of her own intimate, subjective knowledge.

Her fingers could move more loosely, more freely now. The ravine had become a great river, like a dried-up wadi suddenly swollen with the seasonal rains, the channel leading from it had become bigger, more accommodating and the hips were moving and bobbing against hers, brushing her flesh with another's exciting, strange flesh.

Breathing hard herself, Lucrezia moved her finger out of the hole and fastened it on the hard little clitoris which had reared up with its first touch from an alien hand.

Carlotta cried out and then spread her thighs in complete, won-over invitation as the finger bit into that little stem of sensitive flesh. She was wriggling incessantly, her mouth wide open, gasping for air.

'Oh God, oh God!' she exclaimed.

Lucrezia worked furiously and delightedly on the clitoris which expanded at her touch, grew harder, longer. She could feel passion growing in it as her finger and thumb pinched it, tweaked it, stroked it, masturbated it. There was only one thing left to make Carlotta's initiating delight into utter rapture.

Lucrezia slid down her body, revelling in the tight, straining pressure of flesh against hers. Her wet lips followed the swells and hollows of the body in their descent. She withdrew down to Carlotta's thighs with them. She ran her lips down the thighs, kissing tantalizingly on their buttery, yielding insides. The thighs twitched, clasped her head, relaxed. She heard the fury of Carlotta's moans washing down upon her ears like the continual flow of waves against a reef.

Her thighs clasped and unclasped, tensed and untensed continually; her hips wriggled like fish on a hook and she was fastened to the bed with her own overwhelming passion which was no longer timid but demanding.

Sliding her lips up the thighs, Lucrezia met first the slippery ooze of fluid glossing the tops of the legs. She lapped it like a dog. It represented the passion of a lovely girl—nothing unpalatable about that.

Over the swamp and to the very brink of the ravine, a plunge of the tongue and she was kissing and licking in that inundated wadi which squirmed and pressed against her and squashed its side flat against her mouth.

She searched, her tongue leading her blindly in the wadi until she found that steep, stiff monument. She grasped it in her lips and Carlotta's hips went mad, writhing and twisting so that Lucrezia had to hang onto her prize as if she were on a wild horse. But she clung to it, sucking it voraciously while a thin whine of passion, broken often by a deep moan, crashed down on her ears from the tortured face high up above her.

Her hands grasped those slim hips. How slim they were compared to her own. They made Carlotta seem that much more girlish, innocent, helpless.

She slid her hands under the hips and ran them all around the firm, tense balls of bottom. What an excellent little bottom.

She squeezed and worked its pliable bulk as she sucked and licked. The buttocks tightened and relaxed in her hands, swinging wildly in torment. The girl had become a raging form of sexuality. There seemed nothing left of her except a moaning, writhing mass of sensual flesh.

Lucrezia pulled the buttocks apart forcibly. They were hot in the crack between them. There were a few young hairs and then a sweating smoothness. Her fingers slipped over it like little snakes.

The anus nestled there, unprotected now and she rifled it with her fingers the way she'd liked her father to intrude in hers. And Carlotta had no reticence any longer. She didn't even try to press her backside cheeks together. On the contrary she pressed them wide and back so that Lucrezia's finger actually penetrated the anus, the tight little ring of flesh, near to her sucking lips.

She used her tongue on the clitoris which seemed so big as to be unreal. There was a taste of salt and parsley in her mouth; the liquid was running over her face, growing into a torrent.

Above, out of sight, she heard Carlotta's sob.

'Oh, oh, it's here, it's here,' she heard her cry, out of control.

She sucked even more furiously, jabbing her finger deeply into the tight, tearing hole. She was terribly excited herself. She got a vicarious pleasure from the girl's helpless passion.

Following on her gasped out words, Carlotta twisted first one way and then the other in a quick, shivering convulsion. Her mouth opened wide and a long, continuous moan of sound exploded from it as she clasped her thighs around Lucrezia's head and squeezed.

The grip on Lucrezia was strong and suffocating, but she bore it until it slowly relaxed and the thighs fell away.

She straightened up, realising just how hot her loins had become. A little longer and she'd probably have come herself.

She looked at Carlotta. The girl seemed to have collapsed in a coma. She lay with her head thrown back dramatically, her arms wide out beside her head. Her eyes were closed, her breasts heaving in a great swell of emotion.

Lucrezia lay down alongside her and kissed her shoulder. After a while she spoke.

'Wasn't that worth a year in a convent? Isn't it worth anything on earth?'

Carlotta's eyes opened slowly, sleepily. She'd lost all trace of her early embarrassment.

'I feel purged,' she said softly. 'I feel satisfied and purged of all the frustration and not knowing that I've ever felt.'

Lucrezia smiled at her and kissed her bare arm.

'You obviously enjoyed it,' she agreed. 'Your enjoyment was so infectious that I almost had a climax myself.'

Carlotta opened her eyes again and looked at her. Realisation had dawned that there were, of course, two of them, that Lucrezia had given her undreamed-of pleasure, that it was now up to her to reciprocate.

'I'm not at all expert,' she said. 'I shan't know what to do.'

Lucrezia began to quiver with anticipation.

'Just do what I did,' she said with a break in her voice. 'And that will be wonderful.'

'I have got to get my breath back a moment.'

They lay together for a few minutes longer. Lucrezia could hardly wait and she kept pressing her round belly against Carlotta's side and tensing her pelvis against her.

'God, I want it very badly!' she muttered.

At that Carlotta turned over toward her and she fell backwards on the bed. She lay there staring up at the ceiling concentrating on herself, looking inward at the sensation inside her.

She felt the warm face come down on her breasts. To Carlotta her breasts were enormous in comparison with her own. They just asked to be nestled against, to be used as a pillow in which to bury one's face.

The face brushed against the tight, hurting points of her breasts, piquing her with a spearpoint of ecstatic pain that rushed straight to her genitals. And then those cool, well-defined lips closed on her nipple in a soft, fondling grip that made her squirm already.

They began to suck, drawing her pear of breast into the mouth, drawing it in, in, swallowing it, sucking it, pulverizing it with sharp, needed pain.

Lucrezia's legs began to jerk in spasms and the unknown fingers slid down her body, the image of her own, and went straight to the spot which played no timid games with them but waited, wide open like a trap, thighs wide apart and squirming.

Lucrezia held her breath waiting for the contact, expecting it, but still jumping with delight when it came. Cool fingers caressed her long, deep cleft which was stinging as the juices were washed into it from her inner regions.

The fingers explored like timid animals—and everywhere they touched and slid they left a burning, a prickling sense of near-destruction.

Lucrezia groaned. She liked to groan. She let the groans escape from her mouth—not that she could really have controlled them—to show her appreciation of what was being done to her.

Then with a sudden jump she felt the fingertips find her little erection. That was too much. She squirmed her hips in a movement that was almost circular, that was wild, exaggerated.

And the fingers were relentless. They pressed there, loved there, pinched there, gave no quarter although her moans became helpless sobs of passion.

Lucrezia felt her hole growing wide. The love-juice was swamping, too, and her belly was in unbearable torment. There couldn't be much more to go.

'Your mouth, your mouth!' she pleaded.

The fingers came out of her sultry cleft giving her a brief respite. But they were replaced immediately by a pair of cool lips which seized on her clitoris, sending a shock through her whole body.

'Oh, wonderful, wonderful!' she gasped. She could hardly utter the words. They tumbled out in a rush of sound which was mostly escaping breath, wheezing out like steam from a hot spring.

The mouth was working hard, giving her no chance to catch her breath. She was out of breath as if she'd been running hard.

And then the hands, remembering, slid around her hips and dug handfuls from her big buttocks, rummaging between them to find the anal orifice.

'Wonderful, wonderful!' she breathed again, lost and helpless.

She felt the heat like a great wood fire down in her passage. It was as hot as a lump of smouldering charcoal, felt ready to splinter into pieces at any moment.

'It's coming . . . it's . . . coming . . . oh!' she gasped, more as an outlet for her feeling than as a warning. She jerked her legs this way and that as if they were puppets and she held the strings. Speech was now impossible. The sounds from her mouth were animal noises, enlarging in abandon with every lick of that tongue on her erect little organ.

She clamped her legs around Carlotta's head and squeezed her loins up at her face, forcing, straining, arching. She felt the burst, the splintering and she cried out, stifling her cries with her fist as the last suck drew her liquid passion through her channel.

A new and regular activity was begun in the quiet haven of the convent.

My Secret Life

One night soon after this, I met at the Argyle rooms Helen M and was struck with her instantly. My experienced eye and well trained judgment in women, as well as my instincts told me what was beneath her petticoats and I was not deceived. I have had many splendid women in my time, but never a more splendid perfect beauty, in all respects.

Of full but not great height, with the loveliest shade of chestnut hair of great growth, she had eyes in which grey, green and hazel were indescribably blended with an expression of supreme voluptuousness in them, yet without bawdiness or salacity, and capable of any play of expression. A delicate, slightly retroussé nose, the face a pure oval, a skin and complexion of a most perfect tint and transparency, such was Helen M. Nothing was more exquisite than her whole head, tho her teeth were wanting in brilliancy—but they were fairly good and not discoloured.

She had lovely cambered feet, perfect to their toes; thighs meeting from her cunt to knees and exquisite in their columnar beauty; big, dimpled haunches, a small waist, full firm breasts, small hands, arms of perfect shape in their full roundness. Everywhere her flesh was of a very delicate creamy tint, and was smooth to perfection. Alabaster or ivory, were not more delicious to the touch than her flesh was everywhere from her cheeks to her toes.

Short, thick, crisp yet silky brown hair covered the lower part of her motte, at that time only creeping down by the side of the cunt lips, but leaving the lips free, near to at her bumhole, a lovely little clitoris, a mere button, topped her belly rift, the nymphae were thin, small, and delicate. The mouth of the vulva was small, the avenue tight yet exquisitely elastic, and as she laid on her back and opened her thighs, it was an exquisite, youthful, pink cunt, a voluptuous sight which would have stiffened the prick of a dying man.

Her deportment was good, her carriage upright but easy, the undulations of her body in movement voluptuous, and fascinating; every thing, every movement was graceful; even when she sat down to piss it was so—and taking her altogether, she was one of the most exquisite creatures God ever created to give enjoyment to man.—With all this grace, and rich, full, yet delicate of frame, she was a strong, powerful woman, and had the sweetest voice—it was music.

I saw much of this in her at a glance, and more completely as she undressed. Then the sweetest smell as if of new milk, or of almonds escaped from her, and the instant she laid down I rushed lasciviously on her cunt, licked and sucked it with a delight that was maddening. I could have eaten it. Never had I experienced such exquisite delight in gamahuching a woman. Scarcely ever have I gamahuched a gay woman on first acquaintance, and generally never gamahuched them at all.

As I went home with her in a cab I had attempted a few liberties, but she repulsed them.—'Wait till we get home, I won't have them in the cab.'—Directly we arrived I asked what her compliment was to be.—No she had never less than a fiver.—'Why did you not tell me so, and I would not have brought you away.—What I give is two sovereigns, here is the money, I am sorry I have wasted your time'—and was going.—'Stop,' said she—'don't go yet!'—I looked in my purse and gave her what I could—it was a little more than the sum I'd named—and promised to bring her the remainder of a fiver another day. Then I fucked her.—'Don't be in such a hurry,' I said, for she moved her cunt as women either do when very randy, or wishing to get rid of a man. That annoyed me, but oh my God my delight as I shed my sperm into that beautiful cunt, and kissed and smelt that divine body, and looked into those voluptuous eyes. I had at once a love as well as lust for her, as my prick throbbed out its essence against her womb.—But *she* had no pleasure with *me*.—She was annoyed and in a hurry, she had another man waiting in another room in the house to have her—as she has told me since.

What was in this woman—what the specific attractions, I cannot say, but she made me desire to open my heart to her, and I told rapidly of my amatory tricks, my most erotic letches, my most blamable (if any be so) lusts; things I had kept to myself, things never yet disclosed to other women, I told *her* rapidly. I felt as if I must, as if it were my destiny to tell her all, all I had done with women and men, all I wished to do with *her*, it was a vomit of lascivious disclosures. I emptied myself body and soul into her. She listened and seemed annoyed. She did not like me.

Nor did she believe me. Two days afterwards, I took her the promised money, she had not expected it, and then deigned to ask if she should see me again. No. She was far too expensive for me—not that she was not worth it all.—Yea more—but blood could not be got out of a stone.—I had not the money and could see her no more.—'All right,' she replied very composedly and we parted. As I tore myself away, my heart ached for that beautiful form, again to see, smell, to kiss, and suck, and fuck that delicious cunt, to give *her* pleasure if I could. Tho I saw her afterwards at the Argyle rooms—even went to look at her there, I resisted.—What helped me was the belief that I was distasteful to her, why I could not tell, and a year elapsed before I clasped her charms again.

On leaving her that day, I could think of nothing but *her*, went to a woman I knew, and shut my eyes whilst I fucked her, fancying she was Helen M.—'You call me Helen,' said she. 'You know a woman of that name I suppose,'—I told her it was the name of my sister. Not the only time the same thing has happened to me, and in exactly the same manner with other ladies when fucking *them*, but thinking of *another*.

One night at the Argyle rooms, Helen spoke to me. I had several times been there solely to look at her, each time she seemed more beautiful than ever, yet beyond nodding or saying, 'How do you do,' we held no conversation, for she was always surrounded by men. I used to sit thinking of her charms with swollen pego, then either found outside a lady, or once or twice selected one in the room, so that Helen could see, and ostentatiously quitted the salon with her. I felt a savage pleasure in doing so.—A species of senseless revenge.

Sitting by my side, 'You've not been to see me again.'—'No.'—'Why?'—'I'm not rich enough.'—'Nonsense, you've got some other woman.'—'None.'—'Come up.'—'No, I'll let no woman ruin me.'—We conversed further, she got close to me, her sweet smell penetrated me, and in spite of myself I promised to see her next day.

She had changed her abode, had a larger house, three servants and a brougham. I had a sleepless night thinking of coming felicity, and on a lovely spring afternoon, hot as if in the midst of summer, she was awaiting me with an open silk wrapper on, beneath it but a laced chemise so diaphanous, that I could see her flesh and the colour of her motte through it. Her exquisite legs were in white silk, and she'd the nattiest kid boots on her pretty little, well cambered feet. She was a delicious spectacle in her rooms, through the windows of which both back and front were green trees and gardens.

'Say I'm not at home to any one,' said she to the maid. Then to me, 'So you have come.'—'Did you doubt me?'—'No, I think you're a man who keeps his word.' Then on the sofa we sat, and too happy for words I kissed her incessantly. She got my rampant cock out and laughing said, 'It's quite stiff enough.'—'Let me feel *you* love,' said I putting my hand between her thighs.—'Why don't you say, cunt?'—again I was silent in my voluptuous amusement, kissing and twiddling the surface of her adorable cleft. 'Oh let us poke.'—'Why do you say poke—say fuck,' said she moving to the bed and lying down.

'Let me look at your lovely cunt.' She moved her

haunches to the bedside and pulled her chemise well up, proud of her beauty. Dropping on my knees I looked at the exquisite temple of pleasure, it was perfection, and in a second my mouth was glued to it. I licked and sucked it, I smelt it and swallowed its juice, I could have bitten and eaten it, had none of dislike to the saline taste which I've had with some women, no desire to wipe the waste saliva from my mouth as it covered the broad surface of the vulva in quantity, but swallowed all, it was nectar to me, and sucked rapturously till, 'That will do, I won't spend so—fuck me'—said she jutting her cunt back from my mouth.

Quickly I arose and was getting on the bed when, 'No—take your things off—all off,—be naked, it's quite hot—I'll shut the window,' which she did, and throwing off her chemise sat herself at the edge of the bed till I was ready.—'Take off your shirt.'—As I removed it, she laid on the bed with thighs apart, the next second my pego was buried in her, and our naked bodies with limbs entwined were in the fascinating movements of fucking. What heaven,—what paradise!—but alas, how evanescent. In a minute with tongues joined, I shed my seed into that lovely avenue, which tightened and spent its juices with me. She enjoyed it, for she was a woman voluptuous to her marrow, my naked form had pleased her I was sure, not that she said that *then*, she was too clever a Paphian for that.

We lay tranquilly in each other's arms till our fleshy union was dissolved. She then—as she washed—'Aren't you going to wash?'—'I'll never wash away anything which has come out of your cunt you beautiful devil, let it dry on, I wish I could lick it off.'—'You should have licked me before I washed my cunt, you baudy beast,'—she rejoined, laughing.

She then came and stook naked by the bedside.—'Aren't you going to get up?'—fearing her reply. 'Let me have you again,'—I said.—She laughed and gave me a towel—'Dry your prick—you can't do it again.'—'Can't I,—look?' My pego was nearly full size. She got on to the bed, laid hold of it, and passed one thigh over my haunch, my fingers titillated her clitoris for a minute, and so we lay lewdly handling each other. Then our bodies were one again, and a fuck longer, more intense in its mental pleasure, more full of idealities, more complete in its physical enjoyment to me, was over within a quarter of an hour after I had had her the first time.—Nor did she hurry me, but we lay naked, with my prick in her lovely body, in the somnolence of pleasure and voluptuous fatigue, a long time, speechless.

Both washed, she piddled (how lovely she looked doing it), put on her chemise and I my shirt. Recollecting my first visit and her hurry, 'Now I suppose you want your fiver and me to clear out'—said I bitterly and taking hold of my drawers, for I felt a love almost for *her* and sad that I was only so much money in her eyes.—'I didn't say so, lie down with me.'—Side by side on the bed we lay again.

She was not inquisitive. Hadn't I really a lady whom I visited, she knew that I'd had Miss * * * * * * and Polly * * * * I had had, she'd spoken about me to them.—Why didn't I see *her*. Hadn't I a lady, now tell her—I only repeated what's already told.—Then the vulgar money business cropped up.—No, she never had and never would let a man have her, for less than a fiver. Going to a drawer, she showed me a cheque for thirty pounds and a letter of endearments. 'That's come today, and he only slept with me two nights.'

She'd soon again my soft yet swollen cunt stretcher in her hand, and fingered it deliciously, never a woman more deliciously. I felt her clitoris, and kissed her lovely neck and cheeks almost unceasingly.—'Give me a bottle of phiz,' said she after a minute's silence—I complied.—'It's a guinea mind.'—'Preposterous, I'm not in a bawdy house.'—'It's my price, my own wine, and splendid.'—Of course I yielded, who would not when such a divinity was fingering and soothing his prick? It was excellent, we drank most of it soon, and then she gratified me after much solicitation, by lifting her chemise up to her armpits and standing in front of a cheval glass for my inspection, pleased I fancied by my rapturous eulogiums of her loveliness—and exquisite she was.—'You know a well made woman when you see one,' she remarked.—Then quickly she dropped her chemise,—she'd not held it up a minute,—it seemed but an instant,—and refused in spite of my entreaties to raise it again.—'You have seen quite enough.'—Again on the bed we sat, again our hands crossed and fingers played on prick and cunt,—silent, with voluptuous thoughts and lewd sensations.

Then came the letch—'Let me gamahuche you.'—'I won't you beast.'—'You did the other day.'—'Be content then, I won't now'—and she would not. But I kissed her thighs, buried my nose in the curls of her motte, begging, entreating her, till at length she fell back, saying, 'I don't like it, you beast.'—Her thighs opened and crossed my arms, whilst clasping her ivory buttocks my mouth sought her delicious scented furrow, and licked it with exquisite delight. She at first cried out often, 'Leave off, you beast.' Then suddenly she submitted. I heard a sigh, she clutched the hair of my head—'Beast—Aha—leave off—beast —aherr'—she sobbed out. A gentle tremulous motion of her belly and thighs, then they closed so violently on my head, pinching and almost hurting me,—she tore at my hair, then opened wide her thighs—a deep sigh escaped her, and she had spent with intense pleasure. (That vibratory motion of thighs and belly, increasing in force as her pleasure crisis came, I have never noticed in any other woman, when gamuhuching them, tho most quiver their bellies and thighs a little as their cunt exudes its juices.)

With cock stiff as a rod of iron, with delight at having voluptuously gratified her, wild almost with erotic excitement,—'I've licked your cunt dry—I've swallowed your spending my darling' (it was true), I cried rapturously. 'Let me lick your cunt again.'—'You beast, you shan't.'—But as she denied it, lustful pleasure was still in her eyes.—'Let me.'—'No, fuck me.'—At once I laid by her side, at once she turned to me—grasped my pego, and in soft voice said, 'Fuck me.'—'You've just spent.'—'Yes—

fuck me—go on.'—'You can't want it.'—'Yes, I do, fuck me, fuck me,'—she said imperiously. I didn't then know her sexual force, her voluptuous capabilities, did not believe her. But I wanted *her*, and she was ready. On to her sweet belly I put mine, plunged my pego up her soft, smooth cunt, and we fucked again a long delicious fuck, long yet furious, for though my balls were not so full, I felt mad for her, talked about her beauty whilst I thrust, and thrust, and cried our bawdy words, till I felt her cunt grip and she, 'You beast,—beast,—Oh—fuck me——you beast—aher'—and all was done, I'd spent and she with me.

And as she spent, I noticed for the first time on her face, an expression so exquisite, so soft in its voluptuous delight, that angelic is the only term I can apply to it. It was so serene, so complete in its felicity, and her frame became so tranquil, that I could almost fancy her soul was departing to the mansions of the blest, happy in its escape from the world of troubles amidst the sublime delights of fucking.

Then she wished me to go. But only after a long chat, during which she laid all the time in her chemise, her lovely legs, her exquisite breasts showing, she was curious and I told her more about myself than I'd ever told a Paphian. 'When shall I see you again?'—'Most likely never.'—'Yes I shall.'—I told her it was impossible. 'Yes, come and sleep with me some night.'—Laughing, I said,—'I can't do it more than three times.'—'I'll bet I'll make you.'—Then with sad heart, and almost tears in my eyes, I repeated that I should not see her again.—'Yes—you will—look—I'm going to the races tomorrow'—and she showed me a splendid dress.—'I'm going with * * * of the 40th.' How I envied him, how sad I felt when I thought of the man who would pass a day and night with that glorious beauty, that exquisite cunt at hand for a day and night.

Helen and I now began to understand each other (tho not yet perfectly). She knew I was not easily humbugged, so abandoned largely Paphian devices, treated me as a friend, and her circumstances compelling her to avoid male friends, and not liking females much, and it being a human necessity to tell someone about oneself, I became to some extent her confidante. She then had a charming, well furnished little house, replete with comfort, and her own. I have eaten off her kitchen boards, and the same throughout the house. She was an excellent cook, cooked generally herself and liked it, was a gourmet. It was delightful to see her sitting at table, dressed all but a gown, with naked arms and breasts showing fully over a laced chemise, with her lovely skin and complexion, eating, and drinking my own wine, she passing down at intervals to the kitchen. We ate and drank with joy and bawdy expectation, both of us—for she wanted fucking.—Every now and then I felt her thighs and quim, kissing her, showing my prick, anxious to begin work even during our dinner.

Afterwards adjourning to her bedroom, we passed the evening in voluptuous amusements—we had then but *few* scruples in satisfying our erotic wishes.—Soon after had *none*.—How she used to enjoy my gamahuching, and after a time abandoning herself to her sensations she'd cry out, 'Aha—my—God—aha—fuck spunk'—and whatever else came into her mind, quivering her delicious belly and thighs, squeezing my head with them, clutching my hair, as her sweet cunt heaved against my mouth when spending, till I ceased from tongue weariness. Sometimes this with my thumb gently pressing her bum hole, which after a time she liked much. Then what heavenly pleasure as I put my prick up her, and grasping her ivory buttocks, meeting her tongue with mine, mixing our salivas, I deluged her cunt with sperm.—Never have I had more pleasure with any woman, with few so much.

Resting, we talked of *her* bawdy doings and *mine*—of the tricks of women.—We imagined bawdy possibilities, planned voluptuous attitudes, disclosed letches, suggested combinations of pleasure between men and women, and woman with woman—for Eros claimed us both. In salacity we were fit companions, all pleasures were soon to be to us legitimate, we had no scruples, no prejudices, were philosophers in lust, and gratified it without a dream of modesty.

One day I told her again of the sensitiveness of my pego, that with a dry cunt the friction of fucking sometimes hurt me, that my prick at times looked swollen and very red, unnaturally so.—French harlots—more than others—I found washed their cunts with astringents, which my prick detected in them directly, so when I was expected, I wished H not to wash *hers* after the morning, her natural moisture then being so much pleasanter to my penis.—No saliva put there, is equal to the natural viscosity, mucosity of the surface of a vagina.—But from her scrupulously cleanly habits, I had great difficulty in getting her to attend to this.

That led one day to her asking, if I had ever had a woman who had not washed her quim after a previous fucking. She then knew my adventure with the sailor, that at Lord A's, and at Sarah Frazer's—but not the recent one at Nelly L's.—I told her that I had not with those exceptions.—'I'll bet you have without knowing.' She told me of women where she had lived, merely wiping their cunts after a poke, and having at once another man and of its not being discovered; of she herself once having had a man fuck her, and his friend who came with him, insisting on poking her instantly afterwards.

We talked soon after about the pleasure of fucking in a well buttered cunt, and agreed that the second fuck was nicer if the cunt was unwashed. I racked my memory, and recollected cases where I had had suspicions of having done so. Helen who always then washed her quim, again said it was beastly.—I said that if more agreeable to me and the woman, there was nothing beastly in it; nor cared I if there was, fucking being in its nature a mere animal function, tho in human beings augmented in pleasure, by the human brain. 'So why wash after, if the two like it otherwise?'

About that time I found I had not quite as much sperm as in early middle age, testing that by frigging myself over a sheet of white paper, and wished to see what a young man spent both in quality and quantity. We chatted about this at times, and one day she told me she had a man about thirty-five years old, who visited her on the sly, but very occasionally; a former lover who had spent a fortune on her (I know since his name, his family, and that what she told me was true). She let him have her still, for gratitude. He was very poor but a gentleman, and now he helped her in various ways. It struck me she liked him also, because he had as she told, a large prick. I found she had a taste for large pricks, and described those of her former friends who possessed such, in rapturous terms. This man spent much, I expressed a desire to see it, and after a time it was arranged that I should see this cunt prober, him using it, and her cunt afterwards, but this took some time to bring about. In many conversations, she admitted that she had not more physical pleasure from a great prick, than from an average sized one. 'But it's the idea of it you know, the idea of its being big, and it's so nice to handle it.'

I was in her bedroom as arranged, he was to have her in the adjoining room. She placed the bed there, so that when the door was very slightly opened I could see perfectly thro the hinge side. We were both undressed, she with delight describing his prick, repeating her cautions to be quiet, and so on.—A knock at the street door was heard. 'It's his,' said she, and went downstairs.—Some time passed, during which I stood on the stair landing listening, till I heard a cough,—her signal—then going back and closing my door, I waited till they were upstairs and I heard them in the back room. Opening mine ajar again I waited till a second cough. Then in shirt and without shoes, I crept to their door which was slightly open.

They were sitting on the edge of the bed, she in chemise, he in shirt, feeling each other's privates. His back was half towards me, her hand was holding his large tool not yet quite stiff; but soon it grew to noble size under her handling. Then he wanted to gamahuche her, she complied, being fond of that pleasure as a preliminary. He knelt on the bed to do it, tho he'd wished to kneel on the floor.—She insisted on *her* way, to keep his back to me.

So engrossed was he with the exercise, that when her pleasure was coming on, I pushed further open the door (hinges oiled) and peeping round and under, saw his balls, and that his prick was big and stiff—I was within a foot of him.—But he noticed nothing, all was silent but the plap of his tongue on her cunt, and her murmurs. When she had spent once, he laid himself by her side, kissing her and feeling her cunt, his stiff, noble pego standing against her thigh,—she pulling the prepuce up and down, and looking at the door crack. After dalliance prolonged for my gratification, he fucked her. She pulled his shirt up to his waist when he was on her, so that I might contemplate their movements. I heard every sigh and murmur, saw every thrust and heave, a delicious sight; but he was hairy arsed, which I did not like.

Then said she, 'Pull it out, he'll wonder why I have been away so long; you go downstairs quietly, and I'll come soon.' He uncunted, they rose, I went back to my room. He had been told that she was tricking the man then keeping her, and knew that a man was then in the house, and *he* there on the sly was happy to fuck her without pay—for he loved her deeply—and not at all expecting or knowing that his fornicating pleasures, were ministering to the pleasure of another man.

Then on the bedside she displayed her lovely secret charms—a cunt overflowing with his libation.—It delighted me, my pego had been standing long, I seemed to have almost had the pleasure of fucking her as I witnessed him, and now to fuck her, to leave my sperm with his in her, came over me with almost delirious lust. 'I'll fuck you, I'll fuck in it,' I cried trembling with concupiscent desire.—'You beast—you shan't.'—'I will.'—'You shan't.' But she never moved, and kept her thighs wide apart whilst still saying, —'No, no.'—I looked in her face, saw that overpowering voluptuousness, saw that she lusted for it, ashamed to say it. 'Did *you* spend?'—'Yes.'—'I will fuck.'—'You beast.'—Up plunged my prick in her.—'Ahaa'—sighed she voluptuously as my balls closed on her bum. I lifted up her thighs which I clasped, and fucked quickly for my letch was strong. 'Ain't we beasts,' she sighed again.—'I'm in his sperm, dear.'—'Y—hes, we're beasts.' The lubricity was delicious to my prick. 'Can you feel his spunk?'—'Yes dear, my prick's in it.—I'll spend in his spunk.'—'Y—hes—his spunk.—Aha—beasts.'—All I had just seen flashed thro my brain.—His prick, his balls, her lovely thighs, made me delirious with sexual pleasure.—'I'm coming—shall you spend, Helen?' —'Y—hes—push—hard—ahar.'—'Cunt—fuck—spunk,' we cried together in bawdy duet—her cunt gripped—my prick wriggled, shot out its sperm, and I sank on her breast, still holding her thighs and kissing her.

When we came to, we were both pleased.—'Never mind Helen if we are beasts—why say that if you like it?'—'I don't.'—'You fib, you do.'—After a time she admitted that the lasciviousness of the act, had added to the pleasure of coition greatly—to me the smoothness of her vagina seemed heaven.—I was wild to see all again, but circumstances did not admit of it then, yet in time I did, and one day after he and I had had her, 'Go down to him,' said I, 'don't wash, and let him have you again on the sofa.'—The letch pleased her, he fucked her again, and thought he was going into his own leavings. When she came up, I had her again, I was in force that day.—Her taste for his lubricity then set in, and stirred her lust strongly,—she was in full rut—I gamahuched her after she had washed, thinking where two pricks had been, and half an hour after she frigged herself. Whilst frigging, 'Ah! I wish there had been a third man's spunk in it.'—'You beast—ah—so—do I.'—She rejoined as she spent, looking at me with voluptuous eyes.

We often talked of this afterwards, and agreed that the pleasure of coition was increased by poking after another man, and we did so when we could afterwards with her friend and others. Sometimes it is true she shammed that she allowed it only to please *me*, but *her* excitement when fucking told me to the contrary. She liked it as much as I did, and it became an enduring letch with her.

Whether Helen or any other woman—I've known

several who liked it—had increased physical pleasure by being fucked under such pudendal condition, it's not possible to say.—With me owing to the state of my gland, no doubt it did. But imagination is a great factor in human coition, and by its aid, the sexual pleasure is increased to something much higher than mere animalism. It is by the brain that fucking becomes ethereal, divine, it being in the highest state of excitement and activity during this sexual exercise. It is the brain which evokes letches, suggests amatory preliminaries, prolongs and intensifies the pleasure of an act, which mere animals—called 'beasts'—begin and finish in a few minutes. Human beings who copulate without thought and rapidly *are like beasts*, for with them it is a mere animal act.—Not so those who delay, prolong, vary, refine, and intensify their pleasures—*therein is their superiority to the beasts*—the animals. What people do in their privacy is their affair alone. A couple or more together, may have pleasure in that which *others* might call *beastly*—although *beasts* do nothing of the sort—but which to them is the highest enjoyment, physical and mental. It is probable that every man and woman, has some letch which they gratify but don't disclose, yet who would nevertheless call it *beastly*, if told that others did it, and would according to the accepted notions—or rather professions—on such matters, call all sexual performance or amusements *beastly*, except quick, animal fucking. But really it is those who copulate without variety, thought, sentiment or soul, who are the *beasts*—because they procreate exactly as *beasts* do, and nothing more.—With animals, fucking is done *without brains*—among the higher organised human beings, fucking is done *with brains*—yet this exercise of the intellect in coition is called *beastly* by the ignorant, who have invented a series of offensive terms, to express their objections.—Their opinion of the sweet congress of man and woman—which is love—is, that it should be a feel, a look, a sniff at the cunt, and a rapid coupling—*very like beasts that!!!*

H had still two servants, but who were changed often now

›r some reason or another, I guessed to facilitate intrigue. Iore frequently than otherwise her female relative—the :out—in whom she had great confidence, together with ›me very young girl and a charwoman, did the work of ıe house, this looked also suspicious, and the ·rangement as if made to favour intrigues. Indeed H .ughingly admitted almost as much. She now was ;sumed to have quitted gay life for good, and to have ›nsecrated her temple of love to one sole worshipper. I :rtainly believe that she was inaccessible to men (myself ıd a lover excepted), was never seen at the haunts of the ·ail ones, nor at theatres or other places of amusement, ıd she had cut nearly every Paphian acquaintance of old ays. I enquired of women, and at places when they ought › know, but none had seen her. One thought she was ill, ıost that she was being kept.

H spoke well of her protector. She was proud of his ersonal appearance, of his being a gentleman, an Oxford ıan, well born and so on, all of which he was. She said she ›ved him. She was fond of her home and even of domestic uties. She was a very active woman, was very clean, and ıose duties and reading occupied her. She was very clever, ıd indeed had most of the qualities which go to make a ›od wife. She was a gourmet, and most extravagant in her ›od, liked cooking it herself, would give five shillings for pint of green peas or other choice food, even if she had to orrow the money to pay for them—but she much referred going into debt. This is an illustration of, I elieve, her sole extravagance. She could write well, ›mpose charades, and even write rhymes which were far ·om contemptible.

But her nature was luxurious, her sexual force so great ıat it conquered. One man could not satisfy her. Altho ·hen with her protector he fucked her twice daily, and she ·igged herself twice or thrice as well—did it even before is eyes she told me—and I who saw her weekly fucked her vice or thrice and between our love exercise often times ıe frigged herself—no sham, not done to excite me, there ·as no object in that—such was her strong appetite for voluptuous delight, the craving of her flesh. She delighted in bawdy books and pictures, and generally in all voluptuousness—yet for all this she was not a Messalina quite.

Sometimes now she was left alone for a week or two or longer by her friend, tho he idolized her,—but he couldn't help his absence. Then the strong promptings of her carnality placed her in great temptation. Frigging did not satisfy her, her cunt yearned irresistibly for the male. My talk, she averred, so excited her, that when she thought of that alone it led to her giving way to her passions. That I don't believe, tho it might have added fuel to the flames.—She took a fancy after a time to another man. This came about through going to see a dashing gay woman whom she'd not seen since she'd been in keeping. The man therefore was a mere chance acquaintance. He was known in Paphian circles for his physical perfections, and the desire for his very big prick really was the reason for her wishing once to see him, and then for a time her taking to him. But more of this hereafter.

I afterwards witnessed him using his tool. It added greatly to her pleasure to know that I was a spectator. The deed done, he gone away, she came to me, her eyes humid with recent pleasure—still lustful. We fucked, and talked. The idea of my prick being in the avenue his had quitted increased the pleasures of us both when fucking—hers I think more even than mine. Soon after our eroticism entered on even a higher phase of luxuriousness.

When she had thoroughly made the acquaintance of the man with a bigger prick than that of her lover—the biggest she had ever known, she said—she described it rapturously and the delight she felt when it was up her. The gentleman with whom she lived as already said poked her twice daily when there, her poor lover fucked her frequently, I gave her my doodle then once a week, besides gamahuching her which I never failed to do, and in addition to all this she frigged herself nearly every day.—Yet all this did not give her an excess of sexual pleasure, with all her fucking frigging, and gamahuching, she looked the very picture of health and strength, and had both.

She had met as said this man by chance, was told about him, and it was the idea of his size which affected her sensuous imagination.—He was, she found in the long run, a mean hound, who enjoyed her lovely body yet was often half fucked out before he had her, and scarcely made her the most trifling presents. The size of his prick had made him notorious among gay women, she discovered at last, and he got more cunt than he wanted for nothing. I often advised her to cut him, for she told me all about her affairs with him; not that I preached morality but saw that it was a pity to risk an evidently good chance of being settled comfortably for life. Yet if she wanted another man—if variety was essential, 'Have him but beware,' I used to say.

I expressed one day a wish to see his pego of which she was always talking. She was proud at that, her eyes glistened voluptuously as she told me of the arrangements for my view. She had long liked telling her letches to me—a willing listener who had no canting objections.—Tho I cautioned her to take care not to be caught by her protector.—She used to reply—'What have I to live for except it.—Philip and I have no society, we can't afford it now—it's a year since I've been to the theatre,—there is nothing but my house, and playing at cards and fucking, to amuse me.'—'My darling, fucking is all in life worth living for, but be prudent.'

The plan of her house then, owing to the way she and her protector occupied the back bedroom, did not favour a secret peep at her with the man, who had become knowing and wary in such matters, by passing most of his time with harlots, and she had a difficult task in humbugging him. It was to come off in the parlour. I at a signal was to go downstairs from her bedroom barefooted, peep thro the parlour door left ajar, was not to make the slightest noise, and retire directly the consummation was effected.

On the day, I was waiting expectantly in her bedroom, heard footsteps enter the parlour, went down cautiously to the half landing—heard:—'Ahem'—went lower—heard bawdy conversation and then, 'It's right up my cunt.' Knowing from that that my opportunity had arrived, I pushed the door slightly more open.—She was on the top of him on a sofa, her face hid his from seeing me.—She was kissing him, her chemise was up to her armpits, her bum moved slowly up and down showing a thick prick up her. 'It's not stiff,' said she angrily. 'You've fucked before today.'—'I've not fucked since yesterday.'—She'd uncunted him as she spoke, and out flopped a huge prick not quite stiff.—There she lay over him thighs wide apart—cunt gaping wide—his prick underneath it.—It was a dodge of hers to gratify my sight, to show me the procreator she was proud of enjoying.

Then she got off, and stood by the side of him, still leaning over and kissing him, to hide his eyes whilst she frigged him. His prick soon stood and a giant it was. She got on to him again, impaled herself, and soon by the short twitching shoves of her buttocks, and the movement of his legs (in trousers) I saw they were spending—In a minute his moist tool flopped out of her cunt, and I crept upstairs leaving them still belly to belly on the sofa. She had told him that her sister was in the bedroom, to which I soon after heard her coming up, and him going down to the kitchen. Oh the voluptuous delight in her lovely face as she laid on the bedside to let me see her cunt, and the delight she had as my prick glided up it softened by his sperm, and her lewd ecstasy as my sperm mixed with his and hers in spasms of maddening pleasure—for now she delighted in this sort of copulation, said it made her feel as if she were being fucked by both of us at once.

This spectacle was repeated afterwards on a bed in the garret—but after a time she sickened of him and saw him no more.—She however still had her large-pricked poor lover. She had at various times with string measured the length and circumferences of both of these pricks. The way to get proper measurements was carefully discussed by us. I have the lengths and circumferences of the two pricks, and of Phil's all measured when stiff, round the stem half way down—and from the centre of the tip to where the prick joins the belly.

This big-pricked man was a coarse looking fellow tho stalwart and handsome. He would stop at the house and feed at her expense, and scarcely give her a present, yet he was not a poor man, but a man of business as she knew, and as I took the trouble to ascertain. H told me soon all about him. I was certainly the only confidante she could have in this letch.—He was reckless enough to let a youth from his place of business bring him letters whilst at H's and she got acquainted with the lad.

H told me one day that she was in bed with big-tool, when the youth brought him a letter. They both lewd, began chaffing the boy, asked if he'd ever seen a woman naked, and pulled the bed clothes down so as to show her naked to her waist. She permitted, nay liked the lark, and admitted to me she hadn't then seen the prick of a lad of that age, stiff or limp.—'Show her your cock and she'll show you her cunt,' said big-tool. The boy, glowing with lust approached the bed. H opened her thighs invitingly, his master got up and pulled the lad's cock out of his trousers as stiff as a horn, she opened her thighs wider, the man gave the lad's prick one or two frigs, and the sperm squirted over H's thighs.—This, as I happened not to be there, was told me the day after it had occurred.

The next time I saw H we talked over this masturbating frolic with the lad. She had been fucked by him twice, and the letch gratified, desired no more of him. But his youth and inexperience started in me a wish to see him fucking, to be in the room and then for us all together to do what we liked erotically. Before I left it had all been planned.

On the evening about a fortnight after, H looked lovely in laced chemise, crimson silk stockings, and pretty slippers.—As she threw up her legs showing her beautifully formed thighs and buttocks, the chestnut curls filling the space between them, relieved by a slight red stripe in the centre, never had I seen a more bewitchingly voluptuous sight. Rapidly my cock stood stiff and nodding, tho I was a little out of condition.—What a lovely odour it had as I gently licked her clitoris for a minute. But we had other fish to fry. 'Harry's here,' said she. I stripped to my shirt, then be came up, a tall slim youth now just turned seventeen. Quickly *he* too stripped, for he knew the treat in store for him. I laid hold of his long thin tool, which was not stiff, and he seemed nervous.

How strange seems the handling of another's prick tho it's so like one's own. 'Show him your cunt.'—Back she went on the bed exhibiting her charms. The delicious red gap opened, his prick stiffened at once, and after a feel or two of his rigid gristle, I made him wash it tho already clean as a whistle.—I'd already washed my own. Then a letch came on suddenly, for I had arranged nothing—and taking his prick in my mouth I palated it. What a pleasant sensation is a nice smooth prick moving about one's mouth. No wonder French Paphians say that until a woman has sucked one whilst she's spending under another man's fucking, frigging, or gamahuche, that she has never tasted the supremest voluptuous pleasure. Some however had told me that they liked licking another woman's cunt, whilst a woman gamahuched them, better than sucking a prick in those exciting moments. But erotic tastes of course vary.

I laid him on the side of the bed alternately sucking or frigging him.—H was lying by his side, and he put his left fingers on her cunt.—I had intended to let him have his full complete pleasure in my mouth, but changed my mind. Then we laid together on the bed—head to tail—making what the French call sixty-nine or *tête-bêche*, and we sucked each other's pricks.—He was pleased with the performance.—H laying by our side said she should frig herself. Whether she did or not I can't say, being too much engrossed with minetting his doodle.—He did not illuminate me with skill, and after a little time we ceased and his prick drooped.

Then I mounted his belly as he lay on his back, and showed H how I used to rub pricks with Miss Frazer's young man, and putting both pricks together made H clutch them as well as she could with one hand.—But two ballocks were too large for her hand.

Helen's fingers had been feeling her own quim, almost the entire time since we had all been together, and her face now looked wild with voluptuousness.—She cried out 'Fuck me, fuck me' and threw herself on the edge of the bed, thighs distended, cunt gaping. But I knew my powers were too small that night to expedite my pleasure crises, and wished to prolong the erotic excitement, so would not fuck her nor let him.—But I gamahuched her. Then he did the same. She lay full length on the bed, he knelt between her legs, and whilst he plied his tongue upon her vulva, I laid on my back between her legs and his, and took his prick in my mouth. I felt her legs trembling and heard her sighs of delight, she was entering into the erotic amusement with heart and soul, cunt and bumhole as well, as I knew by her movements, ejaculations, and then tranquility. She spent just as a rapid ramming of his prick between my tongue and palate, told me he was about to spend also. So I rejected his tool quickly.

With rigid prick and incited by H he continued licking her cunt till she spent again. Then I laid them both side by side on the edge of the bed, he began frigging *her*, and I frigging *him*.—'It's coming,' said he, and at the instant out shot his sperm in four or five quick spurts, the first going nearly up to his breast.—How the young beggar's legs quivered as his juice left him. Helen leant over and looked as he spent.—His sperm was thinner than it should have been, tho he said he had neither fucked for a fortnight, nor frigged himself for a week. I believed he lied.—My sperm would have been at his age thicker after a week's abstinence. The last time he had fucked her before me it was much more and thicker. He reaffirmed that he had not spent for a week, and she declared he had not fucked *her*, so I suppose it was true.

He washed and pissed, again I played with his doodle and questioned him. He had he said buggered a man once, and frigged one.—Now he had a nice young woman, who let him have her for half a crown when he could afford it, but he only earned a pound a week and had to keep himself out of that. His prick was soon stiff again.—He gave her cunt another lick, and then we went to work in the way. I had arranged with her when by ourselves. He did not know our game.

H in our many conversations on erotic whims and fancies, had expressed a great desire to have two pricks up her orifices at the same time. She wanted to know if it were possible, if sexual pleasure was increased by the simultaneous plugging of cunt and bumhole, and wondered if it would increase the pleasure of the man. I had shown her pictures of the positions in which the three placed themselves for the double coupling, and we arranged to try that evening. He was not now to know what we were at, his inexperience coupled with his excitement at being fucked by a most lovely creature, were calculated to leave him in the dark as to the operations at her back door. But we were obliged to be cautious.

He laid on the bedside his legs hanging down, whilst she standing with legs distended and enclosing his, leant over him—I watched the operation from the floor kneeling, and saw his doodle going up and down her cunt. Then when we knew his pleasure was increasing, I lubricated her bumhole with my spittle, and rising pressed my pego between her buttocks and against his prick, touching it from time to time as she moved her cunt on it. I did this as a blind. Soon after. 'Do you feel my prick?' said I. 'Yes.'—He didn't, for I was then putting my finger against it, but he was too engrossed with his pleasure to notice it. Then she backed her rump artfully, and his prick came out, as she pushed her buttocks towards me, and she kept on talking to him whilst making a show of introducing his pego again to her pudenda.

At the first push my prick failed. It was right in direction—for I had tried the orifice with thumb and finger—all inconvenient nails removed—and knew the road was clear. —Push—push—push with still failure, and then came nervous fear. There were the loveliest buttocks that belly ever pressed, or balls dangled against, smooth, sweet-smelling flesh, an anus without taint or hair, a sweet cunt and youthful prick, and a woman wanting the supremest voluptuousness. Every erotic incitement to sight, touch, and imagination was there, but all was useless. My nature rebelled. Tho I wanted to do what she and I had talked of and wished for, my recreant prick would not rise to the needful rigidity—the more I strove the less my success.

I was mad not for myself but for *her* disappointment—it was *her* letch.—We had discussed the subject many times, and I longed for her to have sperm shed in her cunt and fundament at the same time. Further trial was useless, his prick was again worked by her, and I knew by her manner that she was near her crisis, when anxious to give her other orifice, the pleasure, kneeling I licked her bumhole then thrust my thumb into it, took his balls in my other hand and thumbuggered her whilst I squeezed his cods. She cried out. 'Oh—bugger, fuck,'—when madly excited and both spent. Then his prick flopped out wet and glairy from her cunt into my hand which was still beneath his balls—I arose and so did sweet H looking with bright voluptuous eyes at me.—He lay still on his back with eyes closed and prick flopping down, with a pearl of spunk on its tip. Then too late my damned, disgraced prick stood stiff like an iron rod, and could have gone into a virgin's arsehole or slipped into H's with ease. Sheer nervousness stopped it from doing duty, aided I think by a natural dislike—much as I desired the novelty,—novelty *with* her and *for* her.

The strongest fuckstress, with unlimited capability for sexual pleasure, the most voluptuous woman, the woman with the most thirsty cunt I ever knew, guessed my condition and state of mind. —'*You* fuck me, dear,' said she, and falling back on the bed opened her thighs. Her cunt was glistening with what he had left there.—He'd not uncunted two minutes, nor she finished spending four, yet she wanted my prick—either to gratify me or herself.

Randy enough I went near and pulled open the lips, saw the glistening orifice, pushed fingers up and withdrew them covered with the products of *her* quim and *his* doodle, and looked in her voluptuous eyes.—'Fuck—come on—fuck me.'—'You can't want it.'—'Yes—do me—do it.'—Harry then roused himself, I caught hold of his tool still thickish. 'Wash it, piddle, and she'll suck *you* whilst I fuck *her.'—He* who only had spoken the whole evening in monosyllables, did that quickly. I laid him on the bed and she leant over him standing and bending, laid her face on his belly, her bum towards me.—'Suck his prick, dear'—'I shan't.'—She wouldn't, entreaty was useless, I could not wait, so opening her lower lips for a final look at the sperm, put my prick up her.—Oh! what a sigh and a wriggle she gave as I drove it hard against her womb. Her liking always was for violent thrusts, she liked her cunt stunned almost.—It gives her the greatest pleasure she often tells me. (When at a future day I dildoed her, she liked it pushed violently up her.)

I husbanded my powers, urged her to gamahuche him, hoping she would.—Her refusals grew less positive, and at last into her mouth went his prick but only for a minute.—'There I've done it,' said she.—His doodle had stood, but drooped directly her lips left it.

She'd do it no more, but laying her face on his prick, wriggling her backside, saying,—'Oh fuck me—fuck harder—go on dear.' What a fetch she has when she tightens her cunt round my prick and wriggles her lovely bum, it is almost impossible to stop thrusting!

But I would not finish, pulled out my prick and felt with pleasure its now spermy surface. I turned her round on to her back at the edge of the bed, and put him standing between her thighs. Then belly on belly, cock to cunt, all sorts of postures suggested themselves to me whilst they posed so, and I varied them till I could vary no longer.

Then I made him kneel on the bed over her head, his belly towards me. His prick hung down still biggish just over her head, whilst into her cunt I drove again my stiff stander and fucked, bending my head towards him to catch in my mouth his prick. She laid hold of it and held it towards me, I took it into my mouth and fucked her, holding her thighs and sucking him.—The young beggar's prick soon stood again—went half down my throat.—'Is his prick stiff again?' said she, spasmodically.—'Yes'—I mumbled.—'Oh, we're beasts—fuck me, fuck.'—But as my pleasure came on her mouth pleased me best, I let go his prick, and sinking over her put my tongue out to meet hers, and with mouths joined we spent.—He had slipped on one side when I relinquished his doodle, and when I raised myself and severed my wet lips from hers—our pleasure over—he was looking at us, and she with closed eyes had found and was clutching his doodle stiff still. What a treat for the young beggar.—Thousands would give a twenty-pound note to have seen and done all this. He had the treat for nothing.—All was her device, her lecherous suggestion.

Then we all washed, drank more champagne, and after a slight rest we both felt Harry's pego. Taking it into my mouth it stiffened.—'Can you fuck again?'—'I'll try,' said he.

Ready as if she had not been tailed for a month, her eyes liquid and beaming with voluptuous desire, she turned at once her bum towards him at the side of the bed, and gave him free access. I guided his pego, and the young chap began fucking hard again.—Then I laid myself on the bed, her face now on *my* belly, but in spite of all I could say she would not suck *me*. Was she frightened that *he* would tell Donkey prick of her? Annoyed I arose, and slipping my hand under his belly, frigged her little clitoris whilst he was fucking her on her back, I could feel his prick going up and down, in and out of her cunt, and felt even his balls—which are small.—From time to time I left my post to view the operators from afar, to see his bum oscillate and her thighs move.—It was a long job for him, but *she* spent soon.—The more she spends, the more violent at times seem her passions.—'Ah—don't stop, Harry—fuck— let your spunk come into my cunt,' she cried as she spent. He didn't spend but worked on like a steam engine.—'Spunk—Spunk'—she cried again. Flap, flap went his belly up against her fat buttocks, the sound was almost as if her bum was being slapped by hand.—I thought he'd never spend so long was he in her, till I saw his eyes close.—'Are you coming?'—'Yhes.'—'Ahh—fuck, fuck,'—she screamed again, her whole frame quivered then action ceased, she slipped a little forward fatigued, his belly and pego following with her, and there they still were in copulation both silent and exhausted.—Soon after she uncunted him, and without a word turned onto the bed and laid down—I looked at her cunt and squeezed his prick, felt madly lewd but had no cockstand—I dare not excite myself too much now—I was envious, dull at not being able at once to fuck her again.

She lay with eyes brilliant, humid with pleasure and a little blue beneath the lids, and very red in face. She looked at me intently. 'Do it again,' said she.—'I can't.'—'You can, I am sure'—leaning on one elbow she raised her upper knee, her cunt slightly opening, and I felt it. He was washing.—'Put it in for a minute.'—'It's not stiff .'—Reaching out a hand she gave it a grip.—'You *can* fuck,' said she edging herself to the bedside again and opening her thighs. 'Do it this way just as I am lying.'—I could not resist and put my pego where she wished it—would do anything to bring my prick to touch her cunt.—It was not three inches long—but directly the tip was on her vulva and she rubbed it there, it began to swell. Stiff, stiffer it grew as she nudged it into her cunt. 'It's quite stiff,' said she—I feared a relapse and set to work vigorously, sucked her sweet mouth, exhausted it of spittle which I swallowed and then we spent together, *he* now looking on.—It was an exciting but killing fuck to me—my sperm felt like hot lead running from my ballocks, and the knob felt so sore as I spent, that I left off thrusting or wriggling, and finished by her repeating cuntal compressions and grind, in the art of which she is perfect mistress.—When I first knew her and her cunt was smaller, she never exercised that grip even if she had it—now her lovely avenue tho certainly larger to the fingers, is fatter inside, and has a delicious power of compression.

Harry now was silent, and she at last seemed fatigued, yet sitting by his side began again restlessly twiddling his cock. There were evident signs of its swelling—I felt it, but my lust was satisfied and I cared no more about feeling it. We chatted and drank awhile, and then she laid herself along the bed as if going to repose. Not a bit of it—her lust was not sated yet. She put a hand on to his tool and said, 'Fuck me, dear.' He said he could not. 'Try—I'll make you.' H's eyes when she wants fucking have a voluptuous expression beyond description.—It appeals to my senses irresistibly.—It is lewdness itself, and yet without coarseness, and even has softness and innocence so mixed with it, that it gives me the idea of a virgin who is randy and seeking the help of man, without in her innocence quite knowing what she wants, what he will do, and that there is neither shame nor harm in trying to get the article of which she does not know the use. Her voice also is low, soft and melodious—I was sitting when I saw that she was now in furious rut.—I've seen her so before—and she said to the lad 'Get on me—lay on me dear.'—'I can't do it.'—'You shall,' said she impetuously. 'Lay on my thigh.' The slim youth turned at once his belly on to hers. *He* had now no modesty left—we had knocked that out of him quite.

Wildly almost, she pulled his head to hers and kissed him, her eyes closed, her bum jogged, down went one hand between their bellies, a slight movement of *his* buttocks, a hitch of *her* bum, a twist, a jerk, then up go her knees and legs, her backside slips lower down, and by a slight twist she had got his prick into her. Then she gave two sharp heaves, clutched his backside and was quiet—her eyes were closed—I would give much to know what lewd thoughts were passing through her bawdy brain just then, a flood of lascivious images I'm sure, whilst her cunt was quietly, gently clipping his doodle. She opened her eyes when I said,—'Fuck her well.'—'Fuck dear,' said she to him and began gently her share of the exercise. He began also shagging, but quietly. 'Is your prick stiff?' said I—'Yhes.'—A strong smell of sperm, prick, cunt and sweat, the aroma of randy human flesh now pervaded the hot room,—the smell of rutting male and female, which stimulated me in an extraordinary way. I got lewd, my prick swelled, and for a moment I wanted to pull him off and fuck her myself, but restrained myself and put my hand under his balls to please my lust that way.

If he was a minute upon her he was forty.—Never have I had such a sight, never assisted at such a long fucking scene. She was beautiful in enjoying herself like a Messalina all the time—I squeezed his balls and gently encouraged him with lewd words, she with loving words till she went off into delirious obscenity. With her fine, strong, lovely shaped legs, thighs, and haunches she clipped him, he couldn't if he would have moved off her. Every few minutes she kissed him rapturously crying,—'Put out your tongue, dear, kiss—kiss.—Ahaa-fuck-fuck harder—put your spunk in my cunt.'—Then came prolonged loud cries.—'Ahrr—harre'—and she violently moved her buttocks, her thighs quivered—and after screeching.—'Aharrr'—beginning loud and ending softly, she was quiet and had spent. But a minute after she was oscillating her bum as violently as ever, and crying, 'Spend Harry, spend—kiss—kiss—put out your tongue—kiss—you've not spent—spend dear, kiss'—and her kisses resounded.

I moved nearer to her, and standing, slid my hand under her raised thighs and gently intruded my middle finger up her bumhole.—Her eyes opened and stared at me bawdily. 'Further up,' sobbed she in a whisper, her bum still moving. Then she outstretched her hand, and grasped my prick, and I bending to her, we kissed wet kisses. His head then was laying over her left shoulder hidden, he was ramming like a steam engine, and neither knew where my finger was, nor thought of aught but her cunt, I guess.

Again he put his mouth to hers, their tongues met, and she still holding my pego, on went the fuck. The ramming indeed had never stopped for an instant. My finger was now well up her bum, his balls knocking against my hand, and each minute her bawdy delirium came on.—'Now—spend Harry—spend.—Oh God—fuck—fuck—bugger.—Aharr—aharr.'—Again a screech, again quietness, and as languidly he thrust again she stimulated him.—'Fuck dear, that's it—your prick's stiff—isn't it?'—'Yhes'—'Your spunk's coming.'—'Y—hess.'—'Ahaa—spunk—fuck.—

Ahharr'—she screeched. The room rang with her deliriously voluptuous cries, and again all was quiet. So now was *he* for he'd spent, and out came my fingers as her sphincter strongly clipped it and *she* spent.

I thought it was all over but it was not, her rutting was unabated. 'Keep it in dear—you'll spend again'—'I can't'—'Yes, lie still.'—Again her thighs clipped his, and her hands clutched his backside. I felt under his balls the genital mucilaginous moisture of their passions oozing. His prick was small and I slid my finger up her cunt beside it.—He never noticed it. 'Don't you beast,'—said she.—'Give me some champagne.' I withdrew my moistened finger, gave her a glass, filled my mouth with some and emptied that into hers. She took it kissing me. She was mad for the male tho she murmured after her habit.—'Ain't we beasts?'—'No love, it's delicious, no beast could do what we do.'—He lay now with eyes closed, almost asleep, insensible, half only upon her, his face half buried in the pillow.—She raised her head partially, not disturbing his body, I held up her head, and a full glass of champagne went down her throat.—Then she fell back again and put her hand between their bellies. 'Is his prick out?' said I.

No reply made she—I put my hand under his buttocks, touched his prick which was still swollen, found she was introducing it to her quim and it touched my hand in doing it.—I saw that heave, jog and wriggle of her backside, her legs cross his, her hands clamp onto his buttocks, the jog, jog gently of her rump, then knew that again his pendant doodle was well in her lubricious cunt, and that she'd keep it there.—'How wet your cunt is, Helen,' said I.—'Beast' she softly murmured and began fucking quicker, tho *he* lay quite still.—Her eyes were again closed, her face scarlet. 'Feel his balls,' said she softly.—'Do you like my doing it?'—'Yes, it will make him stiff—do *that* again.'—Her eyes opened on me with a fierce bawdiness in them as she said that.—The exquisite voluptuous look, the desire of a virgin was no more there—delirious rutting, obscene wants in their plentitude was in them, the fiercest lust.—Up went my finger in her bum,—'Aha.—Aha—God'—sobbed she in quick staccato ejaculations.—'Fuck me dear.'

He roused himself at that, grasped her buttocks, thrust for a little time then relaxed his hold and lay lifeless on her. 'I can't do it, I'm sure.'—'You can, lay still a little.'—Still he laid like a log, but not she.—An almost imperceptible movement of her rump and thighs went on, ever and anon her eyes opened on me with a lustful glare, then closed again, and not a word she spoke whilst still her thighs and buttocks heaved.—I knew her cunt was clipping, was nut-cracking his tool,—often times I've felt that delicious constriction of her cunt, as in bawdy reverie I've laid upon her, half faint with the voluptuous delight of her embrace.—Some minutes ran away like this, whilst I was looking at her nakedness, feeling *his* balls withdrawing my finger from *her*, then gently, soothingly replacing it up her bum, frigging my own prick every now and then—none of us spoke.

Then more quickly came her heaves, he recommenced his thrusts. 'Fuck dear,—there—it's stiff.—Ahaa—yes—you'll spend soon.'—'Yes' murmured he.—'Yes,—shove hard—give me your spunk.' All was so softly murmured and with voices so fatigued, that I could scarcely hear them. Again I took my finger from her bumhole (for the position fatigued my hand), on they went slowly, again he stopped, again went on, each minute quicker, and soon furiously rammed hard whilst she heaved her backside up and down thumping the bed which creaked and rocked with their boundings, and the champagne glasses on the tray jingled Up into her bumhole went my finger. 'Aharr,' she shivered out.—'Bugger—fuck—fuck Harry—quicker—aharr—my God—I shall die—y'r spunk's—com—com—aharr—God—shall go mad.'—'Ohooo' groaned he. Her sphincter tightened and pinched my finger out, another bound up and down, one more scream, then both were squirming, another scream from her, a hard short groan from him, and then she threw her arms back above her head, lay still with eyes closed mouth wide open, face blood red, and covered with perspiration, her bosom heaving violently.

He rolled half off her, his prick lay against her thigh dribbling out thin sperm, his face covered with perspiration and again half buried in the pillow and laying nearly a lifeless mass at once he slept. Her thighs were wide apart, no sperm showing: his spend must have been small. Both were fucked out, exhausted with amorous strain.

My strength had been gradually returning, and my prick stood like a horn as I felt again his prick, and thrust my fingers up her lubricious cunt. No heed took either of my playing with their genitals.—I forgot the pains in my temples—cared not whether I died or not, so long as I could again penetrate that lovely body, could fuck and spend in that exquisite cunt. Pouring out more champagne I roused her and she drank it at a draught. 'Am I not a beast?' said she falling back again.—'No love, and I'll fuck you.'—'No, no. You cannot, I'm done and you'd better not.'—'I will.' Pushing the lad's leg off hers—he fast asleep—and tearing off my shirt, I threw myself upon her naked form and rushed my prick up her. Her cunt seemed large and wet but in a second it tightened on my pego.—Then in short phrases, with bawdy ejaculations, both screaming obscenities, we fucked.—'Is my prick larger than his?'—'Ah, yes'—'Longer?'—'Yes—aha, my God leave off, you'll kill me—I shall go mad.'—'Ah, darling—cunt—fuck.'—'Aha—prick—fuck me you bugger—spunk in me arsehole fuck—bugger—fuck—fuck.'—With screams of mutual pleasure we spent together, then lay embracing, both dozing, prick and cunt joined in the spermy bath.

'Get up love, I want to piddle,' said she. I rolled off her belly.—She rose staggering but smiling, kissed me and looked half ashamed. Her hair was loose, her face blood red and sweaty, her eyes humid with pleasure, and puffy and blue the skin under her eyes. She sat on the pot by the bedside looking at me and I at her, and still with voluptuous thoughts she put up her hand and felt my prick.—'You've fucked me well.'—'My God! aren't we three beasts—I'm done for.'—'So am I.'

I'd fucked her thrice, he thrice.—She spent to each of

our sexual spasms and many more times. During their last long belly to belly fucking *she* kept him up to it for *her* whole and sole pleasure, for she was oblivious of *me*.—She must have spent thrice to his once, for her lovely expression of face, her musical cries, her bawdy ejaculations during the orgasm—I know them full well by long experience—were not shammed. That would have been needless and impossible.—The tightening of her bumhole on my finger told the same tale, for the sphincter tightens in both man and woman when they spend.—She'd also frigged herself, been gamahuched by both of us, and spent under all. For two hours and a half, out of the four and a half I was with her that night, either finger, tongue, or prick had been at her cunt and for one hour and a half a prick *up* it.

Impossible as it seems even to me as I write it—absurd, almost incredible—she must have spent or experienced some venereal orgasm—something which gave her sexual pleasure, which elicited her cries, sighs and flesh quiverings, with other evidences of sexual delight, from twelve to twenty times. She may not have spent always, her vaginal juices may have refused to issue, their sources may have been exhausted after a time, yet pleasure she had I am sure. The amusement was planned by us—so far as such a programme can be, jointly for our joint erotic delight.—Harry was but a cypher tho an active one, a pawn to be moved for our mutual delight, and nothing more—tho of course much to his delight—lucky youth.

I thought of the orgy perpetually until I saw her again three days after. I couldn't get to her before.—She looked smiling and fresh as ever, not a trace of fatigue was on her face, but she admitted that she was quite worn out that night, and had spent as nearly as she could tell, twelve or fifteen times, had laid a bed all next day, drank strong beef tea, and that such another night would almost kill her.

The first week of my return from abroad I telegraphed a meeting with H. Getting no reply I went to her house which was empty. I telegraphed the scout, got no response, went there and *she* had flown, but I found that her letters were sent to a neighbouring chandler's shop—I wrote there naming an appointment in the dark and there found H waiting. All was changed, she lived in the country, was not sure if she could meet me, but if so at great risk, didn't know when or where but in a week would let me know. We drove through a park which was on the road to her station and felt each other's carnal agents, I besought her to get out and let us fuck against a tree. She was indignant at the proposal, and it ended in our frigging each other in the cab, face to face, kissing and tonguing, to the great injury of her bonnet, and a little soiling of her silk dress and my trousers. Who would care where sperm fell in such an entrancing ride?

A week after, a place of rendezvous was found, at a convenient snug little house where we met generally.—Before she'd taken anything off but her bonnet and I my hat, we fucked on the bedside with intense mutual delight. Directly I'd uncunted, we both stripped stark naked and got into bed, drank champagne there, and fucked and fucked again till my pego would stiffen no longer; fucked four times, a great effort now for me, but not for her. But frigging and gamahuching always satisfied her as a finish—luckily.

Then our meetings were at longer intervals apart, which only made them more delicious. But I alas, am obliged to husband my strength more than formerly, so the long intervals suit me better.

When next we met, we found that the mistress of the establishment had voluptuous photographs, pictures, and engravings by hundreds, and one or two chests full of the bawdiest books in English and French.—We revelled in them that day for all were placed at our disposal.—We sat feeling each other's genitals between our fuckings, looking and commenting on artistic display of nudities and erotic fancies, and wishing we could participate in such performances ourselves. They awakened ideas which had slumbered in me certainly. She said in her also, but she always declared that I had put desires into her head unknown before. We were well matched.

Living far off now, without a male or female friend with whom to talk about sexualities, more than ever now she looked to our days of meeting, and hours of unrestrained voluptuousness. After hearing all she had done at home even to domestic details—which she was fond of telling as showing her domestic comfort,—lust and love in all its whims and varieties we talked about. 'Did you ever do that?' 'Do you recollect when I showed you * * * prick?'—'When did so and so occur?' So ran our talk. How often he'd fucked her or gamahuched her, how often she'd frigged herself, the sperm *he* spent, and all the domestic bawdy doings were told me with delight, and similar frankness exacted from me.—Then came wishes. 'Let Mrs * * * * * get us another woman, you fuck *her* whilst she gamahuches *me*,' was a request made whilst after fucking, we laid reposing in the bed.—I agreed.—'Let her be stout, I'd like one as stout as Camille.'—These are the very words said funnily enough in a half shamefaced way—for absence and the change in her circumstances, at first seemed to impose some stupid modesty on her.—But both of us liked to call a spade a spade.

All was accomplished. The abbess as I shall call her, we ascertained would procure us every pleasure, tho only cautiously and from time to time she disclosed her powers. A very plump and almost fat, handsome woman of two and twenty was our first companion.—'Don't let *me* ask her, *you* say that *you* want her to lick my cunt—I don't want her to think that *I* wish it,'—said H. So it was done, we had champagne, I stripped the plump one, then asked H to look at her quim—which she was longing to do—and then incited her to the gamahuche. Bawdy talk and wine raising our lust made us friends soon, and Miss R jumped at the idea of gamahuching the other. Then naked all three (warm weather now). Looking-glasses arranged so that H could see all, she laid on the bed-side whilst R gamahuched her. On the bed by H's side I also laid, she frigging me during her pleasure. 'Aha—God—lick quicker.—I'm spending,'—and she spent nearly pulling my prick off during her first ecstasy.

Pausing for a minute, R recommenced, for H likes to continue uninterruptedly at that luscious game, till she has spent at least twice. It was a lovely sight to see H with her beautiful thighs, and the coral little gash set in the lovely chestnut hair, which R held open for a minute to admire. Then her mouth set greedily upon it, her hands under H's buttocks, the dark hair of R's armpits just peeping, her big white buttocks nearly touching her heels. I stooped down this time and peeped along the furrow past the bumhole, and could just see the red end of her cunt with the short crisp hair around it. Then straddling across her waist, my prick laying on her back between her blade bones, I watched the lovely face of H which in her sexual ecstasy is a lovely sight. 'Fuck, fuck her,' she cried to me. But I wouldn't. Next minute saw H's lovely eyes fixed on mine, whilst with soft cries she spent.

A rest, more champagne, a discourse about the pleasures of woman cunt licking woman and of men doing it, and H again was on the bed.—'Oh, I'm so lewd I want a fuck so,' said R—'He'll fuck you, won't you?'—I complied. Further back on the bed now the better to reach her cunt with her tongue, with pillows under her head lay H when R recommenced her lingual exercise on the sweet and fresh-washed quim. I standing up now at R's back.—'Fuck her, and spend when I do,' said H—R's bum towards me was almost too fat a one as she bent, so I made her bend lower, and then between the buttocks went my prick, dividing two well haired, very fat lips of her sanctum of pleasure. She adjusted her height to the exercise when my tip was well lodged, my balls were soon against the buttocks, every inch of my prick up a cunt deliciously lubricated by its owner's randiness.—'It's up her cunt love,' I cried, began fucking and R began gamahuching. All now was silence but the lap now and then of R's tongue on H's cunt. 'She's coming darling—I shall spend,'—I cried at length.—'Oh—God—fuck her, fuck, slap her bum,' cried

H writhing and sighing.—My slaps on the fat arse resounded, as R writhed and shivered with pleasure whilst licking on, and both of us spent as H spent under the tongue titillation. Then with slobbered prick and wet cunts we got up. Soon after standing by the bedside I fucked H whilst she frigged Miss R. Never were there three bawdy ones together who enjoyed the erotic tricks more than we did.

These delightful voluptuous exercises were repeated with variations on other days. R sucked my prick and took its libation whilst I was lying full length on the bed, H kneeling over my head, I licking her clitoris, the looking glasses so arranged that H could see all. Another day I fucked R whilst she frigged H. Then I put my prick into both women and finished in R's cunt, which completed that day's amusement.

Soon afterwards we noticed wales upon R's capacious white buttocks. It was from her last whipping she said. That disclosed what in time was sure to have become known to us. That the abbess was an expert in flagellation, that swells both old and young came under her experienced hand. Questioned, the abbess told us all, was indeed proud of her performances, showed us the varied apparatus with which she either tickled or bled the masculine bums, and women's as well, or superintended men flogging female bums. Such as the fat arsed R's were preferred, tho some she said liked younger and thinner buttocks. Some brought and birched a woman whom they liked and fucked, some a special woman to birch them. They all paid very handsomely for bleeding a fair pair of buttocks.

R told us that flagellation of *her* backside made her lewd an hour after or so. She liked the birch just to hurt slightly the cunt lips. Then if she couldn't get a man, she frigged herself—that some girls said it did not affect them lewdly—others that it did.—We talked quietly with the abbess about this. Both H and I desired to see the operation, and heard that some men liked to be seen by other men when being flogged. If we would come on a certain day, there would be then a gentleman who had a taste for being made a spectacle, and she would arrange for us to see—for pay of course.

We went on the day but the man didn't appear. Two ladies were ready waiting to flog him. The abbess said it didn't matter, something had detained him, that when he disappointed he always paid the money for all concerned. One of them was dressed as a ballet girl, the other only in chemise, such were his orders.—She in chemise, was a sweet faced, dark haired shortish girl of nineteen, with fine teeth. We asked her to our room to take wine, and it ended in H frigging her and my fucking her, then in my fucking H, whilst she looked at the other's quim, and we agreed she would be better for our amorous games than R.—I will call this dark one 'Black.' She had one of the most delicate, refined, cock stiffening, slightly lipped, slightly haired cunts I ever saw: it resembled H's cunt years ago. Black took at once a frantic letch for gamahuching H—and who wouldn't?—When *my* mouth covers it, I can scarcely tear it away from it.

At our next visit the flagellation came off. As H, who'd only had her chemise on, and I my shirt and wearing a mask, entered the room, there was a man kneeling on a large chair at the foot of the bed, over which he was bending. Over the seat and back of the chair was a large towel to receive his spendings. He had a woman's dress on tucked up to his waist, showing his naked rump and thighs, with his feet in male socks and boots. On his head was a woman's cap tied carefully round his face to hide whiskers—if he had any—and he wore a half mask which left his mouth free.—At his back, standing, was one youngish girl holding a birch and dressed as a ballet dancer, with petticoats far up above her knees, and showing naked thighs. Her breasts were naked, hanging over her stays and showing dark haired armpits. Another tall, well formed, tho thinnish female, naked all but boots and stockings, with hair dyed a bright yellow, whilst her cunt and armpits' fringes were dark brown, stood also at his back—a bold, insolent looking bitch whom I one day fucked after she'd gamahuched H—tho I didn't like either

her face, cunt, form, or manner—but she was new to me.

What he had done with the women before we entered we were told afterwards by yellow head, was very simple. He'd stripped both women naked, and saw the one dress herself as a ballet girl, nothing more. Neither had touched his prick nor he their cunts. When the door was closed after we entered, he whispered to the abbess that he wanted to see my prick. Determined to go thro the whole performance, I lifted my shirt and showed it big but not stiff. He wanted to feel it but that I refused. 'Be a good boy or Miss Yellow (as I shall call her) will whip you hard,' said the abbess.—'Oh—no—no—pray don't,' he whispered in reply. He spoke always in whispers. Then he said H was lovely and wanted to see her cunt, which she refused. He never turned round during this but remained kneeling. Then after childish talk between him and the abbess (he always in whispers), 'Now she shall whip you, you naughty boy,' said the abbess—and 'swish' the rod descended heavily upon his rump.

'Oho—ho—ho,' he whispered as he felt the twinge. I moved round to the other side of him where I could see his prick more plainly. It was longish, pendant, and the prepuce covered its tip nearly.—Swish—swish—went the birch, and again he cried in whispers.—'Ho, ho.'—H then moved round to my side to see better.—Yellow head from behind him felt his prick.—The abbess winked at me.—Then he laid his head on the bedstead frame and grasped it with both hands, whilst very leisurely the birth fell on him and he cried. 'Ho—ho.'—His rump got red and then he cried *aloud*.—'Oh, I can't'—then sunk his voice to a whisper in finishing his sentence.—Yellow head again felt his prick which was stiffer, and *he* sideways felt *her* cunt, but still not looking round.

Then was a rest and a little talk, he still speaking in whispers. The abbess treated him like a child. I felt Yellow head's motte, she looked at H to see if *she* permitted *me* the license. Yellow head then took up the birch, and H and I moved to the other side of the bed. Both of us were excited, H's face was flushed with lust, I felt her cunt, and she my pego, now stiff. 'Look as those two,' quoth the abbess. We, and both the women laughed.—The patient had turned his head to look, but could see nothing but us standing.—Swish—swish, fell heavily the rod on his arse, now very red indeed.—'Let me lick her cunt,' whispered he, nodding at H.—She refused.—'I'll give her five pounds,' he whispered. H hesitated, but short of money as usual, at length she consented, beside she was lewd to her bumhole—'I shall spend,' she whispered to me as she got on to the bed and saying aloud, 'Five pounds, mind.'—'He'll pay, he's a gentleman,' murmured the abbess.

Then was the spectacle such as I never saw before nor shall again. H settled on the bed, thighs wide apart, quim gaping, legs over the bed frame, cunt close up to the victim, but too low for his tongue to reach the goal. The abbess, Miss Yellow head and I, pushed pillow after pillow under her lovely bum till it was up to the requisite level, and greedily he began licking it. I moved round him again, looking curiously at his prick which was now stiff.—'Let *him* feel it,' he whispered more loudly than usual. I felt and frigged it for a second. Whilst I did so, swish—swish—fell the rod on his rump, which writhed.—'Um—um—hum,'—he murmured, his mouth full of H's cunt. 'Ahrr,' sighed H, whose lovely face expressed her pleasure, for she was lewd. Yellow head laid hold of his prick, gave it two or three gentle frigs, and out spurted a shower of semen. Then he was quiet with his mouth full on H's open quim, whilst still Yellow head continued frigging his shrinking organ.—'Have you spent?'—said I. 'Damn it, I was just coming,' said H, jogging her cunt still up against his mouth, wild for her spend. But he was lifeless, all desire to lick her had gone.

At a hint from the abbess we went to our bedroom.—'Fuck me.'—On the bed she got, her cunt wet with his saliva, my prick nodding its wants and lust, up I plunged it in her wet cunt, thrust my tongue into her sweet mouth, our salivas poured into each other's, and we spent in rapture, almost before we had begun the glorious to and fro of my prick in her lubricious avenue.

Neither of us had seen such a sight before, never had either of us even seen anyone flogged, and we talked about it till the abbess came up. The man had left, but only gave three sovereigns for H's complaisance. 'No doubt she's kept the other two,'—said H afterwards. The young ladies were still below, would we like to have a chat with them? Our passions were well roused, H at once said 'Yes,' and up they came. We had champagne, giving the abbess some, then all talked about flagellation. The younger woman showed marks of the birch on her bum, and when the abbess had gone, we heard more about the rich victim, whom both had seen before and who was between fifty and sixty. He always had two women, but not always they two, they'd never known him allow strangers to be present when he was flogged, and he wanted to know if H would whip him some day. (She never would.) Then we all four stripped, both women gamahuched H and whilst the younger one was doing *that* I fucked Yellow head, whose cunt I couldn't bear. Then *she* gamahuched H and I without any effort fucked up the other girl and found *her* cunt delicious.—In the intervals we laid pell mell on the bed together, topsy-turvy,—arsy-versy, and any how and in all sorts of ways, looked at each other's cunts, the two women both sucked my prick to stiffness but no further and Yellow head put her finger up *my* bum as I fucked the younger girl at the bedside feeling H's lovely sweet cunt whilst I did so, and as *her* rump was towards me I paid the finger compliment to *her* bumhole.—We had champagne till all were tight, and gloried in most unrestrained bawdiness in act and talk. We all pissed, and I felt their amber streams whilst issuing, and pissed myself against Yellow head's cunt, H holding the basin.—Then fatigued with lustful exercises—H excepted—we had strong tea, and went our ways. A veritable orgy, and an extravagantly expensive one.

Now it was very clear and frankly avowed by H, that our meetings were the delight of her life, that tho happy at home they were friendless nearly, and she looked forward to meeting me with the greatest pleasure, not only to tell me all, but to indulge with me in reminiscences, and have bawdy afternoons with other women. 'And it's your fault, you've told me more than all the men and women together whom I've known.'—But there were hindrances. Sometimes two or three weeks intervened between our meetings at the abbess'; tho each meeting brought some bawdy novelty.

When next we met we had little Black and not Miss R for our companion, and Black and I together gave H her complete dose of pleasure. Two fucks, a frig, and three or four gamahuches, some by me, some by Black, seemed the quantum which she called a jolly bawdy afternoon. All were pleased, for B loved gamahuching H, and being gamahuched by *me*, and tho so young, willingly sucked my pego to its liquid culmination.—H still refusing to do that, or to touch B's quim with her tongue.—What with conversation about fucking in general—of the erotic caprices of men, of money gained and spent, sexual incitements, etc. etc.—in which conversations the abbess joined now at times—we passed most voluptuous afternoons or evenings.—But the cost was heavy—for the abbess' house was quiet and expensive, and champagne and a second gay lady added much to the sum total of the expenses of meeting H.

We from time to time gratified our letches in the various ways already described and epitomised. The conversations we had at other times with Misses R and B and occasionally with the abbess, were delightful. Both told us their experiences, and how, when, and where, pricks first penetrated their unscathed virgins' quims. The abbess told us of strange letches of her clients and of flagellation experiences. So there was nothing erotic that we did not know. Indeed there was little that we had to learn. Looking one day at a print of two women and two men fucking altogether, 'I should like you so to fuck a woman, whilst I am also fucked at your side,' said H. I agreed that it would be delicious. At other meetings on recurring to the subject, we resolved to have that amusement and that Black should be the other woman. 'But who the other man?' The abbess consulted said she knew a gentleman who could be one, but would be masked.—I didn't like that, nor did H, but towards the middle of the summer, H met at a town two miles from her residence, a gentleman who years before when she was gay, had tailed her. She'd talked and walked with him, he got passionate for her, *her* quim she admitted got hot, and forgetting all,—and she risked much,—let him strum her. Then her lusts fully roused, she'd gone to him again. When she told me of this I cautioned her, besought her.—'Oh! He has such a fine prick,' said she laughing, as she drank a glass of champagne. Yet this woman really loved her own man, but as in years before let her passions conquer her.—At church every Sunday after this she felt she was not good enough to be there. Lust is omnipotent.

Then he worried her. She'd refused to let him have her again, unless he'd be one of the party of four (she said). He, wild to possess her agreed, a day was named and Black informed. He was to be without a mask, I to wear one if I liked—for I didn't know what manner of man he might be, tho I'd no fear of a trap or trick on her part.—On the day H was there with Black and this temporary sweetheart, I entered the room masked, we began with luncheon which I had taken, and champagne of very good quality which the abbess kept in stock—for none but gentlemen entered her house,—and when we'd finished two bottles we were all ready for any bawdiness, our talk alone would have roused the prick of a dead man. Both the women had been sitting with chemises only on, we men without coats and waistcoats, for it was a hot day, the sun was shining, the sky clear, all was bright as day in that snug room, the scene of so much love making.

H sat on her friend's knee (Fancy I shall name him), and pulled out his pego, which out of lingering modesty, at the unaccustomed exposure to another male I suppose, was not stiff, tho large and pendant. Black did the same to me, and my tool was in similar condition.—'Make his stiff,' said H laughing, which in a minute the girl did, for the sight of H with her chemise now up to her rump, feeling his pego whilst he fingered her crimson gap, would have stiffened me without the aid of Black's fingers. His was now stiff and in handsome state.—'Isn't it a fine one?' said H proudly.—I'd guessed before that her old letch had made her give herself to the man—a big prick was her delight, her ideal of the male.—His was bigger every way than mine, was, indeed, a noble cunt stretcher. I longed to feel it, but *mauvaise honte* restrained me. H, who from many a conversation knew that I should like, said. 'Feel it—here,'—giving it an inviting shake and looking bawdily at me. Relieving mine from Black's fingers I went and felt it.—At once he grasped mine, and in silent delight we for the minute played with each other's ramrods. 'Let *me* feel it too,' said Black who came close to us and completed the group.—I put one hand between her thighs and felt her hot gap—gap now longing for a stretching, thirsting for the male libation—whilst I handled *his* stiff rod and H handled *mine*. Hands across—a salacious quartet.

Then all stripped to our skin, put the looking glasses so as to reflect us, and in varied groupings viewed ourselves. It was, 'Do this.'—'Lay hold of his prick.'—'Let Black hold it as well.'—'Oh! You hurt my cunt.'— 'Feel H's cunt, Black,'—etc. etc. Not a minute were we in the same position, restless letches were in all of us, bums to bellies, prick crossing prick we men placed them, both pricks stiff as horns. The women delighted, Black knelt down and took my prick in her mouth, her bum towards a glass, incited to that by H. Stooping I took *his* noble tool into mine, and so on, till stimulated by these lascivious preliminaries, 'Oh!—my God—fuck me,' said H. Going to the bed and pushing the glasses into position, she mounted it; in a minute Black followed, and we men were by the bedside ready to cover them.

All had washed pricks and cunts at the beginning, and all were ready for the luscious games.—'No, at the side,' said H changing her mind. There she got, and Black laid by her side. Both opened wide their thighs. H lay with her handsome central furrow, of deeper crimson tint now than years ago, wider spread and fuller now are the curls around it, shining like satin was the surface of the pretty gap. Black's pretty youthful black haired slit shone like coral, showing its tiny nymphae as she lay with finger on her clitoris, put there in her impatient randiness to give incipient pleasure, and make we men more lewd.—'I'll fuck *you* dear H.' 'No, Fancy shall fuck me, you fuck B.'—The biggest prick and the novelty fetched her. I threw myself upon my knees, and licked all over the smooth and pulpy surface of her sweet scented cunt, whilst Fancy seeing my initiative, licked the other's little randy split.—'Oh—Fuck-fuck'—cried H impatiently. Rising I clutched her thighs and drove my glowing prick right up her cunt. 'You shan't fuck me with that mask on,' cried she, and ere I could prevent it uncunted me and drew my mask from off my face. 'Let Fancy fuck me first.'—Reckless now, glad to be rid of the mask which heated my face, I let it lie where it fell, and turning round again I felt his noble shaft, just as he approached the eager slit of H. Then I went to B and drove my pego up her. The next second his balls were against H's bum, his shaft engulfed, and mine up B's little cunt.

This with loud and bawdy talk, then all was quiet. Pleasures too great were ours now for utterances, as pricks and cunts were joined, and we fucked close together, side by side, the women's thighs touching, the glass sideways showing us all. Each could see all—the women's legs held up, the men's arses oscillating with the up and down, and in and out movements of their pricks, in the warm moist quims. Putting one hand out I felt his buttocks.—H tried to put her hand on to B's motte.—'Oh! Look at us fucking,'—cried she. She loves the spectacle of naked copulation, and we never fuck in this house without fixing our eye upon the glasses, where we see our every movement.

She sighed 'Ahaa,'—her belly heaved—B's ivory plump buttocks reciprocated my thrusts, she pushed her legs up higher as she felt my prick's friction.—Rapidly both women's arses now jogged and heaved, as our pricks rammed harder, faster, and wriggled in the cuntal depths. 'Aherr—spunk—fuck,'—cried H.—She loves the bawdy cries. 'Fuck.'—'Are you spending, Black?'—'Aha-yes-spunk,'—cried B sympathetically.—'My spunk's spending in your cunt dear.'—'Aher.'—'Yhes—fuck,' and in a Babel of lascivious cries, bodies heaving, arses jogging, short jogs, cunts wriggling and gripping, bellies and thighs shuddering with the luscious pleasure, out shot our spunk. Then bending over our women, with gentlest movements squeezing our pricks into the cunts gorged to overflowing with the soft mucus, in soothing baths of our blended spendings lay our pricks weltering, all of us quiet, exhausted, dying away after the delirium of the crisis dissolving in the lingering, blissful, soothing voluptuousness of our sexual pleasure, oblivious of all but the blessed conjunction of prick and cunt.

Such bliss can't last forever.—With senses returning we men stood erect, pricks still in cunts, but dwindling in the lubricious emulsion of our making. We talked, still holding up the women's legs, who lay with humid eyes, glad to retain the pleasure-giving implements up them. 'Has he spent much H?'—'Lots, I'm full, it's running out of my cunt,' said H—for I thought of her first.—'Let me see.'—'You shan't you beast,'—laughing.—'Don't let her legs close Fancy,—keep your thighs apart B.'—Fancy entered into the fun and withdrew his dripping pego as mine quitted B's glutenous gap. I closed on H, and saw fat sperm rolling from her heated quim—opaque and thin together.—He'd spent fully, I had deluged B's little tight vulva. H opened wider still her thighs for my inspection. He had left the women, having, it seemed, no taste for the glorious sight, and began washing his tool.

H who knew my letch and had her own, tho saying, 'Beast,' remained quiescent, expectant.—She knew the sight would stimulate my lust, and I felt her lovely lubricious gap with one hand, and with the other B's mucilaginous vulva. How smooth and large cunts feel after their spend, and the male libations are in them.—I plunged for a second my fingers up both cunts, I paddled in the sperm and my prick stiffened, pulsated with desire. Old letches came on me, I put my prick up H. But when half entered, shaking her head silently she pushed me off and winked, looking across at him, who with his rump towards us was still washing. I understood, she didn't wish *him* to see that. Soon after he did.

Then all washed. The women squatting, H beginning to piddle after ablution. I put out my hand and caught the amber stream, at which he laughed.—Naked then all sat down, the abbess brought more champagne, and said it was a pretty sight to see us naked. As we drank, H with one hand was feeling his prick as they sat together on the sofa. Black sitting on my thigh was feeling mine.—'Isn't his a fine prick?' said H. It had swollen again. The abbess felt it, chuckled and said. 'Ain't it a beauty?' Then after feeling mine and patting H's haunches.—'Hasn't she a nice bum?—two pricks standing.—Oh! What a pretty sight,' and then she left the room.

We put on chemises and shirts, for hot as it was, in our climate long continued nudity often causes chilliness. Talk of prick and cunt and fucking them went on, and of but little else, every now and then feeling our pricks and cunts quite indiscriminately, he mine, I his, lifting shirts and chemise at times to gratify our eyes, H now feeling his and mine at the same time, H lolling bawdily on a sofa with him, B and I lolling upon the bed.

More champagne and more pissing. I held his tool to see the watery spout. Then we placed the women against the bedside with bums towards us, to compare the beauty of their notches, then slapping their buttocks with our pricks pulling the hairy lips apart, tickling the stripes with tongues, and other lascivious whims and fancies, our passions were soon roused. H said, 'Let's fuck,'—before we men were ready.—I knew the lot of spending she could give, the fucking she needed when in rut as she was today—the day long anticipated and prepared for.—Again all stripped and went to the soul stirring, delicious, sexual embrace. The embrace when man and woman are angels to each other, tho the power of fucking is the gift of ever ınimal in creation, is the function of a beast. But how Divine the pleasure in body and mind when doing it.

'I won't fuck yet I'll gamahuche,'—said I, wishing to ıusband my sperm. H ready, opened her thighs, and my ·ongue tickled her till she went off shrieking in her ’oluptuous delirium. She was frigging B with one hand, ıolding Fancy's prick—which now again stood nobly— .nd with the other.—H and I suggested all, he seemed ›assive but ready.—'Gamahuche me,' said she to him lirectly I had given her pleasure. Down he knelt and licked ıer vulva which she'd only wiped. She didn't disguise her ›leasure, gave way to it with all its delirium of movements ınd words. 'Oh—God go on—ahrr—feel his prick—is it tiff?' I felt his rigid staff with lascivious delight.—'Stiff as poker.' 'Ahaa,—I can see you—aha—frig it.'—I id.—'Aha, I shall spend—don't make him—spend. -Aha—spunk—fuck,'—and again her cunt gave out its earlyjuices whilst violently she frigged Black who lay on ıe bed next to her with head turned towards, and watch-ıg her raptures.

Up he got with moistened lips, and without a word lunged his big pego up her, she nothing loath. I watched ıem for a while, then looked beneath his ballocks which ere ample in size, well wrinkled, then took it in my hand ıd squeezed it gently. A shudder of delight passed ırough him. 'I'm feeling his balls.—Suck my prick, Black ɜar.'—'I want to frig her,' said H.—'No, come.'—B ıme and stooping took the red tip of my pego into her outh and tongued and licked and played with it, whilst I ɜld his balls, looking at H's face. And he fucked on till ɜr heavenly smile came. Then he groaned lightly and ;ain filled her vulva with his sperm.

Taking my prick from out of B's mouth I pushed it ɜtween his buttock furrow, till it touched his ıllocks—out came his prick, and at once I went between 's thighs, caught up her drooping legs, and rushed my ick now bursting with desire, up her lubricated cunt, 'erflowing again with his mucilage. She laughed aloud ›w, and so did he. Champagne was doing its work, all modesty, if we'd had any, was gone. I thrust and thrust, glorying in its lubricity, in being in the soft avenue his prick had quitted.—B sprang on the bed.—'Show me your bum,' said he.—With her buttocks turned towards him.—'Fuck me so,' said she.—But he'd just spent, and to see *me* fucking was his pleasure. He hadn't washed.—'Let me feel your prick,' said I.—'Let *me* feel it,' cried H with excited eyes. Relinquishing one of her legs I grasped his gummy tool—a fine big handful even now—and pulled him by it close to me. H put the leg I'd dropped up and rested on his haunch. Then feeling him, looking at B's little black haired notch pouting red from between he buttocks, I fucked and spent, and that randy devil H spen again.

'Why didn't you fuck *me*?' said B angrily, as I pulled m prick out of H's cunt. She was a little elevated an quarrelsome.—'Gamahuche her,' said H who sat u looking now fatigued in her eyes—no wonder?—'Yo didn't spend with me,' said I.—'I'll swear I did.'—I kne her force, her stirring lewdness, but liked to tease her so. pushed her back and put my fingers up her cunt, whils watching B, who in a temper pushed Fancy off, who wa gamahuching her. 'You don't do it nice.'—We a laughed.—'Fuck me.'—'I can't yet,' said he.—'I'll fri myself, let me feel your prick.' H got off the bec —B laid herself lengthwise on it, and felt his prick, h standing by her side whilst she frigged hersel Then—'Fuck me, I hate frigging,' and getting off sh rushed to the champagne.—There was none.—'You' had enough,' said H.—'I haven't, and you've had all th fucking.'—'What if I have?'—Then was a wrangle, which H told B she'd come there to help to amuse *us*, ar might leave if she liked.

More champagne, Black got quite screwed and ou rageously bawdy, mad for prick. We were all gettir screwed and Fancy particularly so. An hour ran away, wouldn't minette me or him.—'Gamahuche me B, ar when stiff I'll fuck you,' said I.—'No, you fuck *me* whil I gamahuche *him*.'—H was then handling F's tool b relinquished it. I laid on the bed and B minetted me to rigidity, then I tongue tickled her quim a little, then on the bedside kneeling over her, she sucking *me*, Fancy fucked *her*, looking at my rump, H looking on and feeling his ballocks from behind.

'Suck on,' I cried. But B who had before half frigged herself spent and let go my prick leaving me unfinished.—'He's a fine prick,' were the first words she uttered.—'He has,' said H eulogistically.

More champagne and sweet cakes sent for. The abbess came up, said we were making a dreadful noise, and some friends of hers were below.

A little quieted, soon after we put both our pricks into both cunts, and talked about that. Then we mounted the bed, he fucked H, I fucked Black, both couples side by side and close together. We had fancies even then, and lying on the top of them felt each other's woman, and showed our pricks.—Then encouraging each other bawdily, we fucked till we spent amidst a chorus of lustful words. Just then in came the abbess again, and smacked my rump as I was lying on B, and giving her the last wriggle with my prick.

Then we had tea—then more wine—and again incited each other to further exercises.—Groggy, weary, fucked out all, yet lewd still, we kissed all round and then left one by one, I first, and never shall see the like again.—It *was* an orgy. All the erotic whims which two men and two women could do together in five hours, I think we did.

CARROLL & GRAF